David Finkle has covered the arts for *The New York Times, The New York Post, The Village Voice, The San Francisco Chronicle, The Nation, The New Yorker, New York, Time Out New York, Vogue, Harper's Bazaar* and *The Huffington Post*. David is represented by Julia Lord Literary Management.

The man with the overcoat

David Finkle

Published by nthposition press, 38 Allcroft Road, London NW5 4NE.

First published 2015.

© David Finkle 2015

British Library Cataloguing-in-Publication Data
A catalogue record for this book is available from the British Library

Library of Congress Subject Headings
American fiction – 21st century; New York (NY) – Fiction

BIC Subject Category
FA – Modern & contemporary fiction (post 1945)

ISBN 9780992618520 (paperback)

Cover design by Colin Taylor

THE MAN WITH THE OVERCOAT

"But it is plain you must have a new overcoat."
– *The Overcoat*, Nikolai Vasilievich Gogol

Skip Gerber exited the elevator at 6.18 pm on an until-then ordinary late October Tuesday and took the overcoat handed him by a man standing just outside the intricately tooled brass Amerongen Building elevator doors. Ordinarily, he wouldn't have done such a damn-fool thing, but he was preoccupied – with what thought or thoughts he had no time to recall in the stoked hours that followed.

Was his preoccupation to do with anything that had happened as he left the office where he referred to himself (ironically and, he hoped, humorously) as a "legal eagle"? Were his thoughts concerned with something his administrative assistant Brianna called after him? Something on his calendar he needed to see about? Pick up? Drop off?

Was it some tiresome legal query – or, worse, client – he'd been unsuccessful at pushing to the back burners of his (sometimes he thought) burnt-out mind? Something about his career in general he'd been unsuccessful at ducking? Did it have to do with speculating, as he often did, on how his legal-eagle (no irony necessary) dad, Gabriel Martin Gerber, would have handled similar cases?

Was he trying to recall what information he'd promised to look up for his mother, Bernice Sawyer Gerber – not even for *her*, for her *friend* Gussie Slotnik? (This was his life.) Was he wondering if he'd taken his cellphone? Had he just patted his pockets to verify that he had?

Was he dwelling on his funny (or not so funny) general existence as a guy who used to enjoy being the life of the party but had reached an unfortunate point where he no longer had time for parties, let alone serve as the life of them?

Skip Gerber couldn't say what he'd been contemplating, and as a consequence of his ruminations being elsewhere, he had accepted the unusually heavy, thundercloud-grey overcoat just like that, no hesitation, no questions, no confusion.

He simply allowed someone he'd never seen before in his constantly evolving, and too habitually revolving, days to hand him a coat and say "Here you go, and be very careful with it" in a tone of voice he wouldn't describe as soothing – gravelly, more like.

Why would anyone – he was soon to ask himself innumerable times – take a coat from a complete stranger only because it had been offered? (Foisted off? Unloaded?) Come to that, why would a complete stranger hand him a coat in the first place – as if a night-club patron to a checkroom clerk – and warn him to "be very careful with it"?

When Skip – red-faced as a circus clown with annoyance after realizing what he'd gone and done – tried to return the overcoat to its brash donor, the gesture was futile. The man had boarded the elevator, or Skip assumed he had. The doors had shut behind him and on any other passengers aboard.

Who knows where in the skyscraping Amerongen Building the man was headed? Who knows how time-consuming and complicated it would be for Skip to track down the unasked benefactor and return the blesséd item?

Skip – born Edward Raymond Gerber thirty-seven-years-and-change earlier and nicknamed by Uncle Moe, who got a kick out of his four-year-old nephew skipping all the time – wasn't even certain he could identify the cheeky coat-bestowing bastard. Nor could he count on any of the passengers to verify the culprit. By now they'd all completely dispersed.

Near as Skip could say, the man was of middling height (maybe five-ten, five-eleven), full head of salt-and-pepper hair – Skip was fairly sure of that – had a long face (or was it square-ish), was dressed in a suit and tie. He was of indeterminate age, anywhere between thirty-five and fifty-five, Skip would have estimated.

But screw it all, that description would fit just about every second or third man who charged into or hurtled out of the busy midtown Fifth

Avenue Amerongen Building at any time of the day between 8 am and 8 pm or, for that matter, at odd hours during the late night and early morning.

If pressed further for a police sketch, Skip might have said that in his fleeting glimpse he thinks he noticed the man had a one- or two-day's beard and looked fatigued. But that description, too, could fit almost any of the lean and hungry workaholics populating the no-available-space Amerongen Building.

Middling height? Signs of greying hair? Suit and tie? Thirty-ish? Forty-ish? Workaholic? Good grief, he could have been describing himself, as he often had in his more comically desperate misgiving moments.

All Skip could be sure of – at, checking his knock-off Rolex, 6.21 pm (why buy the real thing when you can get a substitute for so much less?) – was that he hadn't been lumbered with the coat by a woman. Or could it have been a woman gotten up as a man? Probably not. The features he'd scoped for only a split second didn't look as if they were a woman's. No, not a woman's. Skip wouldn't have said that.

Not that he was thinking only about describing the man to anyone as he stood facing the closed elevator doors with the (what's the opposite of "purloined"?) coat in his left hand and his briefcase in his right hand and as people streamed past him or clustered around him waiting for the doors of one or more of the other seven Amerongen Building elevators to part.

Not that he was thinking only of locating the man, either. He was thinking: What the hell! What the hell is this? What the hell do I do now?

Ah-hah, he flashed: ID. There might be some sort of identification in the coat, maybe even a wallet – though he didn't think it was likely. Maybe, failing that, a card saying "If this coat is found, please return to _____ at _____ or call _____ or text _____. Maybe, failing that, a letter addressed to the (disappeared) owner, maybe a name embroidered inside, maybe at least initials, which would give him something, but not much, to go on.

(Skip had read his share of police procedurals and watched them on television enough to understand that having no more information than the manufacturer could serve as enough of a lead.)

He put down his briefcase in order to check the inside of the coat for a haberdasher or a designer. It was double-breasted and made of a sturdy but soft woolen material in an almost imperceptible small herringbone pattern so dark and darker grey it was almost black. The collar and lapels were generously wide. The sleeves ended in wide cuffs and, like the front closings, featured horn buttons. The hem looked as if it would fall just below a man's calves. There was a double seam at the back that, from what Skip could tell, gave it a flare and a flair.

The coat, then, had been smartly styled. At an earlier time, it might have been termed a great coat, or greatcoat, if he was using the word properly. That, in Skip's assessment (which was still rife with agitation), was what rendered it a quality classic. It quietly announced it wasn't just for one cold-weather spell but for many, a big overcoat that would last decades and perhaps had, since it showed only modest indications of wear.

It could be vintage. Yet, there was no label either at the nape of the neck or sewn onto an inside breast pocket that would establish anything of its origin, its provenance, its history – and no evidence that any had been removed.

Skip was taking this in without having stirred from the spot where he'd stopped short. A man brushed by him and said, "*Nice* overcoat you got there." The man kept going a few steps, humming an unidentifiable tune under his breath and giving the impression he was headed to another part of the lobby. He looked back at Skip for a second and threw him a grin reminiscent of Jack Nicholson in *The Shining*, a grin reminiscent of Jack Nicholson in anything.

Skip didn't like it. He didn't like it at all. He liked it even less when the man made a one-hundred-eighty-degree turn, headed back towards the street doors and said, passing Skip for the second time, "Very, *very* nice overcoat. Take good care of it."

Does he think I'm holding it up for display? Skip wondered, as he slipped his right hand into the right-hand front pocket and finding nothing. Or, Skip wondered further, does he have something else in mind? That grin might have suggested the man – who wasn't wearing a suit and tie but a black leather blazer and an open-collar maroon shirt exposing a thick, corded neck – was getting at something else.

It was almost as if the man knew something about the overcoat. Otherwise, why would he say "Take good care of it" right after the first man had made almost the same admonishment?

Did they know each other? Were they in cahoots?

Okay, Skip thought – probing the left-hand front pocket – it's nothing. Why wouldn't he say "Take good care of it." It's a good-looking coat. It deserves good care. This is just a coat that fetches compliments, and that was just a guy who'd come into the building, remembered he'd forgotten something, turned around and, as he left, handed out a bit of friendly advice.

Rummaging in the left-hand front pocket, he felt something soft and something hard. He pulled out the contents. A pair of black kid gloves and an unopened roll of Halls cough drops.

Not too helpful. How many men in Manhattan or visiting Manhattan own black kid gloves? A DNA analysis might definitely point to someone in particular, but Skip wasn't about to get involved with all that. As to the cough drops, what did they convey? That the owner had a cough but had purchased the pack so recently he hadn't had occasion to tear it open yet? That the owner didn't have a cough but was preparing for whenever he might develop one?

Was Skip about to wander through the Amerongen Building floor by floor, listening for a man with a cough – hacking or otherwise? He didn't think so. He returned the gloves and cough drops to the left-hand pocket and resumed his search. Nothing in the breast pocket, either. No wallet anywhere.

But hold it, hold it! The two inside breast pockets each had a double tab secured by two buttons. Skip released the right-hand tab and reached into that pocket. He detected a small rectangular piece of heavy paper that could have been a business card.

He took it out. It was a business card – off-white, printed on one side in a tasteful serif font. (Garamond, Skip thought. Why he couldn't say, and if he were correct, what good would that do him anyway?) On the top line was printed the name "Miles Rogers Havilland," on the second line "Private Consultant," on the third line "9 West Forty-seventh Street, Suite 2200."

That was it – no further information and, when Skip turned the card over, nothing additional on the back other than an ink-stained fingerprint that looked too indistinct, too smeared for corroborating anything.

Skip put the card back in the pocket and invaded the left-hand inside breast pocket with its double tabs and two buttons. These tabs were already undone. He removed a piece of flimsy white composition paper that had been ripped from a larger sheet. It was wrinkled, as if someone had crumpled it up with the intention of discarding it but then decided not to. Or maybe someone had found it and smoothed it out as best he or she could. Written in pencil on it was an address: 1021 Fifth Avenue. Below it, the initials am S.

AM S, Skip thought, A M S. Did anyone's name pop up that might have meaning for him? Nothing occurred to him? Would it be helpful if one did? Then something did come to him: Albert M Schweitzer? Arnold M Schwarzenegger?

That was a big help. One was dead and gone, the other had better things to do than drop a big overcoat on him.

But he did have a start – two starts: two specific addresses. G. d. it, Skip thought, if this guy thinks he can pawn off his coat on me as some stupid kind of practical joke, he'd better think again. I'm not above tracking him to his midtown digs – which happen to be only a five-minute or less walk away – or to his Fifth Avenue crash-pad and returning the bulky item with a curt "Thanks, but no thanks!"

He might even add an equally curt, "Do you think I look like someone who can't buy his own overcoat?"

Knowing where he was bound, Skip draped the coat over his arm and picked up his briefcase. For the first time in the minute or three it had taken him to look through the pockets, he noticed people still eddying around him. He took in that the music floating through the lobby was an easy-listening (Lite-FM?) arrangement of the infectious early nineteen-forties chart-topping "You Are My Sunshine."

As Skip stepped to the weighty bronze-and-glass Amerongen Building doors, humming along with the perky ditty and seeing himself as a wronged man on a mission, he was aware of the overcoat on his arm. It was big, heavy, cumbersome. He'd be better off putting it on.

Yet he hadn't been humming along with "You Are My Sunshine" for more than a few measures – is that the tune the humming man had put in his head? – when the lyrics had him thinking about the weather. Sunny weather. Warm weather. Not greatcoat weather.

Carry the coat? Wear the coat? Carry the coat? Wear the coat? Skip knew from experience – as all men will tell you – that heavy as the coat may be, it would feel lighter worn rather than carried.

He put the briefcase down, put the coat on. When he was holding it up, poking through it, he'd gotten the impression it was a size or two too large for him – but at that, not large enough for Arnold Schwarzenegger's broad shoulders.

At five-feet-ten-inches and one-hundred-seventy-five relatively well-proportioned pounds, Skip normally wore a thirty-eight long suit or overcoat – perhaps, depending on brand idiosyncracies, forty long. But without really giving it much thought, he'd taken the garment for a forty-four long, maybe even a forty-six long.

Now he'd put it on. He'd shrugged his shoulders so the coat would fall comfortably in place. It fit him perfectly. It was as if it had been custom-tailored for him – he hmmmed, not hummed, to himself. It was as if he'd slipped into a bespoke coat, which was something he'd always thought he'd like owning but had never pursued on the assumption he wasn't the kind of man who wears custom-tailored anything.

Still: It is a handsome coat, and I probably look good in it, he thought. Not, he hastened to assure himself, that he intended to keep it. Not that he had any intention of being "very careful with it" for any length of time. He had the two addresses. To unburden himself of the unwanted thing, he'd visit both if he had to. Even if the man who'd palmed it off on him was still in the Amerongen Building and hadn't gone back to the West Forty-seventh Street suite. If he hadn't, Skip would leave it with a receptionist or a secretary – an executive assistant, as they were dubbed nowadays – assuming Miles Rogers Havilland had a receptionist or an executive assistant.

Thinking these things while headed towards the doors, he spotted

Gordon, the lobby man in his gold-trimmed brown uniform. He greeted him and asked, "Gordon, a few minutes ago, did you, uh, notice a man standing by the elevators, um, holding a coat?"

Gordon – whom Skip always credited with high-level job satisfaction for his consistent good nature – said, "You know, I can't say, Mr Gerber. There's lots of men passing by me holding coats, putting coats on, taking coats off. What kind of coat we talking about here?"

Skip felt foolish saying he was now wearing the coat. What would that sound like? He said, "Uh, a coat looking like this one. Give or take."

Gordon took a closer look at the coat. "That's a nice coat, Mr Gerber. Can't say as I've ever seen you in it before. Can't say I seen another one like it here recently. But like I say, lots of coats go through here of a day. Maybe not as many in this weather, but still lots. Why you asking, anyways?"

Skip wasn't ready to answer that one. He couldn't think of a response that wouldn't make him sound, well, *unsound*. He said, "I thought it was someone I knew who I need to find out some information from. Nothing important."

Gordon said, "I tell you what, Mr Gerber. I see a man holding a coat just like that or wearing it, I'll tell him you was looking for him."

"Thanks, Gordon," Skip said. "I appreciate it."

What was he going to say – that Gordon wouldn't see a man wearing a coat just like this one, since this was the one? He picked up his briefcase, pushed one of the Amerongen Building doors open, went through and was almost immediately blinded by the late afternoon sun.

He halted to get his bearings. As he did, he felt the hard impact of another body. "Watch where you're going, bud," warned a husky guy who looked as if he'd played football in high school. Then this fullback in mufti barked with an unmistakable sneer, "What's with the coat? It ain't a bad-looking coat, but you're rushing the season." For what he must have deemed good measure, he punched Skip on his right biceps.

Despite the coat's thickness, Skip felt the uncalled-for blow. Rubbing his arm, he decided to cross Fifth Avenue to the west side of the street. He was smarting from the punch as he stepped off the curb and simultaneously heard the squeal of tires. He looked to his right and saw a black limousine coming towards him.

To avoid it, he leaped backward. The heel of his right foot caught the curb, causing him to fall with a jolt on the pavement. The limo, missing Skip by inches, picked up speed and zoomed past.

As it did, Skip looked up and saw the driver staring straight ahead at the road with a grim and determined look. Through the rolled-down window at the back seat, he saw an older more distinguished man who, Skip would have sworn, was mouthing something while looking (leering?) at him.

What could he be saying? When his mouth was moving, could "overcoat" have been one of the words he was forming? Was it something along the lines of "Take *very* good care of it"?

Coulda been.

Could not 'a been.

Quick, Skip thought as he sat on his bum, which was now additionally padded by the compliment-inviting coat, I'll figure out the make of the car. Who manufactures limousines, anyway? I'll memorize the license plate numbers and letters.

To no avail. The limo turned left into the next cross-town street. It was as gone as the man who'd handed him the coat – as gone as were the devilish grinner in the lobby who'd mock-admired the coat and the lug who'd punched him on the biceps.

Before it vanished, Skip thought he picked out the first letter on the rear plate – F. Big deal. Thousands of New York State license plates begin with an F, Skip happened to know. It was a piece of useless information he'd acquired years back – along with the names of typefaces – but what good did it do him now when he needed it? It was doubly useless.

And what about the black limousine? What about its very existence – how it pulled out going hell-for-leather as he stepped into the street? It was almost as if it were waiting for him. *Was* it waiting for him? *Was* the man at the wheel a seasoned getaway driver? *Was* the man in the back seat leering at him by design?

"Are you all right?" Skip heard. He was so involved with the limo from Hades that he hadn't noticed several people standing around him with fretful looks on their faces – none of them, he noticed, wearing overcoats.

Embarrassed that he was still in full plotzed position, Skip tried to stand but couldn't. Two men offered their hands. He let himself be pulled upright.

"Are you okay?" a second person asked.

"Yes," Skip said, despite his rear-end hurting like hell (never mind the padding), despite his right biceps aching, despite the lightning bolts of pain along the arm he'd put behind him to break the fall, his left arm. He felt obliged to say, "Sorry, I don't know what hit me."

"Don't you mean what didn't hit you?" a woman said. "That car looked like it was coming *right* at you."

"Are you sure no one's after you?" one of the men who helped him up asked. Did they all think that, too? Skip must have pulled a worried face, because the man sniggered and said, front teeth shining in the late afternoon glare, "Just kidding."

But was he? Was he "just kidding"? Was this something to kid about? But who would be after Skip, and why? What had he done to have someone or someones after him? One thing he'd done was accept the overcoat and then put it on, the overcoat he was now rubbing the seat of to brush off any pavement scuzz that had stuck to it in the fall.

"Here," yet another onlooker said, "You dropped this." He handed Skip his briefcase, and Skip had a flash of it flying from his grip as he toppled. Lucky thing it hadn't broken open and sent flying the papers of the unchallenging, downright numbing three contracts he was preparing.

Having anyone pick up your loose professional papers is always an awkward enterprise. But these eye-glazers in particular! He took the briefcase, saying to everyone in general, "I'm okay now. Thanks for your help."

The small crowd disbanded as Skip added sufficient thank-you nods. Before leaving altogether, one of the male Samaritans said with a tilt of his head towards the recently acquired overcoat, "Expecting a sudden drop in temperature?" One of the women said, "You want to take better care of your coat. It's too nice a coat to treat the way you're treating it." Several of them chimed in with remarks about what a handsome coat it was.

Skip saw no reason to respond but once again – this time checking oncoming traffic more vigilantly – stepped off the curb and crossed the street on his three-block journey north along Fifth Avenue.

He reached the other side with no mishaps, but as he was crossing and then as he was walking on the west side of Fifth Avenue sidewalk, he noticed he was doing so with apprehension.

As he thought about it, he could see no convincing reason. Yes, in only a matter of – what was it? five minutes at most – a number of unusual things had happened to him. But even taking into account the acquisition of the coat (he could hardly overlook that), nothing had happened that greatly exceeded mild inconvenience.

As he turned into West Forty-seventh Street, he concluded that if he was sweating – and he was – it wasn't nerves or stress (aside from his high-level everyday stress dosage), it was due to his wearing an overcoat on an Indian-summer day.

But he wouldn't be wearing it for much longer, he reminded himself as he passed several of the sparkling jewelry stores indigenous to the area – the Diamond Center.

Could the coat belong to a diamond dealer? Is that where he was heading? If it did, and there'd been a diamond or two in one of its pockets, that might have been a different story. He patted the pockets again. No diamonds he could ascertain.

No diamond dealer either. Not from the look of 9 West Forty-seventh Street as he reached it and entered a building that resembled any one of a hundred or more buildings in the area without trayfuls of precious gems in their ground-floor shop windows.

Through the metal-and-glass double-doors was a small marble-faced lobby. Directly ahead of Skip on a wall was a directory, one of those black ones into the grooves of which white plastic letters are pushed, sometimes letters from different letter sets. He stopped to look at it. He pulled out the business card to check the name on it against whatever he found on the directory – Miles Rogers Havilland.

He ran his eyes down to the H block. No Havilland. Nor was there any Miles among the Ms or Rogers among the Rs.

Doesn't mean Miles Rogers Havilland isn't here, Skip told himself. He knew commercial real estate and knew how often directories are neglected in these Class B and Class C buildings. Tenants come and go, and often building managers don't get around to updating the directory for months at a time, years.

He turned right a few steps and walked round to two elevators on his left. He pushed the up button. The changing numbers above both elevators' doors – with their wrought-metal, half-circle scrolling – indicated they were going up.

Skip waited until they came down, passing time by betting with himself which would arrive first. Initially, it appeared as if the right elevator would win the competition Skip had concocted. Then the left one seemed to be overtaking the right. Skip put his imaginary money on the right one to regain the lead.

The left one arrived first. Why do I always get the elevator race wrong, Skip asked himself, just like I always get on the slowest supermarket line? Just like I'm getting so much else wrong lately. Whatever happened to my old self? He's gotta be somewhere. What I wouldn't do to get that guy back.

When the doors and then the gate of the left elevator opened, five passengers came out – none with an overcoat to pass off and leaving inside, sitting on a worn metal stool, an elevator operator in a shabby light-grey jacket with soiled white piping.

"Floor?" he said in a bored tone, while Skip – the only one getting on – noticed the operator's jacket was too large for him. Obviously, it was the musty one-size-may-or-may-not-fit-all jacket that the building's elevator operators shared.

"Twenty-second floor," Skip said.

"Twenty-second, it is," the elevator operator said with a slightly heightened lilt. The two rode in a silence broken only by the click of the floors as they went past at a drugged snail's pace. "Floor twenty-two," the elevator operator announced finally and stopped rotating the handle of the lifting apparatus. Taking his sweet time, he pulled open the metal gate and then the doors.

"Thanks," Skip, alighting, said.

"No problem," the elevator operator said as if it had been at the very least a slight problem. Closing the doors and gate as Skip was looking around for Suite 2200, he offered, "Nice overcoat. I like to say so whenever I see one like it."

Then he was gone. What did he mean by that – by "whenever I see one like it" – Skip wondered. How often does he see one like it? Skip answered himself. He's working in a building populated by businessmen. He probably sees them in overcoats like this – or enough like this – to "like," maybe go so far as covet, the kind of overcoat he may not have the wherewithal to buy, even in a resale shop.

Skip let the thought go. He had bigger fish to fry. He'd spotted Suite 2200 just to the left of the elevator and had gone to stand before its door – a wooden door with an unwashed glass panel in its upper half.

Old-fashioned, Skip registered, which was beside the point, really, since on the door were only the remains of letters that for the most part had been scratched out. Not the words "Suite 2200" but the name on the door and the description of whatever services were, or had been, rendered inside.

What was left on the top line looked as if it could have been three names adding up to "Miles Rogers Havilland" but not necessarily. On the line under it, Skip could make nothing out. It looked like either one or two words that could have been anything from "Claims Adjuster" to "County Sheriff" to "Dog Catcher."

Skip doubted it was any of those, nor could he infer anything from what he saw through the window, other than there seemed to be two rooms, possibly more. The room immediately inside the door looked as if it could have been a waiting-room with a place for a receptionist's desk, and behind it, through an open inner door, he could see what must be a larger office space.

But as for a purpose to which the rooms were put, anyone's guess was as good as Skip's. From what he could tell, both rooms were empty. Not quite. A lone piece of furniture stood in the first room, placed in a corner. It was a wooden coat rack, also old-fashioned. It rested on three wooden feet, was about five feet high with six curving wooden arms reaching out like tendrils. It was the type of coat rack that could have been purchased at any time in the first decades of the twentieth century.

Could that weathered coat rack have been one on which, regularly or occasionally, had been draped the overcoat Skip wore?

No way to know. No way to know anything, Skip thought, although he did something he judged stupid even as he did it. He knocked on the door. Virtually certain there was no one inside, he still thought that if there were the slimmest chance of someone's being inside, his not trying to find out would be a mistake.

There was no response to his first knock. He knocked again, and then, even stupider, he tried turning the doorknob. To his surprise and unease, the door opened but, Skip was pleased to note, didn't creak. He entered, still saw nothing but the coat rack in the outer room. He went into the second room and caught sight of something. On the floor – the floorboards of which were worn almost white in some places – and not visible from the front door was a telephone with a rotary dial.

He put his briefcase down and picked up the rotary phone – a rotary phone with a rotary-phone dial in the center of which whatever number had been there was now only scratches made by a sharp object. A pin? A penknife? A letter-opener? The blade of a pair of scissors?

Skip was speculating on that when something odd happened. The phone rang. The obsolete phone in the empty office rang and rang so loudly that he almost dropped it. What was Skip to do? He lifted the receiver on the third ring and said an affectless, "Hello."

"Your overcoat is ready," a man's gruff voice said.

At least, that's what Skip thought the gruff-voiced man said. The words were garbled and seemed to be spoken in a foreign accent. Eastern European? Russian? "Who is this?" Skip asked. "What number are you calling?"

"Your overcoat is ready," the voice said again, thickly. Or had it said, "The older cat is shedding"? Or "The other colt is reddish"? Or "You can't get over that, Randy?"

Skip couldn't be sure.

"Who's this?" he repeated, but all he heard was the click of whoever was at the other end hanging up. He held the receiver away from him and turned slightly. As he did, he saw something else in the room. It was a battered wire wastebasket with something in it.

He put the phone back on the floor and went over to remove whatever it was. He held up part of a yellowed page torn from a newspaper. A New York City newspaper, but which one? Weren't there nine dailies back when it looked as if these two deserted rooms were last occupied?

There was enough of the right-hand side of a right-hand page for Skip to see it was from an August 23, 1925 edition, page 17. But from the *Times*, the *Trib*, the *Daily News*, the *Journal*, the *Herald*? From the what? Good as he was on fonts, he wasn't that much up on typefaces used by newspapers, some of them long-defunct, to know.

He ran his eye over the news stories but was almost immediately distracted from them by an advertisement in the lower right-hand corner. Prominent in it was an illustration, an overcoat that didn't look enough like the one Skip had on to be the same model – for one difference it was single-breasted – but it was close in several other styling details.

The copy read "Top quality for only $79." Expensive for the time, Skip thought. He looked to the bottom of the ad for the name of the store or manufacturer and the address. That information had been torn off, as if – could there even be another explanation? – whoever tore out the page had then torn away the name and location to follow up on. All that was left were the tops of two letters. The first could – *maybe* – have been a capital "I" or "J" or "L," the second a capital "C" or "S."

Lacking further details, Skip wondered what he was inclined to do next. What he was inclined to do was pocket the ad – it went into the right-hand pocket – and get out of the office to head uptown for 1021 Fifth Avenue.

What had he learned, anyway? The only occurrences had been the sighting of a coat rack on which the coat he was wearing had possibly hung, a possibly coat-related phone call on an antique phone and a possibly, if only partially, enlightening advertisement.

He left the office – which had been no more than a tease – closing the door behind him. Noting that the click accompanying the door as it was pulled to close sounded ominous, he went to the elevator and pushed the button with purpose.

While waiting for one of the cars to arrive, he checked the make-believe Rolex – 6.46 pm. He also replayed what had just happened. For some reason, the incident had a familiar ring to it – not a telephone ring, a *déjà vu* ring. Ah, that was it. It was as if he'd just played a scene from a '40s *film noir*, something Humphrey Bogart could have starred in.

I've been thrust into an old movie, Skip thought. A thriller. The Case of the Big Overcoat. Funny thought, too, Skip mused. More interesting than anything else that's happened to me lately.

He had a hearty laugh at that and thought, That's the first good laugh I've had in a while – in too long.

The thought passed when, a minute later, at 6.47 phony Rolex time, one of the elevator cars got to him. It was the right elevator, on which he hadn't bet with himself this time.

The laugh had precluded the bet.

When the elevator doors and gate opened, the elevator operator was the same bored-to-near-catatonia employee who'd previously been in the left elevator. Or was he a twin? What could that mean? If he was a twin, he was also shrinking in a jacket too large for him.

Skip entered, noticing that the elevator operator looked at him with no sign of recognition. "Excuse me," Skip said, while the car began descending, "can you tell me anything about Suite 2200?"

Bogey would have done the same thing, Skip thought and was amused again. Indeed, he not only amused himself, but as he did, he felt something flow through his body. Unidentifiable at first, and then it came to him. I think they call this a *frisson*, he said to himself, and as far as I can tell, I've never had one before – or if I have, it's been so long, I don't remember when.

While he was – what? – enjoying, yes, actually enjoying this frisson, he heard the elevator man reply to his Suite 2200 question. "Like, what do you want to, like, know?" the elevator man said in the bored-out-of-his-gourd tone with which Skip was now familiar.

"Like who the occupant is or was?" Skip continued, Bogey-style.

"No idea," the elevator operator said without turning to Skip. "Somebody – I forget who – once said something about it being a limestone commission headquarters. Whatever that is. But I'm only here a few years, and as far as I know, that space has always been empty. People look at it a lot, but no one ever takes it, as I guess you saw. There's people in and out of here all the time."

"What people?" Skip asked.

"That, I couldn't tell you," the elevator operator said, still gazing in front of him at the gilt-lined, burled wooden elevator wall as if he'd never seen it before. "People like you look at it. You know, the kind of people who want to rent space in a building like this. I never ask them. It's not my job."

He'd reached the ground floor. He said, "This is my job." He pulled the gate back noisily and the doors parted. Skip realized it was his cue to get out. He did and said thanks.

"No problem," the elevator operator said and, "Nice coat. The kind of coat you want to take good care of." He remained sitting on his metal stool with the gate and doors open, since no one was getting on and apparently no one from a floor above had called.

Skip went towards the door to the building. He opened it and stepped out about two feet when another question for the elevator operator crossed his mind, He turned on his heel and stepped back inside to quiz the elevator operator on the additional query.

As he did, he heard through the doors the reverberating sound of something hitting the pavement outside – something crashing into the pavement that he was all but certain would have crashed into him had he not retreated when he did.

For a second, he stood where he was, patting himself with his left hand just to make certain he was all right. Then he swung round again. As he did, he saw a few pedestrians running up to look at the fallen and now shattered object. One of them was wiggling a pinkie-ringed pinkie finger in one ear, as if quelling tinnitus started by the reverberant sound of stone on concrete.

Skip pushed open the door to join them.

They and he were peering at several scattered parts of something. "It's a gargoyle," one of them said. Another added, "A limestone gargoyle." It clearly was a gargoyle, a limestone gargoyle.

(Hadn't Skip just heard the word "limestone"? Isn't life filled with those kinds of peculiar coincidences?)

One half of the limestone gargoyle's body, perched on a thick pedestal with its frightening taloned feet, rested not too many inches from the other half of the body, which had, protruding from the back, a pair of narrow triangular wings. The gargoyle's head had rolled about a foot from both sections of its cruelly severed body. It was still wobbling a bit, but as Skip and his fellow witnesses watched, it stopped, face up.

It glared at them from eyes that suggested this was a gargoyle with an enlarged thyroid. Just as compelling, if not more, was the wide, blubber-lipped mouth. From under a flattened nose, it featured a blood-chilling grimace.

It was a grimace Skip thought he'd seen recently. But where? He knew where. It was the look he'd had from the bruiser in the Amerongen Building lobby and from the man focusing on him from the back of the speeding automobile. It was a look that cautioned, I know something about you, it's not good, and I'm going to do something about that. It was a look that accompanied the "heh heh heh!" of every mustachio-twirling villain in a nineteenth-century melodrama.

But what could be known about Skip that couldn't have been known before this last forty-five or so minutes? And why had this gargoyle seemed to have swooped at him on those two stone wings?

As that thought hit him, he looked up – so did the others, as if in soundless harmony – to see from where the gargoyle came. He and they (and other passers-by, too, wondering what was so interesting above that they had to look) saw a row of gargoyles poking out from just below the building's cornice.

One was missing, of course. No, it looked as if there were spots where gargoyles had been and were now missing. Also missing in Skip's view was any vantage point from which a gargoyle could be pushed or – were a very strong man involved – dropped.

His edgy reverie was interrupted by the elevator man (one of the two elevator men?) who'd come out of the building but hardly on the run. Skip looked at him more imploringly than he would have liked.

"Uh-oh, not another one," the elevator man offered.

"Another one?" the bunch of them sang more or less in unison.

"There was another one, like, recently," the elevator man said.

"You'd think they were migrating south for the winter and lost their bearings," one of Skip's companions inserted, pointing up towards the roof.

"Yeah," the elevator man said without looking up. "The other one fell about this time, too, about three weeks back, but no one was, like, hit. The building management has been talking about seeing to it. Listen, gargoyles are falling all over town. They been at the tops of buildings too long. Age. The weather."

"All over town?" Skip said.

"That's what you hear," the elevator man said. "Other buildings in this neighborhood. I haven't seen them. So I can't say." He looked at the fallen gargoyle again. "I, like, gotta go do something about this. Get the janitor or something. If he's even here."

Without further ceremony, he went back in.

His departure ended the fallen-gargoyle-gazing gathering. The others split off but not without individually and collectively mentioning they admired Skip's overcoat. As they did, they looked around them – and, more to the point, at the surrounding buildings – to make as sure as they could that they were out of harm's way.

Skip was too shaken to move off entirely yet. But in order to think in some safety, he did step under the overhang provided by the receded doors.

Was he safe? he asked himself. If a gargoyle had fallen from 9 West Forty-seventh Street once before, then he couldn't be the target, could he? If they were falling all over town, he'd be even less likely the object of something or another.

Or were the unmoored gargoyles related?

And where did the overcoat, he once again remembered he was wearing – and in which he was now perspiring profusely – fit in? If, while fitting him so commodiously, it did fit in. What was the reason, if there was one, for his current ownership of it?

But wait. Something occurred to him and it was this: What would Bogart do in this situation? Were he Sam Spade, would he worry about his safety?

As Skip Gerber, he undoubtedly would, but, he suddenly realized, being the recent and not-so-recent Skip Gerber had begun to wear on him recently. Why not do something about it? Why not take something

– whatever it was – in his own hands? Or was he already doing exactly that?

He, Skip Gerber, had the Fifth Avenue address, didn't he? He – not Humphrey Bogart, not William Holden, not Harrison Ford, not Matt Damon – would go there. That had to be where he'd find out if and why the wool was being pulled over his eyes, no matter how rich the well-cut wool from which the coat on his back had been constructed.

He ran a hand down the coat's front. It was very supple, the kind of inviting suppleness top-grade material acquires over time.

Giving the broken gargoyle one last gaze and retreating from it, Skip headed towards Upper Fifth Avenue, where, he believed, gargoyles were scarce. Off he trotted to Madison Avenue and a cab, feeling the weight of the overcoat as he did.

He reached Mad Ave, where men dressed like him – but overcoatless – jostled and jockeyed for taxi-flagging positions. Overcoatless women in suits did the same. He waved at a cab someone in front of him grabbed. He waved at another and another, only to be outdone. On the fifth try, an unoccupied cab swerved towards him, cutting off another cab.

Is he coming *for* me or *at* me? Skip wondered.

For him, evidently, because the driver made a graceful last-second careering maneuver, placing the back door right where Skip stood but with sufficient space for Skip to open it.

He climbed in and – when the cabbie said, "Where to, Mister?" – commanded "Straight up Madison Avenue" in a tone he didn't entirely recognize.

(Was it his from a long time back?)

"How far straight up?" the cabbie asked with the merest soupcon of attitude.

"Good question," Skip said, a feeling of magnanimity flowing through him now that he was comfortably settled. "I'm trying to get to 1021 Fifth Avenue. Do you have any idea what's the best cross street?"

"Happens I do," the cabbie said. "East Eighty-third Street."

The answer came so swiftly at Skip in the cabbie's Bronx-thickened speech that he looked more closely at the back of the man's head and what he could see of the profile. He saw curly black hair with only some grey strands in it that flowed over the collar of a bold orange-red-and-green jacket. He saw a low brow, a nose like a baby squash, fat lips, not much of an unshaved chin.

"Okay, my good man, let me off at Madison and Eighty-third," Skip said. (Where, in heaven's name, did the "my man" come from? Skip mused. Had Bogie ever said it wryly? Or William Powell as Nick Charles?) "You really know this town, don't you? I ask you the best uptown cross street. You have the answer at the ready."

The driver had stopped at a red light. He turned to Skip and said, "You won't believe this, but you're not the first dude asked me about that address. Anyways, I think it was that address – or something close to that address."

"What?" Skip asked.

"Swear on my daughter's life," the cabbie said. "You drive a tub like this long enough, you realize it's a town full of coincidences. I can't begin to tell you how many times I've picked up the same people in different parts of town going to the some address I took someone the day before or the day before that."

The light changed, and the cabbie pushed on through the not-so-helpful late-ish rush-hour traffic. "That's right, Mister. I'd say at least three times in the last month, maybe month and a half, two months at the outside, I had fares heading to 1021 Fifth Avenue, I'm pretty sure that's what they said. So I finally figured out the best cross-town street is East Eighty-third. Guys that looked like you, too. Nice-looking fellas in suits, wearing overcoats like you got on or, in really warm weather, carrying them. Then again, this time of day on the East Side, what you mostly pick up is businessmen. Or women. What line of business you in, anyway?"

Skip was thinking about the cabbie having numerous fares aiming to 1021 Fifth Avenue. With overcoats. "I'm sorry?" he said.

"I asked what business you're in."

Skip was still thinking. Sure, it could be coincidence, but what if it wasn't? But what if it was? But what if it wasn't?

They'd come to another red light. "You don't know what business you're in?" the cabbie persisted, turning around to give Skip the fish-eye.

"Oh," Skip said, still distracted. "Lawyer. Real estate law."

"Has to be interesting," the cabbie said. "I'm interested in real estate. Who isn't? Not that I have any."

"Sometimes it's interesting," Skip permitted, "sometimes it's just boring." Skip didn't like lawyers who talked about law being boring. This didn't mean he wasn't bored with it himself. Good as he was at it – and perhaps that was the problem – he was (often?) bored to distraction by it. As a matter of fact, at that particular moment, he felt he was as bored with it as he maybe had ever been.

Was he so bored he'd begun to look to others like the elevator man at 9 West Forty-seventh Street looked to him?

God forbid.

He wanted to cut short any idle banter on the subject. Part of it was that something disturbing was taking place outside the cab. He'd noticed that at the red light, they were next to a black limousine from which he was being watched by both the driver and the male occupant in the back seat.

He was almost certain he'd seen them before. They looked like the same two men in the limousine that had nearly run him over on Fifth Avenue. Uh, they seemed to be watching him, and they seemed to be the same two men. He was *almost* certain but not *absolutely* certain.

The light changed, and the cabbie, eyes once again on the avenue, pulled out. So did the suspicious limo, and as it did, the man in the back seat was mouthing something as he had before – or as the other man, who Skip thought could be this man, did.

Am I being followed by a black limousine or a fleet of them? Skip asked himself. If he were – if someone were on his trail, on his tail – what should he do, and how could the cabbie help? And if he were being followed by a limousine or, wow, a fleet of them, wasn't there something *exciting* about it?

Hey: *frisson nombre deux.*

Should Skip ask the cabbie to speed up or hang back? He imagined himself saying – as they do in the movies that not only Bogart made but all those endless others – something like "I'm being followed by that car. Can you lose it?" But he couldn't imagine himself actually saying it.

What he did say to the cabbie was – thinking it a clever ad lib – "See the black limousine just ahead of us? I think the driver is drunk or something. I know the traffic is dodgy, but why don't you just let it get ahead of us?"

Then – oh, what the hell? – he outright said, "Or it may be following us. Can you lose it?"

"Yeah, I noticed it," the cabbie said. "I notice a shitload of limos on Madison Avenue this time of day, but I didn't see the driver was under the influence. But anything you say. You're the boss."

"Just to be on the safe side," Skip said.

"You're never safe from those mothers," the cabbie said. "I always keep an eye out for them."

Skip had a thought. "Do you ever notice their license plate numbers?" he asked. "Like the one I'm talking about? You didn't get it by any chance, did you?"

"You one of those license plate freaks?" the cabbie asked. "I get a lot of them in this boat, too. No. Me, I know cars. I could care less about license plates – unless they cut me off. Then I look at them and make a mental note. Don't do much about it, though. Who has the time?"

Skip wished the black limo had cut them off. That way, should he need it – he might, who knows? – he'd have a license plate number, thanks to the cabbie. But it had disappeared, something the cabbie must have seen to while Skip was thinking license plate numbers.

The cab was nearing Eighty-third Street. "Right or left side?" the cabbie said, and then again, "Right or left side? You must want the left, if you're going to Fifth. Or I could make the turn. The street goes west."

Skip said, "Leave me at the near corner. That'll be fine."

The cab stopped. Skip got his wallet out of his inside right-hand breast pocket. It was an Alfred Dunhill and not something he'd have bought for himself. It had been a gift some years back from someone. He'd forgotten who. One of his ex-girlfriends, probably.

Not Faye. Faye Reisbach. The current squeeze. All right, she was more than that. His fiancée. His *sort of* fiancée.

Realizing he was flush with cash, he didn't know whether he should be eased or nervous in the circumstances.

Maybe he should be exhilarated.

Why not?

He pulled out a twenty, handed it to the cabbie and told him to keep the change. The cabbie thanked him.

Skip got out, looking around to check if a black limousine was anywhere to be seen.

Nothing. Nowhere.

He started towards Fifth Avenue, once again aware of the overcoat's heft and thinking he'd soon be rid of it. Buoyed by the prospect and those recent inaugural frissons, he quickened his pace. Light was fading and shadows he might not have found portentous on any other early fall evening made him quicken his pace that much more.

On this typical elegant Upper East Side street, he saw nothing out of the ordinary, but he heard something – a weird melody as if from an organ grinder. Wait a sec. He knew the tune – "The Theme from 'Never on Sunday.'" It was his cellphone. He'd brought it with him, after all.

He pushed back the overcoat, which he'd never bothered to button, and reached into the left breast pocket of his suit (Adolfo, purchased at Century 21, a few years old now), pulled the cellphone out and, before he clicked, noticed the caller ID...

Faye Ever-loving Reisbach, the fiancée, or, more precisely, the fiancée by what he and, he imagined, several of their friends took to be tacit agreement. Faye Reisbach, about whom his feelings could be so mixed that they all but blurred.

He knew why she was calling. He was supposed to meet her. Was that what he was thinking about when the elevator was on its way to the Amerongen Building lobby? Maybe, maybe not.

Nonetheless, he knew he was supposed to meet her at a hot new restaurant she'd discovered called, of all things, La Rochefoucauld, where she couldn't wait to be relegated to the bar for an unendurable period of time by a haughty hostess biding her time before snootily informing them that their reserved table was now ready,

He activated the cellphone and said with as much firm nonchalance as he could, "Hello."

"Where are you?" Faye poured into his ear. "You were supposed to be here half an hour ago."

"Complications," Skip said as he continued towards Fifth Avenue and passed another pedestrian speaking into a cellphone.

"What complications?" Faye demanded.

"Nothing important," Skip said, "but too complicated to explain right now."

"If it's not important, how can it be too complic–," Faye started to say, but Skip headed her off.

"Doesn't matter, "Skip said. "It should be cleared up in a matter of minutes. Then I'll catch a cab and be right with you." He was calculating that if he could pass the coat back to its audacious owner or even to a doorman, he could flag a taxi and get to the restaurant on East Sixty-fifth Street with all due alacrity, overcoat adventure over, normal life resuming, Faye presiding.

He pictured her long auburn hair flowing over the shoulders of whatever tailored Chanel or Armani suit she had on. He could hear her tapping the toe of a stiletto-heeled shoe on a polished floor. She'd be darting silent this-is-wacked-out signals at Brenda and Bob Hartley, the couple with whom they were dining.

"Step on it," he heard Faye saying. "We could lose the table, and we had to book too far in advance to have that happen."

Through the cellphone, Skip was certain the nasal voice he was hearing above the background din – the clink of glasses, a pianist diligently resurrecting standards – belonged to Brenda Hartley. "Don't worry," he said. "I'll be there before Bob has the chance to order his second Dewar's on the rocks."

"Straight up," Faye said, easing up on him enough to laugh her peanut-brittle laugh.

"Straight up," Skip said. "Let me go now."

She articulated some sort of agreement, and they both hung up.

As he slipped the cellphone back into the breast pocket from which he'd retrieved it, he rounded onto Fifth Avenue, checking for the marquees and marquee-less doorways.

What he found included a few prewar residential buildings flanking a post-war residential building with a hardly traditional entrance set back from the street by several magisterial (or so some architect must have thought) yards. Casting his glance wider, he took in the Metropolitan Museum of Art, directly across the street, hulking and brooding, even slightly menacing now that it was closed for the day.

What he didn't find in the immediate cityscape was 1021 Fifth Avenue. Near as he could tell there was no 1021 Fifth Avenue. Perhaps, there once *had been* a 1021 Fifth Avenue in a gentle, more pleasingly esthetic time before sedate, not to say, characterless high-rises and the few not-so-sedate high-rises became the *de rigueur* Upper Fifth Avenue thing.

But there wasn't one now. No extant 1021 Fifth Avenue Skip could locate. Perhaps he was mistaken. Perhaps he'd misread the address on the slip of paper he'd found. He reached into the pocket where he'd replaced it, pulled it out and re-read: 1021 Fifth Avenue. There was no mistaking it. Even though the address was written in pencil and therefore could potentially smudge, it hadn't smudged.

Reluctant to accept the confirmation, he walked the length of the block and back again and then back again. No satisfaction. He was beginning to cover the ground yet again, when, passing the post-war, set-back-entrance building, he heard, "Hey, fella."

A doorman in blue livery was talking.

Skip stopped and pointed at himself. "Me?"

"Yes, you," the doorman, who was broad as a boiler, said. "You looking for something on that slip of paper?"

Skip was embarrassed at being caught casing the area by a doorman who clearly regarded himself as an Upper Fifth Avenue vigilante. Nonetheless, he was not to be taken as unsure in any way. No private eye would. So he said with authority, "Why, yes, I'm looking for 1021 Fifth Avenue, but it doesn't seem to be here."

"Or anywhere *near* here," the doorman said with a smile Skip thought was almost a sneer but not quite. "Not for a while, anyway, but you'd be surprised how many people come looking for it."

That took Skip aback, whatever posture "aback" is supposed to assume. "Come looking for 1021 Fifth?" he asked.

"Yeah," the doorman said, "but they're just a few years too late, and by that I mean a few decades. There's no 1021 Fifth Avenue now. There was once." Skip must have screwed up his face in a way signaling gentlemanly confusion. "Yeah, before it was torn down to make room for this monstrosity."

The doorman aimed a gloved thumb at the building behind him. "I know, I know. I should have more respect for the building I'm looking out for, but I've never cared for it. Don't get me wrong. I like the people here – most of them, some of the others are doozies – but the building's no arc-y-techur-al beauty, wouldn't you say?"

Skip hadn't paid much attention to the entire building, he was that wound up with the one he'd hoped to find at 1021 Fifth Avenue. Out of the politeness of the architecturally uninformed, he started to look at it more broadly.

The doorman cut in. "Nope, it's no beauty, and the developers who put up this pile of rocks knew that. You can't see them from here, but there's a line of photographs in the lobby showing the former row of old-time buildings. The two corner ones were originally robber-baron mansions. They tore the ones on this site down to build this place. In the photos there's a house that says 1021 above the old-fashioned door. Maybe hanging up old pictures makes the developers feel better about themselves."

The information was interesting to Skip, but he could feel his mind boggling over what he could or should do with it. He didn't get far into sorting out the challenge when the doorman, squaring his epauletted shoulders to make himself even more commanding, said, "You might think a doorman wouldn't be interested in these things, but I am, and I do have a fair amount of time on my hands during the quieter hours. I've looked at the writing under these photographs. Many times. You might want to read 'em, too. Others going in and outta here have."

Skip had nothing to lose and thought he'd better take advantage of anything that might help him get the God-forsaken (or forsaken by someone other than God) overcoat back to its owner.

"Sure," he said, "yes, okay. Definitely."

Whereupon the doorman gave a small bow and a wave of his gloved hand to show Skip in, then made a couple of fast steps to precede him. Skip went in and down a short corridor where, opposite the elevators, hung six framed turn-of-the-century photographs.

"Take your time," the doorman said. "I better get back to the door."

Sure enough, the photographs showed a stretch of an Upper Manhattan block during the four seasons. The trees in front of the buildings were snow-covered or had leaves on them. In one there were flowers blooming in large pots on austere stoops. Men in top hats and women in long skirts glided along the sidewalks.

The captions beneath them, typed on what Skip took to be an old machine, claimed the photographs had been taken between 1893 and 1907. Skip had no reason to doubt the dates.

One photograph and its caption was of particular interest: "Among the residents on the block was the financier Ambrosius Manley Sturtivant, who lived at 1021 Fifth Avenue. Mr Sturtivant's philanthropies were many and are the reason for a statue of him having been erected along the Central Park Mall in 1937."

Still holding the slip of paper, Skip said to himself, "Ambrosius Manley Sturtivant." He looked at the paper. "AMS," he read again. "AMS. Ambrosius Manley Sturtivant. Could be. Maybe not, but maybe. No, must be."

Realizing he wouldn't be leaving the overcoat at any of the premises on this block – surely not with the friendly but on the *qui vive* doorman here – he figured that perhaps, though it was a long shot, he ought to take the hint and check further into Ambrosius Manley Sturtivant. What else did he have to go on, and what better place to start than by taking a gander at the designated statue?

Consulting his cut-rate homage to Rolex, he saw it was 7.10 pm, and the outside light was fading fast. Skip determined he'd hustle as quickly as he could – that is, as quickly as he could in the overcoat – down to the Mall ten or twelve blocks south and locate the (presumably) bronze Ambrosius Manley Sturtivant.

He double-checked the caption to make sure he had registered the info correctly, turned on his somewhat worn-down tassel-loafer heel and left the building, thanking the doorman as he departed.

"Don't mention it," the doorman said, and touched the bill of his cap with his right index finger. As Skip quick-stepped across the sidewalk to the curb, the doorman called after him, "By the way, it's the one closest to the Naumberg Bandshell."

What does he mean by that? Skip wondered for the split second before what was meant struck him. Dummy, he means the statue. Must be that many people – maybe all, maybe just some – seeing those photographs for the first time head immediately to scope out Ambrosius Manley Sturtivant. The doorman must be used to giving helpful directions. He knew not only to specify the bandshell but to identify it as the Naumberg Bandshell.

As he was going, but, having taken in the earlier lesson on crossing streets without looking first, he did look both ways: two Fifth Avenue buses – one already pulled into a stop at the Metropolitan Museum of Art; myriad cabs, occupied and empty; no suspicious cars, although he was becoming unsure about what he should deem suspicious and what he could comfortably disregard.

The light at Eighty-fourth Street was red. By all accounts, it was okay to cross mid-block even though he'd have to weave through the stopped traffic. He began weaving and was pivoting between two cabs when the one in front of him bumped backward at the same time as the one behind him bumped forward – as if responding in a taxi-cab square-dance *chassée*.

"Hold it," Skip hooted, realizing that if either of the cabs had leapt another six inches, he'd have been leg granola. What are the chances of such an occurrence? he wondered as he edged out from between the cabs and heard a voice yelling over the noise of exhaust and distant honking, "Hello, man in the big-deal coat, watch where you're going!" and another voice shouting, "You wanna get killed, asshole?"

No, he didn't want to get killed. It's what he very definitely *didn't* want. He was on the go here. He was out to accomplish something, and he meant to do it – whatever "it" was.

But did someone else have a different plan for him? He turned to look into the cabs, and saw two cabbies glaring at him. In the back seat of one, a man and a woman locked in an embrace were giving him a pair of what looked like matching sneers.

The thought that went through his jarred mind as he bounded to the Met Museum side of the street was that he'd never been sneered at so often in his life – and such concentrated sneers, as if fiery vengeance was behind every one.

Then again, how many men on missions get used to being sneered at? He didn't know, but he was going to be among them.

Gaining the sidewalk and its milling pedestrians, he stopped to pull himself together and to give some consideration as to how he would travel the ten or slightly more blocks to the Central Park Mall. Should he walk straight down Fifth Avenue, where every passing car would be able to see him – watch him, if that's what, to his bafflement, was taking place? Or when he reached the park entrance at the Met's south end, should he take advantage of it and, in the gathering darkness, enter and leave himself exposed to anyone who might be lying in wait?

For what? For him, because he was wearing the unasked-for overcoat? Because he'd taken the thing? For him, because he was who he was and, for some reason, had suddenly acquired a high-sneerability quotient? For him, because who-knows-what?

Unable to decide, but vaguely invigorated by the developments, he chalked the indecision up to a renewed ringing in his ears. Oh, right, his cellphone. Faye. "Hello."

"Where are you?" she asked in an agitated tone Skip had heard before – and not just during the previous phone call. "The Hartleys are becoming impatient. So am I."

Skip imagined her holding – in the hand that wasn't holding her cellphone – whatever substantial earring she'd removed before making the call. He said, "It's taking longer to wrap things up than I thought. Why don't you claim the table and order? I'll be there as soon as I can."

"As soon as you can isn't soon enough," Faye retorted, "but all right."

"I'll wrap things up," Skip said and rang off but not without hearing Faye start to say something sharpish to the Hartleys. About whom he wasn't that crazy. She was okay, but he – Bob Hartley, who only knew to go on and on about hedge funds.

Yet, the word "wrap" he'd just used gave Skip an idea. He saw himself "wrapped" in the overcoat, and thought he could easily wrap things up by unwrapping himself. He could end his unexpected idyll right there.

He'd come to the park entrance, and without thinking, he'd walked through it. Now that he had, he looked for a bench – not to sit and think but as a handy place to drape an overcoat. Because he'd had a hasty thought: He could just leave the coat here and head directly to trendy La Rochefoucauld, join Faye, the Hartleys, the jolly hedge-fund badinage.

He saw what he was after not twenty-five feet into the park and just outside the children's playground. Making a beeline for it, he took the coat off – it's a heavy mother, he thought – and on the bench (one in a series of only slightly battered park benches with metal memorial tags on them) he folded the coat carefully and, hey presto!, placed it just so.

Now he could walk towards Ambrosius Manley Sturtivant with his briefcase and without a care. But why even walk towards Ambrosius Manley Sturtivant? He was only interested in Ambrosius Manley Sturtivant in relation to the unwanted apparel no longer in his possession, the unwanted apparel he'd conveniently discarded.

Relieved of it, he could retrace his steps to Fifth Avenue, hop into a southbound cab and, yes, greet Faye and the Hartleys, Brenda and Bob, at hoity-toity La Rochefoucauld.

But what's this? He had to acknowledge that joining Faye and the Hartleys, Brenda and Bob, wasn't want he wanted most in the world to do. Or, for that matter, joining Faye were she alone. Some days – and this was turning into one of them – he didn't know what he wanted for himself, what he wanted for the Skip Gerber he'd become.

No, he didn't want the @#.!x?c!*^& coat. That was for sure. He was glad to be rid – uh, relieved – of it. Let somebody else see what light Ambrosius Manley Sturtivant might shed on its origins.

But on the other hand, he found himself thinking, Now I have no excuse not to join Faye, no reason not to get to the contracts I have in my briefcase – the one revising the earlier one inherited from Dad regarding reevaluation of the land leased by the forty-eight-story East Fiftieth Street office building; the one regarding the hotel sale where the buyers are repeatedly delaying the closing for who-knows-what suspicious reasons; the one covering the West Seventy-first Street brownstone where the sellers aren't living up to their commitment to vacate the building.

He thought, Each different from the others, and yet each a variation on exceedingly familiar... Interrupting himself, he had a contrasting thought about what the effect of acquiring the coat was having on him that had nothing to do with Faye Reisbach...

He didn't complete that sentence in his head either. Instead, he halted in his tracks on the other side of a stone underpass he'd just sauntered through, trying to figure out what in hell he did want. While thinking it through, he was slowly tuning into a voice coming towards him. When he had, he heard, "Mister! Mister! Aren't you forgetting something?"

Skip looked behind him and saw at about twenty-five or thirty yards away – and getting closer while racing through the shadowy underpass – a beanpole-thin man of indeterminate age carrying (what's this?) an overcoat, that overcoat, the overcoat.

What do I do now? Skip begged himself. His first impulse was to run, then not to run. He'd proceed hurriedly without looking as if he was trying to avoid this newest apparent pursuer but instead looking only as if he were hastening somewhere he was due and didn't hear the man behind him.

But in which direction should he walk?

Trying to reach a conclusion, he did nothing and now realized there was nothing to do in the way of avoiding the beanpole-thin man who was only several feet away and who, at this shorter distance, looked to be somewhere in his thirties. He had a face as thin as a parenthesis with a two- or three-day beard, sunken cheeks, a thin mouth and piercing eyes.

"Aren't you forgetting something?" the man, stopping in front of Skip, repeated, this time with a heightened accusatory inflection in the "forgetting something."

"I'm sorry, what did you say?" Skip said, attempting to fob himself off as mildly flustered but not in the least annoyed at the intrusion.

The thin man was wearing a cheap suit of an indeterminate dark color with a soiled white shirt open at the collar to reveal an Adam's apple that could have passed for a swallowed hatchet. The sleeves on the jacket were too short, and his thin wrists hung below them. The pants were also too short and were cropped above white socks.

"You left this overcoat on a bench back there," the thin man said. He didn't indicate what he meant by "back there," but Skip knew what he meant, of course.

"Oh, er..." Skip started to say.

The thin man, his mouth becoming wider and thinner-lipped, was not to be interrupted. "Don't try to tell me you didn't. I saw you. What were you thinking? That somebody who needed it more than you would come along and find it. Somebody like me. A little condescending, wouldn't you say? Figuring somebody less fortunate than you would be happy to have a hotsy-totsy overcoat like this here."

He held up the coat for perusal. "Just because you're some kind of freaking bleeding-heart liberal, you don't get rid of a coat so easy, pal. If you want me to have an overcoat, buy me a new one."

With that, the thin man shoved the coat into Skip's chest, grabbed Skip's left arm and forced him to hold on to it. Skip was so startled he said nothing.

"You're not going to *thank* me?" the thin man said. "Just what I thought." He did an unctuous about-face and set off in the direction from whence he'd come.

Skip, clutching the coat to his chest, was nonplussed. This was the second time in – what? – an hour, maybe a little over an hour, maybe two hours, that someone he'd never met had handed him the garment.

Who were these guys?

A word was forming in the back of his mind and had been for a while. It was pushing itself towards the front of his mind like the words "coming attractions" zooming towards the front of the frame in a movie trailer.

The word was "conspiracy!"

Then another word emerged. Not a word, a thought – a thought about having been handed the coat twice, a thought that – could this be? – that he was meant to have it, meant to do something about having it, meant to follow the leads, if that's what they were, to some, some...some whatever.

Or was he just making this up, grabbing onto the notion – he had to smile at this one – because it was a more inviting alternative to dining with (whoopee!) Faye and the Hartleys at La Rochefoucauld?

Skip rejected the concept as fast as it came at him, but it insisted on coming at him again. Again he rejected it. Again it came at him. This time he accepted it. Whatever was going on – whatever was afoot? – Skip knew he couldn't stand there just holding the coat. Neither could he discard it on the nearest bench or even in the nearest bin, given that the thin man or a confederate would sure-as-shootin' pluck it out.

It wasn't just a coat he'd been handed. He'd been handed something else, something much less tangible, less palpable. He couldn't put his finger on it, but he couldn't ignore it. He realized he didn't want to ignore it. Ignoring it meant he was left with Faye and the Hartleys, he was left with his contracts. He wasn't prepared for that, God knows.

Nothing to do but put the overcoat on again and keep going to the Ambrosius Manley Sturtivant statue, which was now only a matter of six or seven city blocks away.

Heading there, Skip was more attuned to his surroundings than was generally the case with him. Not only did he think it wise to keep an eye – peripherally – on anyone he passed or noticed occupying a bench at this crepuscular hour, but he was keyed in to sounds and scents he normally wouldn't register.

He heard the crunch of fallen leaves. He smelled the aroma they wafted after recent rainfalls. What was that scent? A phrase came to him that previously never had. It was the tang of autumn.

He would have almost appreciated the sensations – he would have almost slowed his pace to take it all in – had he not felt obliged to remain on the overcoat-caper trail. But he did feel that obligation and continued to feel it as he reached the plaza dominated by the Bethesda Fountain, the double staircase proceeding from it up to the Seventy-second Street transverse over the tiled underpass through which he could also walk to mount the wide alternate staircase leading to the Naumberg Bandshell and the Cross Park Mall.

Which should he take? If he chose to cross the transverse, a car (cars?) could be waiting for him, cars he maybe wanted to avoid. If he elected to advance through the vaulted underpass, someone (someones?) could be loitering there until he arrived.

I'll flip a coin, Skip thought, and, without thinking further, put his hand into the overcoat's left outside pocket. He'd felt in there before, of course, finding only the black kid gloves and the Halls cough drops, but this time – had he been too hasty earlier? – he located a coin that had apparently escaped his clutch.

He pulled it out. It felt like a penny. He looked at it to affirm its denomination. It was a penny, all right, but it wasn't just any penny. He held it up for closer scrutiny to make sure that in the little light thrown by the lampposts he was seeing what he thought he was seeing.

It was. It was an Indian-head penny. When had Skip last seen one of those? Had he ever seen one of those? Or had he only heard about them? In his huge left-brain store of useless information, he knew that Indian-head pennies were manufactured from 1859 to 1909, no earlier and no later.

It was a lucky penny. He'd pulled it out of the overcoat pocket heads up, which, to his way of silly thinking, made it doubly lucky, not to say valuable. And if it was really lucky – why not decide it was? – then he ought to flip it. Whatever it told him would be the path to follow.

Or would it?

Why not see?

Okay, Skip thought, heads the underpass, tails the transverse.

He flipped but too wildly. When he reached to catch the penny, he knocked it away from him. He heard a muted metallic semi-thunk somewhere near – a few feet to his left, where leaves were littered.

He should look for it, shouldn't he? Or should he? If he bent down to feel for it among the leaves on the plaza's brick floor, would he be vulnerable to – to what? But if he didn't, he wouldn't know what the penny, heads or tails up, instructed him to do.

More than that, he wouldn't have in his possession an Indian-head penny that could be worth a couple hundred dollars. Not that it was his possession. It belonged to the coat. It belonged to whomever the coat belonged to and who must know the penny was there and perhaps knew its potential value. If he was determined to be rid of the coat, to return it to its rightful owner, he couldn't claim rights to anything he found in it, not even as payment for the inconvenience caused.

So here's a howdy-do.

While confessing to himself that he was being superstitious, and accepting, as he'd claimed to do for years, that superstition is foolishness, he wanted to believe – needed to believe – the penny was lucky, that it would bring him luck when he hankered for it, which was right then with the overcoat and its holdings temporarily in his possession.

Walking away from the penny, not returning it to its place in the coat pocket could be opting for bad luck. Retaining the penny was all part of whatever he was caught up in.

Was "journey" the right word? "Wild goose chase"? "Funhouse ride?" "Investigation"?

Yes, investigation. That's what he was committing himself to. Not because he wanted to. Because he must. But because he must, he wanted to. In other words, funhouse ride.

He wasn't just blowing off Faye and the Hartleys.

Or was he?

He'd locate the penny, although the thing to do was not to cast his eyes down for it but to feel for it in the vicinity of where he believed it had come to rest. That way he could keep a lookout for suspicious encroaching activity.

He moved a few feet left, dropped on his haunches. The overcoat billowed around him. His eyes scanning as much of three-hundred-sixty degrees of surrounding park as he could, he began methodically fingering the leaves and the brick floor – as well as taking in the blend of urban-woodsy odors around him.

Touching nothing that felt like a penny, he realized there were other objects he might not want to touch. He didn't want to itemize them, especially if they pertained to dogs on or off a leash. Thinking on this, he wondered whether he should devote too much more time to Indian-head-penny hunting.

Five minutes earlier he hadn't even known it existed, and what he hadn't known, he couldn't miss.

He was about to give up when, lo and behold, he felt something like a penny. He grasped it, picked it up, looked at it. It was the penny, and it was heads up. Only now he couldn't recall to which direction he'd assigned heads up.

He returned the penny to the pocket, and as he did, he heard the sound of laughter. He looked up to see the laughter came from several teenagers – or were they tweenagers? – coming through the underpass.

If they could do it without apprehension, so could he as his new emerging self.

He rose and took, as he now saw it, the path of least resistance. In several blinks of the observant eye, he was at the top of the stairs, looking past the bandshell – the Naumberg Bandshell – and the rows of chairs towards the Mall.

He could spot, if dimly, the statues lining the walk at discreet distances. Some stood on their stone plinths, some sat in chairs on them. The nearest one, the one he took to be Ambrosius Manley Sturtivant, was standing.

He walked up to it. He faced it. He tilted his head up at the bronze stand-in for the man who had lived so philanthropically at 1021 Fifth Avenue. The statue commemorated a tall man who looked at one and the same time dignified and relaxed, although Skip couldn't know what liberties the sculptor was asked to take. Or took it upon himself to take.

Ambrosius Manley Sturtivant was shown in his late fifties or early sixties. He was dressed in a three-piece suit from the post-Great War years. He wore a shirt the collar of which would probably have been detachable were it real. Sturdy shoes. A monocle hung in front of what was visible of his waistcoat. His right arm was akimbo, the fingers of his right hand curving backwards, giving him the stance of a man at ease with himself. His left arm was at his side and in it he held a piece of (bronze) paper that had slightly curling edges.

Skip wondered whether pigeons ever perched on the dignified man. There was evidence they had sojourned on his full head of neatly combed bronze hair, which was parted in the middle as if in a style held over from a former era.

Ambrosius Manley Sturtivant's bronze head was tilted upwards. His face was fleshy. His eyes gave the appearance of taking in as much as they could of a world with which he was reconciled and at which he was smiling.

Those were among the statue's salient features. The most salient – impossible not to notice, certainly noticed by Skip – was the greatcoat draped over Ambrosius Manley Sturtivant's shoulders. It had a wide upturned collar and wide lapels. The sculptor had also used his chisel to suggest by way of delicate economical incisions here and there that it was a herringbone pattern. It fell to just a foot above the sturdy shoes. Of course, it was the color of aged bronze.

On the metal plaque below the patrician figure was:

AMBROSIUS MANLEY STURTIVANT

Financier–Philanthropist

1859–1928

Taking it all in, Skip was thinking that if Ambrosius Manley Sturtivant's coat suddenly dropped from his shoulders and Skip were able to pick it up and compare it more closely to the coat he wore, they would look uncannily alike.

They'd look like the identical coat, Skip was thinking with such absorption that when he heard his cellphone ringing again, he had an inkling "The Theme from 'Never on Sunday'" he'd put on it months before and hadn't gotten around to changing had already been playing for more than a few seconds.

Faye?

He filched the cellphone from the suit jacket breast pocket.

Not Faye.

"Yes, Mother."

"I don't like your tone," he heard the redoubtable Bernice Sawyer Gerber say. He would have wagered she was sitting on the edge of her bed – the bed covered with the designer percale sheets she'd saved "good money" buying on Stanton Street.

Knowing his tone had been sharp, impatient, adventure-tinged, he said, "What tone. Mom?"

"You know perfectly well what tone, Edward," his mother said. "The tone I've heard your entire life when you think I'm getting in touch with you unnecessarily."

"Ma, I'm sorry to tell you I wasn't thinking of you at all." He knew the instant he said it that he shouldn't have.

"Why doesn't that surprise me?" his mother said. "When do you ever think of me? But we'll let that go." Skip heard her take a breath and had a pretty good idea what was coming. "What are you doing anyway? Where are you? It sounds as if you're outdoors."

Skip wasn't about to tell his mother he was in Central Park looking at the statue of a man wearing an overcoat eerily similar to one he'd accepted for no good reason a few short hours earlier. She wouldn't believe him. Who would believe him? He half didn't believe himself.

He didn't fill her in but said – because it was somewhat true – "I'm on my way to dinner."

'With Faith?" his mom asked.

"Faye," he corrected, not for the first time and not, he would have bet the farm, for the last. Bernice made a policy of never hearing the names of the women he dated. He knew it was because she figured there was no need to. They weren't "keepers" – a word she'd never used to him but others had. It was exasperating, and more exasperating is that to date she proved right every fucking time.

She was – the thought went through his head like a shooting star – possibly right this time, too, certainly the way he was feeling about Faith, er, Faye at the moment. If he stopped to think about it – which he made a point of never stopping to do but had been doing for the last jam-packed hour or two – there was plenty about his life he could change besides Faye's presence in it.

Bernice said, "I'm not calling about her. Faye. I want to know if you found that answer for Gussie. She's been hocking me a chinik all afternoon."

"No, Ma, I didn't have a chance yet," Skip said. "I'll get to it when I get to it. I have other things to do with my time."

"What other things?" Bernice prodded, as if the query were a stick and she was poking it into his chest through the airwaves. "I know you better than you think. You have a routine, and you stick to it. You always have."

"Routine." She was right again. The word made him shudder. "Ma!" Skip raised his voice to say, and noticed, as he gazed around, that people nearby were looking at him funny.

Was it what he'd just shouted, or was it something else?

"Gussie!" she repeated. "I'd appreciate it if you look it up for her sooner rather than later."

"I promise," Skip said, "and now I have to hang up."

"Such a macher," Bernice said. "Give my regards to Freya."

She did it deliberately. He knew that. "I will," Skip said.

He clicked off and, having lost his train of acquired-overcoat-related thought, recapped the previous couple of hours. Yes, he'd been looking at the Ambrosius Manley Sturtivant statue and thinking how the man's overcoat resembled the one he was wearing – which was making him feel clammy now that a chillier breeze was stirring the leaves at his feet and the ones left on the oaks and elms.

That the two coats – the real one and the sculpted one – were alike illuminated nothing. Neither did the plaque with its basic facts. Would it help if he did a bit of research? The Museum of the City of New York? The Forty-second Street library?

Too late for any of it.

What about Googling Ambrosius Manley Sturtivant?

Skip was thinking about that when his eye caught the statue's left hand, the hand holding the piece of bronze paper. He wondered what it might be. Again checking around him to ascertain if he was being watched, which he didn't think he was (more than ordinarily), he walked up to the statue and around it to get a better look.

Now he expected to be watched by at least a few strollers, since someone looking so closely at a piece of paper a statue is holding could be expected to arouse at least mild curiosity in someone.

Let them look, Skip thought as he leaned in. He thought – and almost spoke aloud – Adventurers like me *should* be watched. He peered up about four feet at the paper. At first he couldn't discern what it was, although he could see there were lines on it – a drawing consisting of interlocked right-angle rectangles.

To get a better idea, he leaped up about two feet. The piece of bronze paper was meant to depict a blueprint. Ambrosius Manley Sturtivant holds a blueprint. It was a blueprint on which there was writing.

Not caring how many gawkers might observe him jumping up and down alongside a bronze statue in the park, Skip leaped again. Since the print was large enough for him to make out – had been designed by the sculptor to be legible, perhaps as a stipulation of the commission – he read 185 Vesey Street. He also realized the image of a skyscraper had been incised on a corner of the bronze paper.

Skip was looking at the ground-floor plan of a building at 185 Vesey Street in lower Manhattan. As that recognition sank in, it also came to him that the bronze Ambrosius Manley Sturtivant, his head tilted at that angle, had been crafted as if gazing at the building. It was a building that obviously came about at the financier-philanthropist's command. The Sturtivant Building?

Speaking of commands, Skip thought, is Ambrosius Manley Sturtivant dictating another of them right this minute. Am I supposed to return the coat to 185 Vesey Street? I'd better find out, he thought. Checking his, um, Rolex (7:36 p. m.) as part of getting his bearings, he looked around to figure if he was being watched as well as to decide how best to quit the park.

Jogging the straightest line he could, he headed to Fifth Avenue. (When was the last occasion on which he'd actually jogged?) Ready to flag down the first unoccupied cab that might come along, he was making good time when his cellphone went tuneful.

He fumbled for it, thinking "not Faye again." It wasn't. It was someone with whom he was possibly even less eager to chat: his brother Jerome.

Funny how many thoughts go through your mind – like fast-motion headlines around the Allied Chemical Building in Times Square – before you depress the cellphone thingamabob to say "hello." Not to mention the range of inflections that, as a consequence, are packed into that brief "hello."

One of Skip's thoughts was, "Now what?" Another was "Why now?" That one was followed by "Of course, now, when I could use it least." Others compounded those, like his knotted feelings for Jerome. Jerry to him. Jerry, the older brother, whom he'd idolized throughout their childhood, despite being aware – intuitively – that Jerry was the child Bernice Sawyer Gerber favored.

She made no bones about it, even though the favored Jerry had yet to "find himself," as they used to say, and, pushing forty, was still looking God-knows-where.

Never mind.

Bernice talked about Jerry as "special" and found excuses for his string of business mishaps. As she assessed them, they had nothing to do with his shortcomings – "Uh-*uh*," she insisted. They were all tied up with the failings of deceitful others or with unfortunate timing or both.

Often in the same breath, she'd attribute Skip's remunerative career (no matter how little he enjoyed it) to luck. This was nothing unusual to Skip. He'd spotted it more than once in other families where of two sons, the older one was anointed golden boy while the nose-to-the-grindstone younger was deemed to be on an unbroken lucky streak.

Furthermore, every family where he'd noticed this, well, syndrome, was Jewish. Go figure. And go figure why his commitment to real estate law was so largely predicated on getting Bernice Sawyer Gerber to give him a break in the favorites ranking.

"Jerry, hello," Skip said into the phone matter-of-factly, although he didn't feel so matter-of-fact as he surveyed the immediate vicinity for any unusual stirrings that could involve him.

"I hate to bother you," Jerry said. "I wouldn't if I didn't absolutely need to. Urgently."

"What is it, Bro?" Skip said, fairly certain the man heading towards him in shorts, a sweaty T-shirt and wiping a towel on his left thigh was finishing a run rather than coming after him. "What do you need, and when haven't you needed whatever it is you need urgently? I figure it's money, although it would be great if for once what you needed didn't require my writing a check. It sure would be nice if, just for once, what you urgently needed was only an encouraging brotherly hug."

"Can you spare a thousand?" Jerry asked. "I know I owe you the five thousand, and I promise I'll get it to you, but if the extra thou works out the way I'm pretty certain it can, that could mean me paying you back the entire sum even sooner."

Skip didn't have to mull asking Jerry what the money was for. What would be the point? He knew it was some hare-brained scheme. It always was, and Skip always came across with the sum, because Jerry was his brother and he loved him, despite everything. He also admitted to himself that having Jerry in his debt caused him a kind of satisfaction about which he only felt the faintest guilt pang.

Still more deeply than that, he sometimes had to repress the notion that Jerry's unending search to "find himself" was more honest than

Skip's pretending he'd found himself by settling on his increasingly unsettling law practice.

Skip snapped out of his mental diversion and, remembering the oddball fun he was having, said into the phone, "I don't have much time for this, Jerry. "I'm in the midst of something. Where are you?"

"Can you meet me at the southeast corner of Eighth Avenue and West Twelfth Street?" Jerry asked. Skip didn't question this either, since he was accustomed to Skip's street-corner reconnoiterings. "Where are you anyway?"

Feeling no obligation to be specific, Skip said, "Uptown. I'll catch a cab and be there quick as I can." As he clicked off, he heard Jerry say, "You're the best" and start to say something else he knew would be a meaningless declaration of gratitude and remorse.

He realized that other than to shuffle back and forth on his feet, he'd stood still through Jerry's entire once-a-month-if-not-more-often supplication. No time to waste, he thought, and resumed hurrying to a cab.

Nearing an opening in the stone wall bordering Fifth Avenue, he passed a homeless man – or someone looking as homeless as makes no difference – who eyed him and said, "Hubba, Hubba! *Some* coat."

Skip pretended not to hear him but once again wondered why the coat was getting such raves. Did New Yorkers, no matter at what social stratum, have nothing better to do than remark on each other's apparel? Or was something else going on?

And did he hope it was? Or fear it? Or hope/fear it? Or love it?

No time to think about that now. He had a cab to catch to Vesey Street with a stop – he could shake Jerry – along the way.

At Fifth Avenue, he saw, to his mitigated joy, several cabs with their unoccupied lights on. He raised his hand, and the first of them came to a halt. As he was getting in the car, he noticed that a second cab had been hailed by a man standing not fifteen feet behind him.

Why wouldn't there be? People hail cabs all over town. Nothing out of the ordinary about that. Unless there was.

Closing the door, he said to the bald-headed driver, "I'm going to 185 Vesey Street."

"World Trade Center territory," the driver said.

"Right," Skip said, realizing the cabbie had it right. It was the past, present and future WTC area. "But I've got to make a quick stop on the way at Eighth Avenue and West Twelfth Street."

"You got it, bud," the cabbie said and picked up speed to catch as many green lights down Fifth as he could. "Nice night."

"Yes, it is," Skip said and caught himself. "No, it isn't. I mean, it is. It could be. Maybe. Maybe not. I don't know."

"You better make up your mind, bud," the driver said.

Skip thought maybe he better had. Whatever else he decided, he decided he should stop thinking out loud. He did when the tinny bell indicating a text message went off. It was from Faye and read, "We're @ table, tho our 4th hasn't arrived. No need 2 respond." Skip didn't like the sound of that but conceded there was nothing to do about it at the moment.

"I don't mean to interrupt, bud," the driver said, interrupting Skip in his thoughts, "but is there any reason why you might be followed?"

"What?" Skip asked. "What do you mean, 'followed'?"

"What I said," the driver replied, not turning his bald head in order to keep his eyes on the busy avenue. "It could be me imagining it, but there's a black limousine behind us giving me a pain. The limo's so close I can see him and his passenger in my rear-view mirror. I'm getting the creepy feeling they're both watching us. Or you. But like I say, it could be my imagination."

Without stopping to consider the advisability of such a move, Skip looked behind him through the rear window and, sure enough, saw the limousine. Was it the same limousine he'd been seeing? Who's to say, when all black limousines look alike – particularly when their one-way windows are up.

"No reason anyone would be following me," Skip said, although, suddenly aware of the overcoat again, he could think of a possible reason. "Manhattan's lousy with black limousines. All the same, maybe you might try to lose them."

"Not a problem," the driver said and with that careered through a yellow light onto the Sixty-fifth Street transverse, leaving the (stalking?)

limousine at the red light. "I love these challenges. You don't get half enough opportunities for them, I can tell you. It's not like the years I was a cop. A' course, you don't get that many opportunities then, either, not as many as people think from watching too much television."

The guy was an ex-cop. Should Skip say anything about the predicament he was in? That's if he were in a predicament. Recapping in his mind what transpired for the last couple of hours, he sensed that if he recounted them, he'd sound like just another Manhattan paranoia case.

He probably was just another Manhattan paranoia case wearing a coat he'd never ordered. He held that thought as the cabbie/ex-cop took any number of arbitrary right and left turns on his zig-zagging journey south.

Maybe, Skip mused, he could get at his little involvement obliquely. He cleared his throat. "Asking you as a former member of the police force," he said – sounding, he hoped, off-handed, "if a guy, theoretically, were being tailed, how could he know for sure?"

"Most times, you can't for sure," the cabbie said after only a second's hesitation, "until whoever actually tailing you – if, theoretically, someone actually is – makes himself or herself known, one way or another. Usually, it's not a pleasant way and can involve dangerous objects. But one way to defuse it would be to hire someone to follow him."

Skip tried that possibility on for size and brushed it aside. "I see," he said. "So, theoretically, if it was an actual stalker or whatever, you wouldn't rate it as an adventure. More like a crisis."

"'Pends how you define 'adventure,'" the cabbie said. "Way I see it, one man's adventure is another man's nightmare."

Nightmare, Skip thought. He wasn't in the midst of an overcoat nightmare, was he?

"It's all attitude," the cabbie said, "like everything else in life. My attitude is I like being around people. Not much difference, cop or cabbie. Maybe there is. Most people will talk to a cabbie faster than a cop. That's why I'm here and not sitting alone in a warehouse somewhere on security-guard duty."

"Attitude," Skip thought. What was his attitude – his attitudes? Whatever it/they was/were, was it time to rethink them? There's something to chew on.

They were heading out of the transverse across Central Park West, and the cabbie said, "There you go. Whoever they were, they're history now, bud."

History, Skip thought, if only. Yes, if only, but then why was he feeling the merest twinge of a letdown?

The cabbie picked up where he left off. "Tell me this. You looking for someone to do that for you?" the cabbie said and darted a look round. "A tail job?"

Skip saw a pug's craggy face with a smudge of a nose in the middle, a heavy nine o'clock shadow and yet something comforting in it. "No," he said, "Just asking."

"I thought, you maybe being followed, maybe not," the cabbie said, "you might be thinking it over. I happen to do that kind of work from time to time, you know, on referrals usually. Maybe you want to take my card."

"You have a card?" Skip asked, not completely incredulously.

"A guy should always have a card," the cabbie said. "Here we are, bud." The cabbie hadn't stopped for a light all the way down Ninth Avenue. Skip looked out of the taxi and saw they were circling out of lower Ninth and onto where Hudson Street morphed into Eighth.

Skip sighted Jerry there – Jerry pacing a pace Skip had seen many times before.

The cabbie said, "Maybe you should take my card. Whether you need it or not. You don't, you can give it to a friend, like maybe the guy waiting for you here."

"How did you know someone – ?" Skip started to ask but stopped himself. Jerry was hurrying towards the cab, assuring himself Skip was inside.

"That'll be fifteen-thirty," the cabbie said, handing Skip his card.

Skip looked at it. "Dermot McAllister," it said on the top line and under that "All jobs courteously handled," and below that a cellphone number and an e-mail address: mac@mcallister.com.

"Nice talking," the cabbie said, as Skip gave him a twenty and waved away change. "But, hey, we got to talking so much, I nearly forgot this is just a stop on the way to 185 Vesey."

By then, Jerry had opened the taxi door. Skip felt Jerry's arm on his, pulling him from the cab. "Hold your horses, Jerry," he said and then to Dermot "Mac" McAllister, "I'll just be a minute."

"You're the boss," Mac McAllister said.

Skip closed the taxi door and turned to Jerry. He was used to Jerry's impatient and frustrated expression. He'd seen it before on a smooth-cheeked face that resembled their mother's, just as he looked more like their late lawyer father, Gabriel of the thin lips.

Sometimes Skip thought he could trace Jerry's gaze to the year in their adolescence – Jerry was eighteen, Skip was sixteen – when he grew the inch taller than Jerry and then two inches taller. As a consequence, he often conjectured, Jerry compensated by getting wider. Not plump, but wider, huskier and somewhere between casual and slovenly in his dress.

Skip had an explanation for that, too. He'd continued dressing well, thinking that would help obtain Bernice's approval, while Jerry knew no matter what he did, he already had it and would stop at nothing to prove he'd never lose it.

"That took you long enough," Jerry said by way of greeting.

Skip flashed on the joy ride McAllister – Mac to handyman clients – had just given him. "Traffic," he said duo-syllabically.

"And why's the cab idling here?" Jerry went on.

"I asked him to wait," Skip said. "I'm due downtown."

"What am I, chopped liver?" Jerry said. "Only worth a wham-bam-thank-you-sir?"

"I wouldn't be here at all if you hadn't called with one of your usual bail-out requests."

"I wouldn't do the same for *you*?" Jerry said, heavy on the inflection.

"I'm sure you would," Skip said, "but you've never had to."

"You're going to hold that over me?" Jerry said, and Skip saw Jerry's round cheeks get redder. "This is a tit-for-tat discussion?"

"No arguments, please, Jerry," Skip said, "I have enough on my mind right now."

"Like what?"

"Nothing you need to know about," Skip said, "but if it'll make you feel better, I'll let the cab go. I can always get another one."

"Suit yourself," Jerry said, which Skip knew meant, don't suit yourself, suit me. He went to the cab, had Mac roll down his window, told him he wasn't needed after all and paid him with some loose bills he located in one of his trouser pockets. He included another large tip.

Before Mac drove off, he said, loudly enough for Jerry to hear him, "Don't forget, bud, you need something done, you got my card. Use it for whatever, whenever."

Just to get the cabbie/ex-cop on his way, Skip mumbled something about not forgetting.

"What was that about?" Jerry said.

"What was what about?" Skip asked.

"If you need him for anything, et cetera."

"Oh, that." Skip said. "He responds to pick-up calls and is aggressive about it. Now. About the money you need." He put down his briefcase in order to pull out his checkbook.

Recognizing what Skip was doing, Jerry said, "No, no, no, Bro. Cash. No check. Cash."

"I haven't got that much cash," Skip said. "I don't carry that kind of money around with me."

"I didn't think you would," Jerry said and nodded to his left, where, on the side of the corner apartment building, Skip saw a row of three ATM machines. "That's why I asked you to meet me here. You can withdraw the thousand dollars, and don't tell me no. I checked online, and it's one of the FAQs – one of the frequently asked questions. What's the withdrawal limit? By lucky coincidence, it's a thousand even."

Skip dipped into his right hand suit pocket for his wallet to get at his bank card, got it. He picked up the briefcase and walking to the nearest cash dispenser – none of the three was occupied – he said to Jerry, "I'm not even going to ask you what you need a thousand dollars in cash for."

"Glad to hear it," Jerry said, "because I wouldn't tell you if you did. I'm your brother, and like Mother always says, blood is thicker than water. If I need it and you have it, why wouldn't you give it to me? I'm good for it."

Having inserted his card, pushed all the required buttons and begun waiting for the fifty twenties to issue forth, Skip stifled the urge to ask

Jerry how he figured he was good for it when so far he'd allowed his debt to mount up to a cool five thousand.

"Nice coat," Jerry said to pass the time. "I don't believe I've seen it before, have I?"

Skip looked up from the ATM. Jerry was eyeing him with one of his familiar leers, a leer close enough to a sneer to pass for one.

"You look like a million bucks in it," Jerry said. "I bet you paid plenty more for it than the thousand you're about to lend me. Whose is it? Ralph Lauren? Ermenegildo Zegna? Brioni? If you can pay that for a coat, you shouldn't begrudge me a mere thousand."

"'Begrudge'?" Skip said. The thousand dollars coughed out. Skip handed them to Jerry, who started counting the twenties. "Where do you get 'begrudge'? I arrive at a designated street corner to hand you cash – not the first time and not the last, either, I'm sure – without even asking what you need it for, probably because if I knew, I'd get angry. And you're telling me I'm *'begrudging'* you?"

On the "begrudging," Skip put up the index and middle fingers of both hands to signify his italics. Jerry, who'd stopped counting, looked at the gesture with disdain and said, "I said *'begrudge'* because I'm your brother, and you think handing me money – " He waved the thick stack at Skip. " – is all you need to do. For fuck's sake, you even have a cab waiting for you – ."

This was enough for Skip, who said, "I let the cab go."

It wasn't enough for Jerry, who continued undeterred, "You have a cab wait for you so you wouldn't have to spend more than five minutes with me. Did you ever stop to think that if I didn't need a few bucks once in a blue moon, I would never see you? We'd never see each other?"

Skip was thinking over whether to correct the "once in a blue moon" part or point out that Jerry was free to call at any time he didn't need the quick loan.

He didn't get the chance to do either or both, because he was abruptly distracted. A shot rang out from somewhere nearby, possibly a car passing by at a good speed up Eighth Avenue. At least, it sounded like what Skip believed a ringing-out shot must sound like.

He flinched reflexively and so noticeably that Jerry said, "What's the matter, Bro? You afraid somebody's gunning for you?"

Skip tried to pull himself together but – too mired in wondering whether somebody was gunning for him – didn't feel as if he could quite shake the feeling.

"It was only a car backfiring," Jerry said, and then, as if reverting to their childhood when he could always sense Skip's fear and play off it, said, "Anyway, I *think* it was only a car backfiring. Maybe it was a gunshot."

Jerry had hardly finished the sentence when another sound-burst identical to the first split the air. Skip flinched again and looked around for somewhere to take cover.

As he turned, Jerry grabbed him by his left arm, and said, "Holy shit. There could be a bullet hole in a wall near here or in the pavement." He started patting himself and then patting down Skip. "Maybe one of us is hit."

Not comfortable with Jerry's hands on him – on the coat – Skip pushed them away.

"What's the matter, Skippy?" Jerry asked. (Jerry was the only person who ever called him Skippy. Skip hated it and liked it.) "You don't like me touching you? You don't want me touching your expensive new coat? You want to take shelter from a car with a faulty exhaust and me?"

Skip didn't want to answer the question, because the answer was "yes." He didn't quite know why, but it was so. He did know that part of the reason was if someone with a gun was shooting at him, he didn't want to remain standing where he was for another split second.

He was thinking of Jerry, too – to his partial chagrin.

Adventure or no adventure, he hadn't engineered this, but if this was what adventure was starting to mean, was he ready to stand up to it?

Unable to stop himself from brushing the coat's sleeves where Jerry had rubbed them and him, he said, "Look, Jerry, I've got to go. You have the money. I'll call you. We'll have a real talk. You'll tell me if you've heard from Doris and what's going on there."

Skip said this while hurrying into the street to get the next cab he could and face up to (face down?) whatever was coming his way. He snagged one, and as he climbed in, he saw Jerry watching him with a knowing look that rubbed Skip the wrong way, worse than the unsolicited literal rubbing he'd just received.

As Skip was opening and closing the door, he heard Jerry saying, "Nothing's going on there. Anyway, Skippy, since when are you interested?"

Have I been uninterested? Skip wondered. I wasn't aware I'd shown a lack of interest in Jerry's divorce from the grating Doris. Jerry himself had begun to show a lack of interest after the first two or three years of their marriage. He remembered one loan Jerry needed to pay off an assistant – a scheming secretary – with whom Jerry had gotten in over his head. Skip had come through then as always.

But maybe that still didn't make him a good brother. Maybe that made him only a brother using money to buy off fraternal obligations.

"You're headed to 185 Vesey Street, right," said the cabbie, to whom Skip had given no destination and at whom he hadn't looked. He'd been too busy thinking about Jerry and irritated that yet again his errant brother had inserted himself between Skip and something more pressing, more invigorating, more positive despite its negative aspects.

Now he looked at the cabbie to see what kind of driver knows where you're going when you haven't said. Could it be someone involved with the overcoat plot, if indeed there was a plot? Should he be thinking of jumping out at the next red light or remaining exactly where he was?

The prescient driver was Dermot "Mac" McAllister, who threw him a meaty smile and said, "A real coincidence, huh? Okay, it isn't. When you sent me off, I had the feeling you didn't really want to, but the guy you met wanted it. So I drove around the block a few times. Straight to 185 Vesey Street now?"

"Yes," Skip said.

"You got it, bud," Dermot said, "and I'm getting the feeling you've got things on your mind. From here on in I button my lip."

Skip wasn't about to quarrel with that. He still felt funny about the situation and thought that by this time – he looked at the ersatz Rolex: 8:21 pm – he had been feeling funny about whatever the situation was for over two hours. Trust Jerry to insert himself into the midst of something – Skip looked at the coat again, felt it – just when Skip needed to concentrate fully elsewhere.

He wanted to put Jerry out of his mind and hoped time and distance – the time it took to cover the distance between Hudson and Twelfth and World Trade Center territory – would do the trick.

It did, when Mac McAllister, who'd held to his word about keeping mum, said, "Here we are, 185 Vesey Street, the Sturtivant Building."

Hearing the announcement and, particularly, the word "Sturtivant" spoken aloud, Skip was jolted out of the Jerry sidetrack. "What made you say 'Sturtivant'?" he asked Mac. "Do you know the building? Do you know something about Sturtivant?"

"It says 'The Sturtivant Building' over the doorway," Mac said and chuckled. "I know a lot about this town from driving around it every day, but I don't know every last building. Near as I can recall, you're the first fare I ever brought here. Brought many fares to buildings near here, but not here. And speaking of fares, that'll be seven-fifty."

"Oh, yes, right," Skip said. He'd been switching his gaze from the building to Mac but remembered why he was here. All right, he didn't know precisely why he was where he was, but he recalled he was on a quest that could end here and possibly even in an exciting manner.

He got out of the cab, handed Mac a ten through the right front window. Mac nodded thanks and said, "Don't forget. You need my help, you got my card. Don't hesitate to use it whatever, whenever."

"I certainly will," Skip said, just to get the cab away so he could size up the Sturtivant Building. Scanning it from bottom to top, he recognized it was a three-dimensional realization of the rendering on the bronze blueprint he'd seen forty-five minutes or so earlier. Chiseled into a foundation stone at the left corner of the ground floor was the legend "Erected in 1915. Cass Gilbert, architect."

So, Skip said to himself, the idea Sturtivant had was to have the man who designed the Woolworth Building, not much more than five hundred feet away, do something similar for Sturtivant, but what, if anything, did that have to do with the coat?

To the left of the doorway was a brass plaque that said, "The philanthropist Ambrosius Manley Sturtivant (1859–1928) had this building constructed in 1916 by the architect Cass Gilbert. It is one of the finest examples of Neo-Gothic architecture in the city and often considered an improvement on Gilbert's Woolworth Building, completed in 1913. In a concession to its acclaimed predecessor, the Sturtivant Building is fifteen feet shorter. Known for a gentlemanly approach to his life and financial career, Sturtivant allowed Gilbert and the chain-store magnate Frank W Woolworth this humble bow. In many other aspects the 782-feet-high, 54-story, limestone and granite edifice elegantly reflects the prevailing architectural style of the time. Its Moorish lobby and exterior ornamentation are especially noteworthy."

Though Skip found the information interesting, he had no more than a neutral reaction to what he was reading until he got to "limestone." That word, again. And then to "ornamentation."

The word was especially chilling. Neo-Gothic ornamentation. Did that mean gargoyles? He scanned the facade slowly, bottom to top. What he saw wasn't very different from many other buildings of the time. After eighteen or twenty stories there was a set-back and a second set-back after several more stories. At the top, he saw a cupola with slender columns and a spire piercing the ink-blotched night sky.

But what was it he noticed at the corners of the limestone or granite (given his meager acquaintance with architectural niceties, he had no way of knowing) balustrades surrounding the set-backs and presumably the terraces at those two levels?

Gargoyles, that's what he noticed – gargoyles looking to be on the point of flying or leaping in fury from their perches.

Or falling from them.

That put Skip's feet in motion. He'd been thinking his next step – or steps – should be entering the building to see what turns up. He'd been thinking maybe the lobby was where he'd find further clues. Maybe the directory would show an office occupied by Miles Rogers Havilland.

Now he wasn't so sure about the wisdom of advancing. Once he'd spotted the gargoyles, his first impulse was not venturing – or adventuring, as he was calling it in his evolving frame of mind – into Ambrosius Manley Sturtivant's humble nod to Frank W. Woolworth.

Besides – and this came to him as a relief – he'd just noticed that the three revolving doors were locked in place. The building was closed. That was all Skip needed to see before retreating across the street, from where, he reasoned, he'd also have a better view of the building as he gazed up.

The angle was decidedly more favorable. Besides, although he hadn't noticed it before, he was in a small, neatly laid-out square. Little in Manhattan strikes the inhabitant – or certainly the tourist – as pastoral, but this pleasant acre, deserted at this time of a weekday evening, had that effect.

From it, Skip thought, maybe he'd see something in a window that would have meaning for him. Maybe there'd be a sign he could read, maybe a deluxe tailor shop. Maybe, despite the building's appearing to be battened down, someone would signal him from one of the two terraces, which he gauged to be wide enough for occupants' use.

He even had a fleeting fantasy of someone using a lamp or flashlight to send a message in Morse code, the way they do in mystery-island movies. What good that would do Skip, he didn't know, since beyond SOS, he had no grasp of Morse code. For the first time in his life he wished he did.

Starting at the ground floor, he decided to run his eyes slowly from left to right and right to left and from floor to floor. The ground floor housed an otolaryngologist group practice. Skip wracked his brain for any connection between the coat he had on and an ear-nose-and-throat partnership.

He came up with nothing there or in the darkened smoke shop occupying the other ground-floor space.

There was no movement inside either of them.

He scanned upward to no avail until he got to the cupola. Was something occupying it he hadn't taken in when he looked at it the first time? A cupola, if it were accessible, would be a very promising spot for someone to wave and summon – also from which to fire a pistol.

Madmen are always attracted to those kinds of vantage points.

Skip tilted his head far back to examine the cupola more carefully, thinking at the same time that maybe, rather than paying attention to it, he'd be better off hiding himself from it. If someone was up there watching him, he (maybe she) might even have a better vantage point.

While Skip was weighing the pluses and minuses of shuttling himself off – the minuses seemed far fewer than the pluses – he became aware of something happening behind him, scuffling noises he couldn't place but that didn't sound enticing. Or was it simply that paranoia was kicking in more acutely?

He turned around to find out what was going on and saw three people just inside the postage-stamp park's farthest corner. They were engaged in some ambiguous activity.

It didn't remain ambiguous to Skip for long. Two men in street clothes had waylaid a woman in a business jacket and skirt and low heels and were attempting to take her purse.

This wasn't a skirmish in which Skip by dint of initial impulse wanted to involve himself at all. Then again, that was his old Skip Gerber impulse. In the last hours, his tried-and-true impulses were shifting. Right now, he didn't see how he could avoid butting in and maintain his shaky self-respect.

One way to keep out of it was to alert a cop, but looking around, he didn't see one. With the thought "Where are the cops when you need them?" going through his mind as if it were a banner being pulled behind a Piper Cub, Skip did something he wouldn't ever have bet on his pre-overcoat self to do.

He started running towards the entangled threesome, shouting, "What's going on there?" A wayward thought was that the coat might impress them as belonging to someone powerful with whom they wouldn't choose to wrangle.

Perhaps he was someone powerful. He certainly felt a powerful urge propelling him, an urge far surpassing a mere *frisson*.

The men who were attacking the woman – one behind her trying to keep her still while the one in front of her tried to get her to surrender her shoulder bag – looked up without letting go. They took Skip in, conferred with each other by means of slippery facial maneuvers and resumed the struggle.

Skip thought they must have decided he was alone – he was, of course – and presented no problem if they got what they wanted immediately and then fled.

That made Skip angry. He continued towards them, and as he approached, he did something he knew could be foolhardy. He did it anyway. He put his left hand – the one not carrying the briefcase – in the left overcoat pocket, took hold of the Halls cough drops package, pressed it forward and said, as he'd heard it proclaimed in too many crime flicks to enumerate, "I've got a gun."

Then, for good measure, "And I'm not alone!"

What if either or both of the robbers also had guns? He'd be a goner, and so might the woman be, but he'd already committed himself to the act of, for him, unusual derring-do.

He was close enough now for them to see the bump the Halls packet made in the coat pocket and for him to see they were two high-school-age or slightly older kids – one white, one black – in hoodies and running shoes and she was a red-headed woman in her late twenties, maybe early thirties.

The phrase "damsel in distress" danced nuttily through his brain – not that she looked like a damsel, more like a capable woman in a jam. And she and the two young men were looking at Skip with – was it fear? disbelief? hilarity? – with whatever-it-was on their faces.

Skip got lucky. Having given him the wary once-over, the boys looked at each other, let go of the woman and raced out of the park as only their high-priced running shoes could hurry them.

The episode – or that part of it – ended so rapidly that Skip's marveling at his accomplishment was only hazily marred by the thought that the entire incident could have been a setup.

But a setup for what?

He wasn't able to pursue the thought, since the red-headed woman, gathering herself together, was speaking to him. She was also glaring at him. "You could have gotten both of us shot," she said, "if not killed."

Pulling the Halls packet out of his pocket and holding it up for her to see, Skip replied, "This *could've* been a gun. Want one?"

"But it isn't," the woman said. "That trick only works in movies."

"Apparently not," Skip said.

"It worked this one time out of the movies," the woman said. "I'll give you that. So I suppose I owe you thanks. But what if they'd had guns or a wire-cutter they intended to cut the strap on my bag with?"

Skip's immense pride at pulling off the rescue was taking a blow from these questions. "None of that happened," he said, his new-found derring-do deflating, "and now the two thugs are gone, and we're here."

A voice behind Skip said, "Is this guy bothering you, Ma'am?"

Neither Skip nor the woman had heard whoever it was approaching. It was a policeman who stood about five feet five inches tall and may have been at most twenty-five. He *had* a gun – in the holster strapped to his thick belt. His hand was on it.

The red-headed woman spoke first and said, "No, Officer. He was actually helping me."

Skip said, "She was being attacked by a couple of thugs. I scared them off." He pointed in the direction where they'd disappeared. "They went that way."

Skip – who'd almost said, "They went thataway" – half expected the cop to give chase, but the cop stayed where he was and asked, "Do you want to come to the precinct and give us a description, Ma'am? Were they one white kid and one black kid?"

"Yes," she said.

"Both about my size, maybe a little taller, and wearing running shoes and hoodies?"

"They're the ones," the red-head said.

"Yeah," the cop said, "we know about them. They use the same *modus operandi* but not in the same place twice. We'll catch them, maybe sooner, maybe later."

"I hope sooner," the redhead said, "so no one else has to go through what I went through and whoever's gone through it before me." She indicated Skip. "If this gentleman hadn't come along, I could now be without my bag and everything in it."

Skip started to say, "I *pretended* to have a..." but was stopped by the redhead who said, "He *pretended* to be my boyfriend, and look at him in that impressive overcoat. They must have figured he'd overwhelm them. So they took off."

"Okay, then," the policeman said, "I'll see you two out of the park, and we can all be on our way. I'll keep a lookout for those kids, too. One of these days they'll trip up – uh – worse than they did tonight."

They'd reached the street where the cop tapped his cap, said "Have a good night" and left.

Skip and the redhead stood looking at each other. She said, "I think I owe you an apology. I was rude back there. You helped me, and I went after you. I guess I was upset by what had happened and had to take it out on somebody and there you were."

Skip didn't know what to do but thought gallantry might be his best shot. He regretted resorting to the thought of a "shot," but went on. "It's okay. I understand. It's the modern world. Women can take care of themselves. Maybe you had an exit strategy, and I interrupted it because I'm locked into pre-feminist thinking."

At that, the redhead laughed, and Skip realized she was extremely good-looking. In addition to the red hair, she had green eyes, a sloping nose, a wide mouth and pert chin. With the full-bodied laugh as well as, he saw now, the kind of fullness of body he went for, it all added up to something. He would have said she was awesome, if he ever used the ramshackle adjective.

"No, I didn't have an exit strategy," the redhead said. "I was just angry, and now that I'm over it, I realize I'm thrown and, I hate to say it, frightened. Something bad could have happened there." She pointed behind her without turning round. "But thanks to you, my hero, it didn't. Now I think I'm going to start shivering. Not from the cold – well, maybe that, too – but from the delayed shock."

She looked Skip over and then directly in the face with the kind of look that she had to know contained the power to melt a man's heart. She said, "Do you think I could borrow that terrific coat of yours for a minute?"

Skip's unspoken thought was, I've never been called a hero before. Maybe I am – maybe even an existential hero, which from time to time since he was a kid he'd contemplated being, though not quite knowing what constituted being an existential hero.

Then he thought, Is this why I have this coat? To put over this woman's shoulders? Then he thought, Is this what I maybe shouldn't be doing with the coat? Then he thought, Get over the existential hero business, get over the to-be-or-not-to-be with the coat.

The lady needs it.

He set down the briefcase he'd never let go of the entire time, took off the coat and helped put it round her shoulders. As he did, he again felt the heft of the coat and expected it would appear far too big on her, that she'd appear to be shrinking inside it. Not so, though. When she had, as he'd done, shrugged it into place, it looked as if it fit her well enough.

Or maybe it wasn't as large as he'd first thought.

Or maybe it was all in his imagination.

"Nice coat," the redhead said. She folded her arms across her lovely chest and rubbed the sleeves. "*Very* nice coat. You must have paid a pretty penny for it."

Skip was about to say something but wasn't certain what. Should he tell her how he came by it? Somehow, pretending he'd purchased it, that it was part of his wardrobe, seemed to be dissembling – not that he'd had that misgiving with Jerry.

She beat him to it. Apparently seeing his hesitation, she said, "You don't have to tell me. It's not my place to ask. I was just commenting on how nice and warm it is." With that, she pulled it tighter, a gesture that had its own warming effect on Skip.

"By the way," she said, "I think I also owe you my name. I'm Sheryl Sherman."

She reached in her recently threatened bag and pulled out a business card. She handed it to him. He looked at it, read it. It said, "Sheryl Sherman" and under that "Family Advisor" and below to the left, two telephone numbers, one on top of the other. He put it in the coat's right-hand pocket.

"Please, no jokes about the moniker," Sheryl said. "My parents thought it was a poetic name for their little girl. There's nothing I can do about it now. Not even marry, since I am feminist enough not to want to take on a husband's name and be branded like a cow in a rancher's herd. My luck, it's one of the perils of feminism. Fifty years ago, I wouldn't have given it a minute's thought."

The name Skip suddenly saw plastered on a billboard in his brain was Sheryl Sherman Gerber. Nutty, he knew. Faye Reisbach Gerber had never been billboarded there.

Sheryl Sherman paused and inhaled showily. "That's enough of that for now," she said and stuck out her right hand, her left hand still holding the coat to her. "You're?"

Skip was so caught up in what she'd just said and how she looked in the coat – how she looked, period – that he had to think for a second. "I'm, uh, I'm..."

He fumfered long enough for her to say, "You're a figment of my imagination, and so's the coat, although it feels real enough."

"I'm Edward Gerber," he said and shook her hand, "My friends call me Skip."

"What kind of friends would call you Skip?" she said, which Skip wasn't ready for. She saw as much. "And what kind of a person am I to make such a crack on such short acquaintance. Skip is a perfectly nice nickname. My friends call me Sher. Like the singer, but with an 's' instead of a 'c.' There's no stopping them, either."

She was looking directly at him. Skip had no idea what she saw. "But, okay, I'll call you Skip for as long as we're together, which shouldn't be long, since you need your coat back, and I need to get home. No, on second thought, Edward Gerber, I don't know you long enough to call you Skip. We're not full-fledged friends yet. I'll call you Edward for the next few minutes until we are."

That's when she smiled, and Skip (or Edward – whoever) got to see how the wide mouth and the green eyes worked together to charm a guy right out of his overcoat concerns.

If he were looking for adventure, here it was looking him straight in the eye. "No hurry about the coat," he said and then, "Look, we're both a little shook up by what just happened. Maybe you want to go somewhere for a drink or something."

Why was he saying this? He had other things claiming his attention, although no, for the moment he only had this. He only had Sheryl Sherman. He looked at the passing-for-genuine Rolex: 9:22 p. m.

"You're looking at your watch," Sheryl said. "You have to be somewhere. I'm holding you up. So to speak, under the circumstances."

She started to take the coat off, but Skip instantly lunged to stop her. There was an awkward moment when it looked as if he was trying to embrace her. (Was he trying to embrace her?) They both laughed it off in an awkward man/woman way, and she kept the coat on.

She said, "I'd better just get in a cab. Right now, I think I'll feel better in my own surroundings."

Not thinking – or not thinking too linearly – Skip said, "I can't let you go home alone. If you don't mind, I'll see that you get there safely. It's the least I can do. Your hero, you know."

'It's much more than you need to do," Sheryl said, ignoring the "your hero" ploy. She started to take the coat off again but stopped. "This is silly. I'm still shivering."

Good will surged through Skip. He said, "No arguments, please. I'm taking you home, wherever home is."

"I'm way up on the West Side," she said, "surely out of your way."

Without skipping a beat, Skip said, "I was just headed in that direction." He stepped into the street and waved at the only taxi in the area.

It stopped. Dermot "Mac" McAllister was not driving it. He helped Sheryl into the back seat, noticing she lifted the skirt of the overcoat as she got in and slid to the far side. He followed her in and said, "Where are we going?"

She leaned towards the driver and said, "458 West Eighty-sixth Street, please." When the driver repeated the address and Sheryl confirmed it, she said to Skip, "Really, Edward, I could have done this myself." Skip assumed a skeptical look but said nothing. "But I'm grateful to you. I'm grateful you were in the park when no one else was. What were you doing, anyway? Do you work in the area, too?"

Before he knew what he wanted to say and because he was still undone by what was transpiring, he said, "No." Not satisfied with that, he said, "I just happened to be there."

Without Sheryl, who had an enticing way of unconsciously tossing her hair back, saying anything, he thought better of what he'd said. Nobody in Manhattan "just happened to be" anywhere. He wasn't inclined, though, to say he was there in connection with a coat that had been pawned off on him and that he was determined to get to the bottom of finding out why or from whom.

Would she even believe him?

"I mean," he said, "I – um – thought I had a appointment with a client in the Sturtivant Building. I'm a lawyer, see, but when I got there, I saw the building was closed and realized I'd gotten the date and time wrong. So I crossed the street into the park to get a better look up at his office to see if maybe a light was on."

"Why didn't you call?" Sheryl asked. "Presumably, you have a cellphone. I don't know a single lawyer who doesn't."

"Yes," Skip said. "My cellphone. Why didn't I think of that? Of course, the Sturtivant Building itself is so unusual. I also wanted to give it a proper look-see."

"Interested in architecture, are you?" Sheryl asked.

"I am," Skip said. For the moment, he'd run out of things to say, suspecting Sheryl didn't believe anything he'd imparted so far anyway. "You don't believe me?"

Why should she? He didn't believe himself. He faced the fact he'd reached a point in his ambulance-chaser's life that he allowed himself fewer and fewer interests. He really must broaden them.

"I believe you," she said. "Is there any reason I shouldn't? A strange guy comes to my rescue and then lends me his coat. I have every reason to trust anything you tell me."

Skip wondered if she'd trust his saying he was attracted to her but thought that wasn't something he was about to say. He also thought of Faye and how she might have some tart comments to make about his being with Sheryl when he was missing La Rochefoucauld, where, he'd been reliably informed, the French pundit's maxims were installed on the walls in discreet neon.

"Discreet neon." Isn't that an oxymoron? He wondered that but said, "If I were you, I wouldn't trust anything I say." He wanted her to take it as a joke.

"You know," Sheryl said, and Skip could see color coming back into her face, "you're the first guy who's ever said that to me, and the honest-to-God truth is every man you meet hands you some kind of line." She took time to give him a closer look. "But maybe you're different."

All Skip could think of was the number of lies he'd already told her, beginning, when he first saw her and the hoodlums, with having a gun in his pocket. The whopper that loomed in his head, however, was allowing her to think the coat belonged to him. The oddest thing was he had a strong urge to tell her everything but couldn't bring himself to.

(This is on top of the lies he'd fed Faye about his not showing for the Hartleys and her.)

He said, "I'm probably handing you a line, too." As he said it, he thought of something he'd never thought about himself, or, if he had, he'd dismissed as not requiring further consideration: He always handed the ladies lines.

Sheryl was right. Men did that. He wasn't different. He figured it was expected of him – he figured, if you don't go along with the creed, you're letting down the side. Lies were so expected, they somehow ceased to be lies, were only part of the process.

The embarrassment he felt at recognizing that about himself was enough to make him turn away from Sheryl and look out the window at the passing West Side Highway. He hadn't even noticed that's how the cabbie had chosen to go uptown, and here they were, already in the Sixties. Ahead, he could see the towers of the West Side's bilious Trump development coming at him – coming at them – like gargoyles of a different genus.

"If you're handing me a line," Sheryl said to his back, "it's a good one. I won't call you on it."

He turned. She was smiling at him and looking good in the coat. For the briefest instant he was almost gratified that he'd had it to give her. He was beginning to think the coat was truly good for something, after all. What would he have given her to warm her up if he hadn't had the coat? His suit coat, probably, but it wouldn't have been as effective. She wouldn't have looked half so appealing.

Hold it! If he hadn't had the coat, he wouldn't have even been in the pocket park, and what would have happened to Sheryl then? It was almost as if he was meant to be there, as if the whole rigmarole was destined.

Was it? Of course, it wasn't. Or was it?

So much that had happened in something like three hours struck him as unreal. But he was in a taxi with someone calling herself Sheryl Sherman and wearing a coat he'd come by out of the blue and now, looking out the front window, he saw they were nearing the exit that would get them to West Eighty-sixth Street.

"You've gone quiet," Sheryl said. "Thinking of more lines to try out on me?"

"No," Skip said, "I was just thinking."

"Thinking is good," Sheryl said.

"458 West Eighty-sixth Street," the driver said. He came to a stop in front of the building.

"Here we are then," Sheryl said.

"I guess we are," Skip said.

"Then I think you'd better let me out."

Skip was on the curb side. He had to get out first. "Right," he said and swung into action. He got out, and gave Sheryl his hand to help her.

She had the coat around her and had picked up her bag, but on her good-looking legs now, she put it down again and started to take off the coat. "You'd better have this," she said.

"No," Skip said, "keep it on until you're inside the building. I'll take it then."

He began leading her to her door.

"Aren't you forgetting something?" she asked and looked back at the cab.

"Paying the driver?" Skip said. "I thought I'd keep him and get to my next stop."

"I mean your briefcase," Sheryl said. And then, "It seems to me I can't let you go so easily. For your troubles I should at least offer you a drink. Unless you're in a hurry."

Skip was in a hurry. He just didn't know what he was hurrying to or from. But just then, he wasn't in that big a hurry.

"That's fine with me," he said. "A quick, revitalizing drink would be great."

He put down the briefcase he'd picked up at Sheryl's reminder, got out the wallet and paid the driver. It was a good thing he'd been carrying a fair amount of cash, he thought, taking into account the mounting cab rides,

Sheryl had already crossed the sidewalk and was standing in front of her building.

Obeying an impulse he wouldn't have had hours earlier, Skip looked up at the building's top. No gargoyles, although at both cornice corners, there were elaborate stone pots he didn't like the looks of.

Stepping quickly towards Sheryl, Skipped noticed two young men in hoodies and running shoes passing. The white one said to the black one, "Some killer coat she's got on."

Skip looked at Sheryl to see what she made of it, but she'd been distracted by a neighbor who was coming out of the building.

Were the two boys who passed by the same two? They couldn't be. He wasn't sure and therefore wasn't reassured. The hoodies the boys from the park had on had shielded their faces. Though he was slightly throttled, Skip thought better of mentioning his suspicion to Sheryl. No need to upset her again.

What are the chances of seeing two kids so alike within a half-hour, forty-five minutes? Pretty good, actually. This was a town full of young white men and black men in hoodies. Hoodies, baggy pants slung low on the hips and running shoes were the unemployed urban man's uniform.

Skip shook it off and went to join Sheryl. She was standing in her building's antiseptic lobby and taking off the coat. She went to hand it to him and then thought better of the gesture. Instead, she indicated that he should allow her to hold it while he slipped into it.

She said, "It certainly is a nice coat, Edward. You're a man of good taste."

No matter what care he gave to it, Skip never thought of himself that way, not in the wardrobe department – possibly because Bernice was always going on about it. Until he went away to prep school (Choate, at his father's insistence), she'd picked out his clothes. To this day she continued to make unsolicited remarks about what he wore.

So did Faye, he noted.

"I hope you don't mind my calling you Edward," Sheryl was saying. "To me, you're still Edward, not Skip. I think I met you in an Edward mode. From the little I know of you, I'm not convinced Skip would have done the same thing."

Funny, Skip thought, I'm not convinced of it, either. "I don't mind," he said. "I'm usually Edward – or Mr Gerber – to people in my business dealings."

"Which are?"

They were at the elevator. Skip wondered who might get out. No one did. They got on. "I'm a real estate lawyer," he said.

"That must be interesting," Sheryl said. Her green eyes had caught the elevator's clever lighting.

"At one time, it was," Skip said. "I think. It can become routine."

"That's what I was thinking," Sheryl said and laughed. "I guess I was hoping it would be interesting for you. It sounds cut-and-dried to me, but what do I know?"

"You know more than you think," Skip said. "'Cut-and-dried.' That's the word, all right." He thought but didn't say, Maybe I'm cut-and-dried, too.

"You can always get out of it," Sheryl said. "You wouldn't be the first lawyer to do it. To go back to what they wanted to do in the first place. Was there something you always wanted to do in the first place?"

Skip had no quick answer to that. When he was a kid, he played the trumpet and thought he might become a musician, but not with Gabriel Martin Gerber and Bernice Sawyer Gerber frowning on the prospect, not when Gabriel Martin Gerber had once said, "When I was a kid, I thought I'd be a writer, but my father talked me out of that cockamamie notion fast enough."

They'd reached Sheryl's floor, and the doors opened. A woman in a robe and a bandanna on her head was passing with an empty bin. She'd been to the incinerator. She looked at Sheryl and then at Skip and said, "Hello, Sheryl." To Skip she said, "Some swell coat you got on. Wear it in good health."

"Hello, Annie," Sheryl said.

"Don't mind me," Annie said, "I'm just getting rid of trash." She indicated her bin. "If I was smart, I'd leave this at the incinerator door and throw myself in."

She continued left, while Sheryl, saying "Good night, Annie," went to a door at the end of the corridor. She unlocked it with a key she located in the depths of her pocket, waved Skip – Edward to her – in and said,

"Give me your coat – to hang up this time – and make yourself at home."

If I only could, Skip thought, as well as, Shouldn't I be on my way – returning to this coat caper? Then, getting a load of a living room obviously decorated for comfort and not necessarily for show (as, for instance, Faye's was), he thought, Maybe I could make himself very much at home here.

He removed the coat, handed it to her.

She went to a closet just inside the apartment door and hung the coat on a padded hanger. "There," she said, "safe."

If only, he thought, and settled onto the end of a couch with an earth-colored shawl draped over it. Then he thought maybe choosing one-half of a couch would be too suggestive. He got up and moved to a chair upholstered in a burnished red-and-grey pattern.

"What can I get you?" Sheryl, who'd come in from the bedroom where she'd left her suit jacket, asked. "I can give you anything you want." She realized what she'd said, and when the realization crossed her face, Skip realized it, too, but sensed it was best not to confirm it.

"Scotch," he said. "Not much and not on the rocks."

"Coming up," Sheryl said, going to a breakfront at the far side of the room that served as a dry bar.

She prepared his Scotch and whatever it was for herself, handed him his glass, saying "To your health, Edward," and went to sit not too near him and not too far away in a matching upholstered chair at the other end of the couch.

What ensued – with Skip only occasionally wandering away from their conversation to the overcoat and what he was going to do about it – was on the surface a neutral exchange. They talked about his law practice (which she reiterated he could choose to change), her work (she was a fund-raiser for a recently organized children's charity, which explained the "Family Advisor" phrase on her card) and their attitudes towards the city and the arts. They talked about the plays and movies they'd seen. She'd seen more than he had.

They did not, Skip noticed, talk about the restaurants they frequented – La Rochefoucauld did not come up for discussion.

That was on the surface. Underneath was a different story. Skip was experiencing the kind of attraction for her he hadn't felt in he didn't know how long. Nor was he sure he'd felt it for Faye on even their first dates. He also thought Sheryl might be having the same feelings for him. He'd been told somewhere, or had read, that when a woman, talking to a man, continually pushes her hair back, it's an indication she's interested.

Sheryl kept pushing her hair back.

This had gone on for some time – well over an hour and a half when Skip checked the Canal-Street Rolex: 11:27 p. m.

Sheryl saw him looking at it and said, "You've got to be going. That came out wrong. You had to be somewhere, and I've kept you. Sorry, Edward." He loved the sound of her saying "Edward." "I've got to get to bed, too." She actually blushed when she said that.

Skip thought he might be blushing, too, since at the mention of bed, he imagined her with nothing on, her breasts, her legs, her reddish pubic hair. He feared his mouth would start watering. He imagined himself entering her. He fought to squelch further fantasies.

"It's a school night, you know," she said.

She was getting up, and Skip knew he had to, too – in such a way as to disguise the beginnings of an erection. He did so as gracefully as he could, not knowing what to say, knowing he wanted to say he'd like to see her again but also knowing that was out of the question.

Faye.

Or was it?

Could it be arranged?

After a pause during which they looked at each other – presumably aware they were looking at each other with thoughts they didn't feel comfortable expressing – Sheryl said, "I'd better get your coat."

Skip started to follow her to the closet but stopped. Sheryl retrieved the coat, shut the closet door and, something having struck her, put the coat on.

"I just want to wear it one last time," she said. "You don't mind."

Skip said, "Why would I?"

Sheryl said, "When I think of you, Edward, I'll think of you coming at me and those jerks. I'll see you with your left hand in your left-hand pocket holding your Halls cough drops pistol.

She put her left hand in the coat's left front pocket, patently having fun mocking his cavalier's cavalier gesture. Skip's impulse was to put his arms around her, devil take the hindmost, but before he could act on it – or not – Sheryl's expression shifted.

"Hello," she said, pulling out the black kid gloves and the Halls cough drops and stuffing them in the empty right hand pocket where her card resided. She pulled out the Indian-head penny and said, holding it up before putting it in the right-hand pocket, "Hello, what's this? A lucky penny. I hope it brings you luck."

When she said that, her green eyes twinkling, Skip's thought was, Maybe it just has.

He could see her continuing to feel around in the pocket. "How new did you say this coat is?"

"I didn't say," Skip said. He couldn't. He didn't know.

Sheryl said, "It's old enough for this pocket to have a hole in it. You didn't know?"

She took her hand out and walked over to reach for his. He let her take it and put it in the coat pocket. Were they both thinking of the sexual implications? Skip knew he was, but then he wasn't. He'd located the hole and was thinking, What's this? What's this?

Sheryl let go of his hand and backed a few steps away. "Do you think," she asked, "something has fallen through it? Have you been missing anything?"

Skip didn't want to say that nothing of his could be missing in the coat and only said, "Nothing's missing I know of."

With both hands Sheryl had grabbed the coat just below the pockets and was jiggling it. She said, "Something could have fallen through and gotten caught in the lining. Funny those cough drops didn't fall through or your lucky penny. When I had the coat on before, I had the feeling there was something heavier on one side. This side, I think. You've never noticed it?"

Skip didn't think he had but then recalled that somewhere along the way he had had a vague feeling there was an imbalance on one side of the coat's bottom. He'd just thought it was the way the coat had been tailored.

"I guess I didn't."

"Here," Sheryl said, taking off the coat and handing it to him. "See for yourself."

Skip took the coat by its substantial collar and shook it. Now he did have the feeling that something about the heavy coat felt heavier than it should.

"Try this," Sheryl said. She picked up the hem of the coat and began running her fingers along it where anything that had fallen through the hole would have settled. "Yes," she said, gripping something and showing the lump of whatever she'd located to Skip, "there's something here."

Skip felt it. It was something lumpy. "What do you think it is?" he asked.

"I have no idea," Sheryl said. "It's your coat. You don't remember missing anything?"

"Nothing," Skip said. "What should I do – cut the lining free?"

"Don't do that," Sheryl said. "Maybe we can work it out through the hole."

Suddenly embarrassed about the situation, Skip said, "It's probably nothing." He had a thought he kept to himself. He'd found the Halls cough drops in the pocket. Perhaps there'd been a second pack, and it had fallen through the hole. He probed the lump for length and width, but no, it didn't feel like anything Halls manufactured.

He repeated, "No, probably nothing," and started to put the coat on.

"Don't be foolish," Sheryl said. "You want to get it out of there. If it has sharp edges, it could tear the lining or even the wool. Give me the coat. I have smaller fingers than you. I might be able to work whatever it is up and grab it."

Once again taken over by the overcoat, bamboozled by the hold it had gotten on him and the chase it was leading him on – including this warm-and-fuzzy Sheryl Sherman development – he handed Sheryl the coat. Not handing it to her would likely have led to his explaining why he didn't want to. Explaining how he'd come by it and where it had led him was still something he wasn't ready to do.

"Thank you," Sheryl said, sitting on one of the upholstered chairs again, putting the coat over her lap, pushing the object up with one hand and inserting her other hand into the pocket. "I'm getting it," she said. She'd furrowed her features, but to Skip she looked even more like someone he could go for – if he was in the market to go for anyone.

Was he?

"I've got it," Sheryl said. "Let me just pull it through the hole." She stretched the verb "pull" to let him know the effort she was happy to put into it. "And here it is."

She held it up.

"What is it?" Skip said.

"You don't recognize it?" Sheryl said.

I should recognize it, shouldn't I? Skip thought. At least I should if I were the owner of the coat. But I'm not, and I have no idea what it is.

"You mean someone else put this..." Sheryl held it up higher. "... in your pocket when you weren't looking?"

Skip thought, Yes, that's what happened. Whoever owned the coat – presumably, the man at the elevator who'd handed it to him – had put it in the pocket and must have forgotten about it.

Whatever it was.

What, for God's sake, was it?

Sheryl was holding up a rock for his scrutiny. A rock! The way she was holding it – upright with left thumb and forefinger – it was approximately two inches high, perhaps not quite two inches. At its widest point it was perhaps an inch and a half. It was shaped like a jar that narrowed at the neck and then flared to a lip not as wide as the widest part.

Was "amphora" the word to describe what it resembled? A tiny amphora. He motioned to Sheryl that he'd like to see it at closer range.

She handed it to him. Holding it now only a foot or so from him, he saw the stone was a mottled grey and brownish yellow. Was it sandstone? Skip had never had the slightest interest in geology – other than to know Manhattan was for the most part built on gneiss, shist and marble. Was it limestone?

The grey section which ran from the middle of the top to the bottom – looking somewhat like the state of Illinois – was smooth and contained various shaped spots of white. The brownish parts were like an amorphous frame around it.

The stone's make-up wasn't its most compelling feature. Skip hadn't examined it for more than a few seconds when he decided he saw a face carved into it. Yes, towards the bottom of the stone, as if the top were an ornamental headpiece, was a stern face. Its mouth was a downward turning thin-lipped frown. Just above it the stone flared into a broad, flattened nose. To the left of the top of this seeming nose a brown dot within a flat grey oval that came to a point at both ends looked like a right eye. There was nothing to suggest a left eye, but just to the right of where it would be was a totem of three short and equal-length rolls that gave the impression of a clenched fist.

The entire effect was that of an ancient civilization's god (a Mayan god? Aztec? Incan?) regarding anyone who looked at him – and more pointedly, at whom he looked – with unalloyed disapproval, with a gargoyle's disapproval.

The question in Skip's mind was whether this curiosity dug from the depths of the overcoat was something that had formerly been dug from other depths.

Was this an artifact?

Sheryl said, "What do you make of it?"

"I don't know what to make of it."

"You've never seen it before? It isn't something you thought you mislaid."

"No," he said.

"Do you have any idea who might have put it there?"

"No, but now I realize I'd better get going. I'm keeping you up on a school night." While he was saying this, Skip was rubbing the back of the stone with his left forefinger. It was a nervous gesture, he knew. He felt he was on the spot with Sheryl and at the same time wanted to get going with this new – was it a clue?

While running his forefinger along the stone's other side, he felt something there, too. He turned the stone over. It was mottled grey and brownish-yellow as well, although the grey predominated and in it were odd markings. He raised the stone to see if he could make them out.

At first he could discern nothing other than crude scratchings.

Looking even closer, he saw they formed a name – Harold something.

Now he was squinting, and Sheryl noticed. "What are you trying to see?"

"There's writing here. I think it's a name. Harold something."

She held her hand out to him. "Let me see it."

He gave it to her with reluctance, although he hoped he was hiding that.

She took it, looked. She moved closer to a lamp at her left. "I see what you mean. Barely legible. Harold. Harold. I think it says, Harold Smith. Harold Smith! Do you know anyone named Harold Smith?"

She handed Skip the stone so he could look again, confirm what she'd seen. He took it and, stepping over to the lamp, squinted again. It did seem to say "Harold Smith." Maybe "Harold Smits." He said to Sheryl. "I don't know any Harold Smith."

"Everybody has to know a Harold Smith," Sheryl said. There must be a million of them in the Manhattan phone book alone, and that's only the listed ones."

Why did Skip know that thirty-seven percent of New Yorkers with phones were unlisted? It was another of the factoids he had stored in his confounded legal brain that weren't much use except at an unpredictable time like this when they were discouraging – discouraging because he was thinking about how he was going to turn up a Harold Smith, any Harold Smith, the right Harold Smith.

And that didn't take into account the ones with no landline, only a cellphone.

Did the coat belong to someone named Harold Smith, who'd put a stone in its pocket that fell through the hole?

How was Skip to verify that?

And why was he thinking that going through these frisking motions with Sheryl was, well, just this side of enjoyable? No, make that the other side of enjoyable, the enjoyable side.

Sheryl said, "Don't you think you should see about returning the stone to Harold Smith?" She was standing up. "I'll get the phone book."

"Please don't do that," Skip said. He was thinking fast. Much as he might like what was going on here, he couldn't get her involved.

Telling her as much as he knew and had gone through already was too much for him to undertake. "You've done enough. Besides, it's late. I've kept you up, and I don't think it would be wise to wake up anyone named Harold Smith at this hour. I'll try to reach him – or them – in the morning." He thought for a second. "And find out how and why a stone with his named etched into it got into the – my – coat pocket."

"Your big beautiful coat pocket," Sheryl inserted.

He was reaching for the damn thing and looking at his make-believe Rolex. Could it be 11:42 p. m.? It could and was. "I think I've missed my appointment," he said, as he went to the door.

"That's my fault," Sheryl said. "I shouldn't have kept you."

Skip said, as she opened the door for him. "That's all right. It wasn't really an important meeting. Besides this was worth it. Meeting you. Perhaps we'll meet again."

"Next time I'm being held up, I'll expect you to be there," she said. "Edward Gerber, my Lochinvar."

She did have a smile that could steal a man's hardened heart, Skip thought.

And then thought, "Edward Gerber, my Lochinvar." The gentle, even affectionate, mockery she'd infused in the remark had the sound of finality for Skip, who was standing in the doorway and, like a sap, began to hear an old Jimmy Durante song his not usually song-loving father occasionally croaked, "Did you ever have the feeling that you wanted to go but still have the feeling that you wanted to stay?"

He didn't know what to do. He knew what he wanted to do. He wanted to kiss her good-bye. If he did, he wouldn't want to stop there.

He held out his hand. Sheryl held out hers. They shook hands, It was as if they'd just concluded a business deal. Very unsatisfying to Skip, and as he turned to go, he couldn't tell if she felt the same way about him but hoped she did.

He continued down the hall to the elevator.

As he reached it, he heard her say, "Don't forget you've got my card," and then heard her door close. When it did, he felt as if something important had ended that should have only just begun.

But there he was, in his newly acquired but, he hoped, temporary overcoat, his briefcase in one hand and a stone that looked as if it could be a museum piece in the other, an object that tipped him to someone named Harold Smith or possibly Harold Smits.

Getting into the empty elevator – his, um, Rolex said 11:47 pm – he'd resumed rubbing the back of the stone as if he'd be able to turn it over and find the name Harold Smith clearer or even, by some magic, find additional clarifying information.

Skip had told Sheryl he thought it out of the question to call Harold Smith at this time of night, but he didn't intend to hold to that. He'd known he wouldn't as he said it, and when he reached the empty lobby, he put down his briefcase and studied the mottled stone again.

The (was it a?) god appeared as disdainful as before, just as disdainful as the broken gargoyle outside 9 West Forty-seventh Street. When he turned the stone over he found nothing new, just "Harold Smith," as if it had been roughly cut into it by a school kid using an old, rusty nail. Or, he wondered, looking at it again, did the scratchings now look more like "Harold Smits."

Thinking he'd be happier ferreting out Harold Smits than Harold Smith, Skip looked up. He was facing the 458 West Eighty-sixth Street front door, which had a wrought iron grill protecting the glass.

Pressed against the glass he saw a face. A man had pressed his face to the glass so that his features were flattened. He'd raised his right fist to his cheek. In that absurd position he looked like nothing so much as the face on the stone Skip held, or was it the face of the fallen gargoyle?

Skip told himself it isn't anything, it's coincidence, it's a drunkard making his way home. He'd return the look, without flattening his features with his hand but with the same derision. He did, but when he did, he became uncertain as to whether the man was even looking at him but was just pressing his face to the glass for an unspecified reason.

The man backed off, walked away.

Manhattan at night could be like that, Skip tried to convince himself, while also musing that these were the elements that made the nighttime city appealingly unpredictable.

He decided to take stock of where he was and what had brought him there. He rubbed the coat. Having met Sheryl Sherman – having gotten her out of that jam – altered his attitude towards the blasted thing. Yes, he remained irritated that he'd taken possession of it, but returning it was having an effect on him he didn't fully understand. On the other hand – the one holding the stone – he felt instinctively that he might, that he would, come to some understanding, if he continued the, uh, scavenger hunt.

Okay, he wouldn't walk outside immediately. The drunkard could be skulking. He'd wait a few minutes and while he waited, he'd look into the Harold Smits business. He put the stone in the right-hand pocket – the one without the hole and with the black gloves, Halls cough drops, the Indian-head penny, Sheryl Sherman's business card.

He pulled his cellphone out to consult it for any Harold Smits(es) he might find in the New York City telephone directory.

What he found immediately was a text. He opened it. It said, "Sorry about last message, Angry. Over it. F."

Faye.

She says she's over it, Skip thought.

Am I?

He thought of the woman upstairs. Doing nothing to stop himself – maybe because it was so late and he was impatient – he texted back, "Maybe you shouldn't be over it. Maybe you should be over me. Think about it." He signed the text "Skip," backed up and shifted that to "Edward."

Had he been rash? Maybe there are times, he decided – taking into account how typically his routines were tempered – when it paid to be rash. Maybe after being unrash all these years, he was getting an out-of-the-past lesson in the benefits of rashness, of risk.

Risk – how often did that thought pepper his average day?

Just about never.

Anyway, he had Harold Smits to think about. Inside of a minute, he was in luck. Among the listings he scanned, there was only one for a Harold Smits – at 124 Avenue A. The other side of town, the other side of way downtown. Hardly convenient, but what so far in this coat chase had been convenient, even when – as with Sheryl Sherman – it had its upside?

Since Skip was cooling his hot heels in the 458 West Eighty-sixth Street lobby anyhow, waiting for the dipso with the flat Mayan face to move completely out of range, he thought he'd call the Smits person first, forget the hour. Harold Smits might be up. People in that part of town kept late hours.

Matter of fact, Skip thought, if Smits had anything to tell him about the store or, more than that, knew something about the coat, was perhaps its rightful owner, he deserved to be called at midnight. Macht nichts whether he was wide awake or in a deep slumber.

Skip dialed the number, which, tellingly, had a 646 area code – tellingly, because that indicated there was a good chance he hadn't been at his Avenue A location for long. It could have meant Harold Smits was one of the younger crowd who'd been moving into the gentrifying neighborhood and paying enormous rents for spaces that only ten or twenty years earlier went for peanuts.

Smits might be someone who'd own a coat like the coat Skip once again had on. Smits could be the rightful owner of this coat.

The phone was ringing. What was it Lily Tomlin said in her classic Ernestine sketches – "one ringie-dingie, two ringie-dingies"? There were three ringie-dingies and then four.

The phone was picked up. A man's groggy voice came on, "Hello. Who's this?"

Skip said, "Is this Harold Smits?"

"Yes, this is Harold Smits," the voice said. It was a harsh voice Skip thought he'd heard recently though he couldn't place it. "Who is this? Do you know what time it is?"

"Never mind the time," Skip heard himself have the unmitigated gall to say. "I'm calling, because I want to ask you about a stone I found that has your name on it." Skip was holding the stone up to look at the scratched "Harold Smits" name. "Do you know anything about it?"

"Who is this?" the voice said. Skip thought he could place the voice. It didn't speak with a foreign accent, but it sounded not at all unlike the voice he'd heard on the phone at the office Miles Rogers Havilland no longer occupied, if he had ever occupied it. "Are you crazy calling me at this time of night to ask me about a stone?"

"You're saying you don't know about a stone you might have lost?" Skip said. "What about an overcoat with a wide collar in a herringbone pattern? The stone was in the pocket. Well, not in the pocket. It was in the lining. It must have fallen through a hole in the pocket."

"Are you cracked," the voice said, "phoning me at this ungodly hour, asking about a stone and a herringbone overcoat?"

Skip heard the voice, and the exasperation in it, but he thought he'd found a likely suspect and wasn't going to let up. He wasn't in the mood to let up on anything, and it wasn't a mood he was often in, if ever.

Even if maybe he hadn't found a likely suspect. Even if maybe he'd called some innocent shlub, who happened to have the same name as the one on the stone he was gripping like a crazy person. And that's if Harold Smits was even the correct name, if the scratching on the stone even formed an actual name.

Maybe he should let up. He was closing in on doing as much when the voice, less grinding now, said, "Hold on a second. You're looking for Harold Smits, right?"

"Right," Skip said, "and you said you're Harold Smits."

"Yeah," the voice said, "I'm Harold Smits Jr My father was also Harold Smits."

"Your father?" Skip said, incredulous but not much more incredulous that he'd been about anything that had been going on for what was now inching into its second day.

"My late father," the voice said. "He's dead seventeen years, the old bastard." Skip thought he heard another voice in the background. He couldn't be sure if it was a man's or a woman's. Then he heard Harold Smits Jr say, not to him, "Some guy calling about my dad. What am I supposed to do, hang up on him?" Then he said to Skip, "What do you know about my dad?"

"I don't know anything," Skip said. "That's what I'm calling you about."

"You're saying something about a stone and an overcoat that belonged to my father?" the now more alert voice said. "If they did, and I'm not saying they did, but if they did, what are you doing with them?"

"That's what I want to know," Skip said.

"I can't tell you anything about them, can I?" Harold Smits Jr said, "until I see them."

Skip saw an opening and seized it, feeling almost cocky about his new itches to be proactive.

"Proactive"? Where did that thought come from? He'd never used the word – certainly not about himself, certainly not about his behavior. He'd never liked the word, but now he had a new respect for it.

"Do you want to see the coat? The stone?" Skip asked Harold Smits Jr.

"If they had to do with my father," Harold Smits Jr said, "about whom I knew very little, I'd be glad to look them over." He then again said something to someone else apparently nearby. "Some objects that belonged to my dad – or may have belonged to my dad." There was mumbling and then, "Of course, I want to know more." And then into the phone, "When do you want to let me see them?"

"What's wrong with now?" Skip asked.

"Now?" Harold Smits Jr said. "Nothing, I guess." More mumbling in the background, which elicited, "Yes, I know what time it is, but how often do you get a call like this?" Then into the phone, "Let me give you my address."

"I have your address," Skip said. "It's in the phone book. I'm taking a cab there right now."

"What's your name?" Harold Smits Jr asked.

Skip gave it and, saying he was catching a cab right away, rang off. Pocketing his cellphone (not in the pocket with the hole; he had a flash of Sheryl extracting it from the lining), he picked up his briefcase, opened the building door, stuck his head out and looked both ways.

All he saw was a man of about forty-eight or fifty in a cardigan walking a Scottish terrier. A little late for walking the dog, Skip thought, but not worth worrying about. Maybe the guy worked a late shift and had just gotten home. Maybe the dog was on a farkakteh schedule.

He stepped out of the building towards the curb where he saw no cabs and debated whether to turn left towards Riverside Drive or right towards West End Avenue and Broadway, where cabs might be more plentiful.

He decided to go towards Broadway. As he did, the man with the terrier now choosing the curb as an ideal spot to urinate looked up from the pet at Skip and said, clearly as a honking vehicle, "You're a lucky man."

Skip kept walking and picked up his pace.

The man spoke again and said, "You're a lucky man." Skip was walking faster but hadn't yet broken into a run. Neither did he turn around to see if the man and the dog were scurrying after him.

"Do you want to know why you're a lucky man?" Skip heard shouted behind him, as he broke into a run. "Because you can afford a nice overcoat." Though the man's voice was getting dimmer, the man repeated what he'd said. "Because you can afford a nice double-breasted overcoat in a masculine herringbone tweed."

The terrier, putting an exclamation point on the man's observation, barked twice. Then silence, except for the swish of the one or two cars he dodged as he crossed West End Avenue.

At Broadway and Eighty-sixth, Skip got a cab quickly. Again the cabbie wasn't Mac McAllister. This one was a Sikh. That's what the headgear announced, and the licence said Singh, Fateh. He spoke with a distinctly plummy accent, and once he got the destination from Skip, he did the rest of his speaking on a rasping intercom. It wasn't a new thing, Skip thought, as the man called Singh took the lights as if going to a fire, while keeping up his end of, of all things, a baseball conversation complete with statistics. Near as Skip could figure, he was with a rabid Yankees fan.

Just to keep Singh cognizant that he had a passenger, Skip – massaging the stone until he thought he might rub out the "Harold Smits" – uttered the occasional "That's right" or "I agree" or "You don't say" or "I'd totally forgotten he pitched that game."

As there was little traffic, Skip was deposited no more than twenty minutes later at 124 Avenue A, saying, "If it's not the Yankees and the Red Sox, I'm probably not going to get to the World Series, after all." He paid the sixteen-fifty, got out – briefcase, overcoat, stone and all – missing what the baseball enthusiast spouted in parting salutation.

Looking at the building, he saw a man huddled inside the first of a pair of double doors with glass in their upper halves. He was a young man in a thick terry-cloth robe that had seen better days. He hadn't bothered to comb his carrot-top hair and had certainly not shaved for the encounter.

When the young man – Skip would have guessed his age at twenty-five, twenty-seven, somewhere around there – satisfied himself he was looking at the man who'd called, he opened the door and whizzed out to intercept Skip on the sidewalk.

"You're the man who just called me?" he said. "You're Chip somebody?"

Skip saw that the man (whom he assumed had to be Harold Smits) had shoved his feet into rubber boots with loose and flapping Velcro-strap closings. "Edward, uh, Skip Gerber," Skip said, putting out his hand, as he walked towards the building. "You're Harold Smits?"

"Junior," Harold Smits Jr said, taking Skip's hand. "I'd invite you up, but it's not a good time." Skip recalled hearing the other voice through the phone. "Too messy. My apartment. I don't like anyone seeing it like that."

Skip stopped where he was, wondering how many men actually cared if their apartment was messy. He never did. (Anyway, he had housemaid Chaka to clean it up.) Instead, he had the impression he was being lied to, which further irritated him, because he didn't like standing in the street.

Too exposed.

He looked around for anything that could offer shelter and spotted another doorway only a few feet away recessed enough that he'd feel better in the shadows it provided. He nodded towards it and then moved that way.

Following him, Harold Smits Jr said, "I'm sure we can do whatever business you have in mind right here. You said something over the phone about a stone and an overcoat?" He screwed up his flushed face. "Is the overcoat you got on the one you think belonged to my father? It doesn't look like any overcoat I ever saw him wear. Of course, I never saw much of my father, the late, great Harold Smits Sr."

As Harold Smits Jr said that, he sneered, adding one more to the sneer parade that had been marching past Skip at a steady pace.

"I didn't say the coat belonged to your father," Skip said. "I don't know who it belongs to."

Harold Smits Jr sneered again – he's a very sneer-y guy, Skip thought

– and said through his sneer, "You're wearing it. Wouldn't you say it belongs to you?"

Skip wasn't going to explain why he was wearing it and how he'd come by it – not to anyone, not even to Sheryl Sherman, who may have deserved an explanation.

Then he thought better of it and relented somewhat. He had gotten this guy out of bed fairly late. (It had to be pretty near 1 am by now.) Maybe Harold Smits Jr had a right to sneer when asked to examine a coat that turned out to be no coat he'd ever seen before.

Skip changed his tactic. He pulled the stone from the right-hand pocket and aimed it towards Harold Smits Jr but held on to it. "Would you mind looking at this?" he asked.

"How do you expect me to see it?" Harold Smits Jr asked. "There's no light here."

Skip couldn't argue with that. He moved out of the shadowy doorway to where the streetlights offered enough illumination for Harold Smits Jr to study, at first, the carved surface.

"What is this?" Harold Smits Jr asked. "Some stone you picked up off the street? You got me out of bed and down here to look at a *stone* that for all I know you picked out of the gutter? Is this some kinda *joke*? Did one of my piss-ant friends put you up to this? Did Einar Westfelt cook up this little scheme, because Ramsay is sleeping with me now and not him?"

"I have no idea who either Einar Westfelt or Ramsay are," Skip said and shook the stone in Harold Smits Jr.'s face. He said, "Look at the stone more closely. You don't see a face there?"

Harold Smits Jr made a show of looking at the stone. "What face? It looks like a stone to me."

"You don't see a mouth? Nose? A right eye?" Skip insisted. "You don't see that little clenched fist on the right side?"

The questions appeared to intrigue Harold Smits Jr He looked closer and after a few seconds taking more than his previous cursory look, he said, "Yeah, maybe I see some of that, but what if I do?"

"Doesn't it hit you like it might be valuable?" Skip asked.

"What? Like it's some Peruvian relic or something? What's it to me?"

"Now look at this," Skip said. They were still in the light. He turned the stone over. "Can you see writing there? Can you read it?"

While Skip held it, Harold Smits took Skip's hand and pulled it to him. He twisted Skip's hand an inch or two this way and that to get a better look. Skip was looking at the top of Harold Smits Jr.'s unkempt carrot-top mane. "Looks like a name, I think."

"Go on," Skip said. "What does it say?"

"I don't know," Harold Smits Jr said, looking up at Skip as if he were a child dissembling before a disciplinarian parent. All Skip saw in those eyes with the bushy reddish-brown eyebrows caterpillaring over them was vacant space. "It looks like Harold – I don't know – Harold Smith?"

"You don't see Harold Smits?" Skip said, beginning to lose patience.

"It could be Smits," Harold Smits Jr said. Little gleams of light came into those eyes. "Uh-oh. Now I get it. This is a scam. You pick a name out – from the phone book or somewhere – scratch it on a stupid rock and then try to get the bozo with that name to buy it off you."

"Did I say anything about selling you the stone?" Skip asked.

"I bet you were just about to," Harold Smits Jr said, "but I'm not falling for it. What would I want with a stone anyway? I couldn't care less if it's – whadya call it? – a museum piece. I don't collect stones. Go find Harold Smith and work your sicko con on him."

For a dizzying moment, Skip viewed himself from outside himself: trying sometime around one in the morning to convince a Lower East Side man he'd never met that a stone retrieved from the lining of a coat he'd never bought had some special meaning.

"You're not getting my point here," he said. "You may not collect stones, but you said you're Harold Smits Jr What about Harold Smits Sr.? Maybe he had a collection." He'd freed his hand from Harold Smits' and was holding the object up. "Maybe this stone was your dad's."

The remark had an effect on Harold Smits Jr He stood upright, tightened the robe around him, planted his rubber-booted feet on the ground and said, "Come to think of it, my father did have not one but many collections. Collections were his big hobby. He was always with the collections. Not with us. Not with my mom and not with my brother Sidney or me. He'd come home, go into his study – where the rest of us weren't welcome – and futz around with his collections."

The way Harold Smits Jr was gathering steam, Skip could tell he'd struck a nerve. He also could tell now wasn't the time to interrupt the fellow.

"That thing you're holding in your hand could come from one of my father's collections or it couldn't," Harold Smits said, "but if it did, I wouldn't want anything to do with it. He didn't have time for us, and now that he's dead and gone, I don't have time for him or anything to do with him. And, buddy, that's all I have to say to you. As far as I'm concerned, you can take your stone and shove it where the sun don't shine. And if you think that's my dad's coat, I wouldn't wear it in a million years. The only thing I'd do with it is feed it to the moths."

The Oedipal peroration ended (and making Skip think much better of Gabriel Martin Gerber than he had for a while), Harold Smits Jr turned on his boot heel, took a key ring dangling maybe a dozen keys out of the robe pocket and went back to the building door and – taking no time at all to locate the key – through it.

Skip couldn't think of anything to do but stand on the street and watch Harold Smits Jr go. He knew he had to think of something, though, and decided to think of it not under the bright – relatively bright – street lights but in the shadowy door he'd repaired to before.

Noticing by his trusty fake Rolex that it was 1:11 a. m., he decided his interview with Harold Smits Jr was inconclusive, and that was putting the best face on it. On the other hand, he didn't think he'd soon forget Harold Smits Jr.'s face – the eyebrows, the unkempt hair, the sneer-prone mouth.

Perhaps Harold Smits Sr did own the stone, did have it logged in some artifact collection or other? He'd never know for sure.

Or would he? A bulb clicked on in his head. If Harold Smits Sr was a collector – or if even Harold Smith or one of the many Harold Smiths in the Manhattan phone book or any phone book was a collector – he would have had to purchase the stone for his collection, wouldn't he? If that were true, then it followed logically that he bought it from another collector or from a dealer in rare Mayan (Aztec, Incan, name-the-lost-civilization) objects.

Furthermore, if Harold Smits Sr – or any of the Harold Smiths – had amassed a valuable collection, it's possible other collectors knew about it, museums knew about it.

It was possible a curator, or curators, at the Museum of Natural History or, maybe even better, a dealer in South American – or any kind of antiquities – knew about the collection and, more than that, knew about this stone.

Skip was clicking on all cylinders, but it was 1:15 a. m, fifth-rate Rolex time. I'm not about to visit any dealer and certainly not anyone at the Museum of Natural History – not at, checking, 1:16 a. m.

What was he to do? he was thinking as he stepped out of the doorway. Propelled into pondering his next move – patting down the overcoat again for hints; he'd overlooked the hole earlier and the stone to which it led; what else might he have overlooked? – he wasn't heeding his surroundings.

He'd neglected to cast another of the beacon-like glances he'd gotten used to beaming round him. And he was only peripherally aware of several loud, low-pitched masculine voices coming his way on the generally deserted street.

The owners of the voices were aware of Skip.

"There's one, ladies," a low-pitched masculine voice rang out. "So well dressed, too, in that big *faaaabulous* coat," another low-pitched masculine voice agreed. "Let's *join* him," a third, low-pitched masculine voice said. "Or have *him* join *us*," a fourth low-pitched masculine voice joined in.

Still paying little attention to the low-pitched masculine chorus because steeped in thoughts of his next move, Skip was only jarred from them when he realized he'd been gripped by both arms and, in the old phrase, had been swept off his feet.

Barely able to utter alarm, Skip looked at his new traveling companions. His momentary surprise lessened when he remembered he was on Avenue A, where anything of this nature can't be dismissed as unlikely.

The two people holding him up and the two others, one who grabbed Skip's briefcase, were dressed in the kind of garish finery that only men in drag wear out of some need to dress – if they're going to dress as women – in the extreme, to dress as *ne plus ultra* women, to dress so *ne plus ultra* that they can't shop in stores like Bloomingdale's or Lord & Taylor or in any sort of Madison Avenue or Fourteenth Street boutique, stores catering to actual women.

They must shop in drag-queen specialty stores or, the way things were changing these days, online. This quartet surely had done one or the other or both. They were fireworks of glitz and glitter wrapped in feather boas. They teetered on huge high-heeled shoes.

They were all well over six-feet tall and each of them weighed at least two-hundred-fifty pounds, Skip observed to himself as he was dragged (in more than one sense of the word) along.

Even though the night had gotten progressively chillier and Skip had long since ceased feeling overheated in the coat, his new companions were adorned skimpily. Under the boas were short-hemmed dresses exposing thick thighs. Hairy chests, hairy arms and hairy legs abounded.

Holy hell, Skip thought, these guys are a football coach's worst nightmare, and his best efforts to free himself from them – even in his new, energized condition – were useless. All he was able to summon repeatedly was, "What do you think you're doing?"

"*Calm* yourself, child," one of the two gripping him, who had a black star pasted to his rouged cheek, said. "You can't fight us."

"And if you can't fight us," the other one gripping him, who featured a rhinestone tiara on his shaved head and a full beard, said, "you might as well join us."

"You should be *proud* to be with us," a third with red bee-stung lips and holding Skip's briefcase, said. "You'll be able to tell your friends you were specially selected by the Bad Mama Bears."

"To be our Goldilocks for the evening," a fourth one, holding a canvas tote bag that promoted "Whole Foods," appended." Having said that, he pulled a Goldilocks wig out of the Whole Foods tote bag and, the two holding Skip stopping, arranged it on Skip's head.

Though he was trying to free himself, Skip recognized futility when he looked it square in the mascara-laden face. He was able to say, "I'm not about to be anybody's Goldilocks. I'd appreciate it if you'd let me go and give me my briefcase. I don't have time for this."

He didn't. He had a mission to go on that was looking that much more enticing just then.

The Bad Mama Bear with the black star said, lowering his voice to an even lower pitch, "Listen to this, Ladies, he doesn't have time for us. He doesn't have time for Lulu, Zelda, Gigi and me, Gertrude." He pointed at each of the others with an index finger weighed down by a ring the size of a small hubcap.

"He's a busy, busy Goldilocks," Zelda, the one in the tiara, said. "How busy can he be not to have time for some fun with a few lovely ladies of the night?"

Lulu, the tote bag carrier also holding the briefcase, said, "Why not let's see what keeps him so busy?" He bent down to set the briefcase on the sidewalk, balancing on his high heels with his actual chapped heels protruding an inch over the platforms. He released the latches on the briefcase.

"Please don't do that," Skip, who was still being held, said. "Those papers are important. They can't be mixed up."

Lulu paid him no mind but said, "A lot of mumbo-jumbo here. Hold it. Here's a business card." He looked it over. "Ladies, say hello to Edward Raymond Gerber, attorney-at-law."

As if conducted by a choirmaster, the ladies said a choral, "Hello, Edward Raymond Gerber, attorney-at-law."

"And here," Lulu continued, "must be legal." "Oooh, legal briefs," the others cried, and Lulu added, "We love briefs."

Gertrude said, "We love boxers, too."

Ignoring the intrusion, Lulu said, "Gigi, you're the lawyer. What do you make of them?"

The red bee-stung-lips Bad Mama Bear squeezing Skip's left arm let go but not before motioning Bad Mama Bear Zelda with the tiara to take over. He went to look at the briefs. "I'm a trial lawyer, Lulu. You know that, and these look like they have something to do with real estate. They're *contracts*, for fuck's sake. Bo-ring."

He elongated the "boring" so that it resonated around them, turned to Skip and, picking up the short hem of his skirt to hold it out, curtsied and said, "You're in real estate law? You should be kissing us for taking you out of those dreary doldrums." He let his skirt drop and returned the contracts to the briefcase.

"We're such a god-send," tote-bag-carrying Lulu said. "Should he be kissing us? Zelda? Gigi?" "On our cheeks?" tiara-wearing, full-bearded Zelda said. "On our lips," red bee-stung Gigi said.

"I think he should," Lulu said. He tottered to Skip, leaned over and kissed him full on the mouth. Skip clenched his lips against Lulu's thick and probing tongue, trying to feel nothing. He smelled a strong perfume he hadn't detected before.

As Lulu kept his lips pressed to Skip's, Zelda and Gigi kissed him on his cheeks. Gertrude leaned in and kissed him on his chin.

They all reeked of perfume, enough to make Skip think he might collapse from the invisible weight of it. He was so woozy he wasn't sure he could think straight, although "straight" may not have been the adjective most relevant to his position.

The men calling themselves Lulu, Gertrude, Zelda and Gigi completed their sloppy osculation, but then Zelda reached into the fringed purse he carried over one hairy forearm and got out a flask.

"You must try some of this," he said. "Sure as shit, he must," Lulu said, followed by Gertrude and Gigi saying, "He must, he must" in bass-baritone sing-song.

The next thing Skip knew – "experienced" was more like it – he was swallowing something strongly alcoholic. But that was about all he knew for sure. Otherwise, he couldn't even determine where he was or how long he was being hauled about like a straw figure to the jangling of cheap jewelry and the click-clack of size-thirteen heels pocking the pavement.

Was he still on Avenue A, or was he being led along one of the streets that ran east-west?

Because it was so late – maybe 2 a. m., or later by then, though he couldn't see his not-Rolex – there was little traffic wherever they were. So during the soused promenade, he and his escorts encountered very few pedestrians.

One or two passed by and laughed not just at the sight of the outlandish quintet but at Lulu or Gertrude or Zelda or Gigi when one or more of them said something along the lines of "It's his birthday. We're celebrating the way he asked us to celebrate."

All that Skip could muster the energy to say a version of from time to time was, "Please give me my briefcase. Please let me go. I'm not Goldilocks. I don't even have blond hair. I'm Skip Gerber. I'm Edward Raymond Gerber, and I need my briefcase."

He said it one too many times. Lulu, the Bad Mama Bear carrying the Whole Foods tote and the brief, finally said, "Don't you think Goldilocks is too attached to his briefcase?"

Zelda said, "Abso-fucking-lutely, Lulu, dear." "No one wearing such a handsome overcoat should be so dependent on a sad little briefcase," Lulu said, and Gigi said, "We really need to do something about it,"

Lulu said, "We know what to do with it, don't we, Ladies? We need to – ." He paused so the others, seeing where he was going with this, could join in with a low-pitched chorus of, " – *get rid of it.*" This was followed by a chorus of "I'll do it, let me do it"s.

"I'm holding it," Lulu said. "I'll do the honors."

"Please, please, don't," Skip repeatedly said. To no avail. Within seconds he heard the sound of what he knew had to be leather hitting metal. It was plain to him, even in his liquor-and-perfume-inebriated state that his briefcase was now resting in a trash can somewhere on the Lower East Side.

How and when would he be able to retrieve it in what he knew, or had heard, were still the wilds of Manhattan's Loisaida? Would he ever retrieve it and all the contracts, et cetera, that may have been the bane of his existence but were nevertheless the *sine qua nons* of his working life?

"You shouldn't have done that," he said. "You shouldn't have done that."

"Don't be silly," Lulu said. "Wait and see. You'll thank us."

"I won't," Skip said. "You just threw away my livelihood."

But how bad was that, really? Skip wondered, as the toes of his shoes scraped along. Maybe that's what I want, he thought.

"If you think your whole livelihood is in that briefcase, Goldilocks," Gertrude said, "you better start looking around for another livelihood. Am I right, Ladies, or am I right?"

"You're right," the others echoed, and Lulu said, "Ladies, I'm beginning to think Goldilocks isn't registering very high on the Bad Mama Bears fun-o-meter. What do you think?" Zelda said, stroking his beard, "Dolled up in that overcoat, he sure looked like he'd be a great Goldilocks." "Maybe we need to find another Goldilocks," Gigi of the red bee-stung lips said. "No maybe about it," Gertrude of the black-starred cheek said.

"Shall we take a Bad Mama Bears vote?" Lulu said. "May I see a show of ringed hands and braceletted arms, Ladies?"

Skip was too out of it to see how the vote went but learned soon enough. "It's unanimonious. Edward Raymond Gerber is no longer Goldilocks."

Through blurring eyes, Skip saw and felt the Goldilocks wig wrenched from his head. "Now," Lulu said, "he's just Edward Raymond Gerber, the real estate lawyer in an overcoat too good for him." "Maybe we should relieve him of it," Gigi said. Zelda said, "Not a good idea. By now it might be highly contaminated by negative vibes." Gertrude said, "Let's leave it on him, wherever we leave him."

Skip, still gripped by two of them, heard some mumbling and sensed a decision was being reached. He felt himself being lifted up by the four of them and carried several yards away.

He heard Lulu say, "Gently, Ladies, gently. When dumping a Johnny – literally dumping him – we must be as gentlewomanly as we can be."

Then he felt himself hitting something round and hard. He was suffering the same fate his briefcase had. He had, he easily but not happily ascertained, been deposited, rear-end first, in a trash receptacle – and too far in to force his way out.

As the Bad Mama Bears clattered away, their voices growing dimmer, Skip heard Zelda say, "What time is it, anyway, Ladies?" "It's nearly three in the fucking a. m.," Gigi said, "time to get home for porridge. I'm in court tomorrow." "I'm flying to Atlanta," Gertrude said. "I'm sleeping in," Lulu said. "The dealership ought to be able to get along without me for a day." Zelda, heard faintly, said, "I'm not sleeping at all. I'm due in surgery at six. Oops!"

Skip heard no more, and wriggling in the metal can like a cockroach on its back – like something out of Kafka's *Metamorphosis* – he was left. He thought that maybe if they'd relieved him of the overcoat – the thickness of which was part of his inability to dislodge himself or do anything better than cram himself in more tightly – he'd have been released from this waking nightmare.

On the "waking nightmare" phrase, however, he heard what sounded like a young man behind him say, "Look at the man, man." He tried twisting around to see who was talking but was impeded by the way he was wedged in the can.

"We ought to help him out of his misery," a second adolescent voice said.

"You're right," the first said. "He needs us to do that."

"Maybe that stick over there will do the trick," the second voice said.

Their exchange was over fast, but led Skip to believe he was about to be rescued by one of the newcomers using whatever stick they'd found as a lever to remove him from his ungainly pose and by the other grasping his arms to pull him from it. He also thought he might have heard those voices before – hot-footing it away on Vesey Street, scuffing along on West Eighty-sixth Street.

Wondering if all the city's troublemakers sound alike, he caught a thunderclap of rowdy laughter and felt a dull knock on the top of his head and then – even as he thought he was losing consciousness – felt himself grabbed by each arm.

What a relief! Whoever they were (there seemed only to be two of them), they were going to pull him from his buffoon's perch.

No, they weren't.

One of them said in a growl, "Nothing on this wrist." The other said in a higher growl, "Something on this one. A Rolex." The first said, "Fuckin' *awesome*." The second one said, "Forget it. It's a knock-off." The first one said, "Yeah, but maybe we can unload it to someone as stupid as this guy." The second one said, "Not worth our time." The first one said, "Cheap bastard. The coat's probably a knock-off, too. But if he likes knock-offs, this oughta make him happy."

Skip felt another cranial thud. Then nothing, then a blaze of falling stars. He regained consciousness slowly, thinking sequentially "Where am I? Wherever I am, why am I here? Who am I?" He also thought, "Why is the light so bright?" and "What is that face looking at me? Why is that face looking at me? Whose is that face looking at me?"

"You're finally coming to," a male voice that struck a distant chord said.

Skip tried to make out the man's features but couldn't.

"It's me, bud," the voice said, "Dermot McAllister. Mac."

Whoever Mac is, Skip thought, his features are coming into focus. It was a clean-shaven, craggy face with not much more than a dot for a nose. It was a boxer's nose, Skip thought and, "It's the cab driver. What's he doing here – wherever here is?"

"Don't be alarmed," Mac said.

Yes, it came to Skip that Mac was someone he knew he knew. The person known to him was wearing a grey sweat shirt and sweat pants, had a towel around his shoulders like a trainer and was holding a brush of some sort.

Mac went on to say, "You're out of danger, and if you're wondering, you're at my place." He held up the brush. "I've just been in the other room getting the dirt off that big coat 'a yours. Not much damage to speak of."

Skip tried to raise himself on his elbows to look around, but Mac said, "Not yet, bud. Just lie there for a few more minutes."

"Where is your place?" Skip asked, though the words didn't come easily to him.

"Astoria," Mac said, "Queens. You ever been out here before? Not counting JFK?"

As Skip took in what he could see – mostly ceiling with a water stain marking one corner like a rusty tide coming in – Skip tried to remember if he'd ever been to Queens. He knew he had but couldn't recall the occasion.

He couldn't recall much of anything. He knew he was Skip Gerber – Edward Raymond Gerber. Beyond that he had to wrack his brain, which, now that he realized it, wasn't feeling too conducive to being wracked. Might that have something to do with the slight bump he discovered when he felt on the top of his head?

He tried nodding that not unfamiliar head to let Mac know he'd been to Queens, even if he hadn't, but his neck didn't seem to respond to his bruised and aching brain's commands. He let his head fall back – but tenderly as he could – against whatever he was lying on. He would have said it felt like a bed with a pillow, but he wasn't prepared to draw any hard-and-fast conclusions.

"Why don't you take it easy for a few more minutes," Mac said, "and let me talk while you're getting your strength back."

In his present condition, that sounded like a good idea to Skip, who didn't even think about nodding again. His head was hurting like a son-of-a-bitch. He resumed surveying the ceiling.

Mac, sounding as if he were sitting in a chair somewhere nearby, began to talk, saying, "You're probably wondering how you happened to end up at my humble abode. It's like this. When I dropped you off to meet that guy at Hudson and Twelfth, I had a feeling something wasn't right. Truth to tell, I'd picked up something about you all the way to Hudson and Twelfth from the Upper East Side. That's why when you paid me and sent me off, I had a hunch I ought to drive around the block a couple times."

That's why he picked me up the second time, Skip remembered.

"That's why I picked you up again. It wasn't no coincidence. When I dropped you off at 185 Vesey Street, that wasn't the end of it, neither. I don't mind telling you I followed you ever since – up to West Eighty-sixth Street and down to Avenue A. I just didn't want to pick you up again, 'cause I didn't want you to think I was stalking you. It's just I kept having the feeling something was wrong with you. You can take the cop out of the precinct, but you can't take the precinct out of the cop. Hunches are my business."

While Mac was talking, Skip was beginning to get his strength back – not a lot of it but enough to move his head right and left on the pillow. Yes, it was a pillow with, he was pretty certain, a red-white-and-blue pillowcase on it. He was in a bedroom on a bed with metal poles for a headboard. It was a small room with pea-soup green walls and a window that looked out on another building. Through the window he saw a brick wall and a window with a white lace curtain in it.

In the rest of the room, he saw a closet with no door and inside, clothes jammed together. Other clothes were piled on a wooden chair. There was another non-matching wooden chair painted a lima-bean green. Mac was sitting on it. On the wall opposite the window and to his right was a crucifix.

If only Bernice Sawyer Gerber could see me now, Skip thought, under the care of Jesus. Of course, if she could see me now, he further thought, she'd want to know if I've uncovered the information Gussie Slotnik claimed she needed.

Mac was still briefing him with, "And you can count on the fingers of one hand and still have a few fingers left over the number of times my hunches have let me down. A good thing, too, because if I hadn't been following you the way I was, I never would have found you in that trash can when I did. I would have gotten there sooner, but I have to own to making a few misjudgments. Not wanting you to make me, I lagged behind a certain distance wherever you were, and I wasn't counting on a bunch of drag queens taking you on that hike. What a bunch of what-are-theys they were. But that's New York City for you.

"So in Alphabet City I lost you for a while. I had to drive around for longer than I expected and finally saw you in the trash can with two hoods in hoodies frisking you. I jumped out of the car and scared them off, but not before they'd located the wallet on your person. When I came after them with the truncheon I keep on the front seat of the cab in case anybody gets frisky, they made it out of there on their Nikes and dropped your wallet on the way. I picked it up and shoved it in my pocket before I got you out of the can, which was no easy job. Those two shitheels dumped you in there but good."

Skip was listening, but something about the last part didn't sound right to him. For the life of him, he couldn't remember what it was. The last thing he remembered was meeting a carrot-top guy somewhere on Avenue A. Whatever happened between then and his lying on this bed with a pillow under his throbbing noggin and the old wooden cross to his left was a blank to him.

Mac wasn't finished. "I got you out eventually, slung you over my shoulder, stuffed you into the cab and brought you here. I looked in your wallet. That's how I know you're Edward Raymond Gerber and where you live, but I didn't think I should take you there. If there was a doorman or no doorman but only a nosy neighbor, I didn't think you'd want them to see you like this. I got you out of most of your clothes – suit, shoes, shirt, tie, that heavy overcoat you didn't seem to want to get out of, even though it got a little roughed up."

He stopped and started. "Everything's in the living room. Your wallet, with, near as I can tell, everything in it, in case you're worried. Yeah, and your briefcase, too. It's not often you find a guy and his briefcase in two different trash cans. I found it where you or somebody left it. I don't suppose you're the one who threw it in a trash can."

What did he mean by that? Skip wondered, and then he knew. His memory was coming back. At least partially. He remembered something happening with his briefcase he didn't want to happen. Someone else had it and was threatening to discard it.

Did discard it.

It was more than one someone. Now he got it. He had an image of four big men in dresses abducting him, putting a wig on his head, calling him "Goldilocks."

No, he had to be making that up, but he couldn't be. Why would he make up something that preposterous? And then all sorts of things came back to him. That's what Mac meant by "a bunch of drag queens." There were four of them. They called themselves Bad Mama Bears.

And before them there was a majorly attractive actual woman who called herself Sheryl. There was a Mayan (or maybe Aztec or maybe Incan) stone he had somewhere. How about the Central Park Mall? Yes, there was that and a statue of a financier. Even before that there were a few chases his head ached too much to spend time reliving.

Most of all, there was an overcoat. Yes, an overcoat. That's what Mac must have meant when he referred to a coat Skip didn't want to get out of. Why didn't he want to get out of it? It came to him, as if he'd been slapped in the face, that he hadn't wanted it in the first place – had to get rid of it, would get rid of it, would now refocus himself on getting rid of it. Get it to the rightful owner before who-knows-what does him in.

He'd get on with the great exploit that had been dropped in his lap.

Just when he needed it, he said to himself. But no, it hadn't been dropped in his lap. It had been put in his hand, draped on his shoulders.

He reckoned he'd been deterred from it for some hours now. And by whom, by what? By four steroided drag queens and two hoodlums. By his lying in a strange bed watched over by a Savior.

Now he was incensed, riled, pissed off. He tried sitting up again. This time he was able to. He swung his legs over the side of the bed, which, since he was swaddled in a blanket like a newborn, was more difficult than he signed up for.

"Whoa, there, Mr Gerber, bud," Mac said. "One thing at a time. I know it's one small step for man, one giant leap for mankind, but I don't think you're ready for any giant leaps yet."

Mac was right. If Skip even tried to walk, he'd pitch over, and since he felt bum from top to toe, he'd best sit where he was for a few minutes.

Assured that Skip was stationary for the time being, Mac said, "Anyway, I better tell you that although I have your briefcase, I don't know about all the stuff in it. When I saw it lying on the ground next to a trash can, I'd been driving around looking for you, and there it was. I figured it might be yours. Who else would be carrying an expensive-looking briefcase around the Lower East Side in the middle of the night? When I knew your name was Edward Raymond Gerber, I knew the initials on the briefcase matched yours."

"Anyway, I'd pulled over, stopped the cab, got out and went to pick it up. Sorry to say, it had been opened and the papers in it were scattered around. Probably some homeless person or a couple of kids were hoping for something they could sell or pawn, and when they saw there was nothing in it but papers, got mad and threw them around.

"I rounded up what I could, but I can't say some of the papers didn't blow away or were maybe trashed by whoever went through them. Could of been those kids in the hoodies. Could of been anyone who happened to come along."

Skip tried to remember what he had in the briefcase. There were the three contracts. He needed them, but they weren't what you'd call classified information. If he was being tailed, it was unlikely those were what he was being tailed for. Didn't matter. Brianna could duplicate them at the office. The office! He couldn't go to the office looking and feeling as he did. Was Brianna even in the office?

What time was it? When that question went through his tossed-salad brain matter, he progressed from sitting position to standing as fast as that. He began unwrapping himself from the blanket into which Mac had secured him. He had no idea how long he'd been here, how long he'd slept – or if he'd slept. He could have been unconscious the whole time.

"What time is it?" he asked as he was getting himself unraveled.

"Take it easy, bud," Mac said. "It's about eight-thirty, quarter to nine. Anyway, you're not going anywhere until I say so. I'm not going to be responsible for you passing out on the staircase or anything."

Free of all tethers now, Skip looked down at himself and saw he was still in his underwear, and his legs looked purple in spots. He only wore Calvin Kleins because women laughed at Fruit of the Loom, and, yes, he wore the real thing, not rip-off CKs – though he would if he could ever find any.

Being plunked into trash cans definitely bruises a guy, Skip observed. He wondered what the back of his thighs and calves looked like. Not so good, if they looked the way they hurt.

"What time did I get here?" he asked Mac, who'd also gotten up, as if to restrain Skip, should it come to that.

"I must have discovered you about three, maybe a little after," Mac said, "and by the time I got you back here, it had to be three-thirty, thereabouts. So you been here close to five hours, five hours plus change, something like that. Not enough time to be up on your pins. Why don't you sit back down like a good boy while I make you some breakfast?

"You're looking at a former short-order cook. That was my first job when I was fourteen and my uncle needed help at his greasy spoon, and the family needed someone else bringing in bread. So it'll be good. How do you like your eggs, and do you take your coffee black or with milk? I only keep skim milk."

"Scrambled, like my brains," Skip said, "and coffee with milk. Skim milk. I need to look at whatever's left in my briefcase."

"You stay seated," Mac said. "I'll bring it to you. You can look over whatever's there, while I'm in the kitchen – anyways, what my landlord calls a kitchen."

Mac left the room.

Skip, sitting on the edge of the bed like a good boy, seized the opportunity to give the room a second once-over and, among less compelling items of a standard nature, noticed on an old bureau a pistol in a holster attached to a wide belt. He looked at it with alarm and wondered if Mac had been wearing it during the cab ride(s) or had it with him.

Mac returned with the briefcase and saw Skip gazing. He nodded and said, "I never need it. Okay, *hardly* ever." He emitted what could only be called a chortle that made his craggy face craggier. "Just kidding. Here's your briefcase. I'll go scramble some eggs. That's what you said, wasn't it? Not poached or sunny side up."

Mac disappeared, humming an unidentifiable tune under his breath. Was it "You Are My Sunshine," and if it was, why did that hit a familiar chord? Skip put the thought aside, laid his briefcase on his lap and snapped it open. He faced partial disarray. Mac had tried to square off the papers into a manageable stack but had only been partially successful. Skip found the contracts with which he was involved at the moment – or parts of them.

His Chapstick was there, along with his Rolaids and Binaca. His copy of "The Firm" was there, only slightly the worse for wear. John Grisham must not have been of interest to anyone rifling the briefcase. Not fiction readers, apparently. Maybe just not legal-thriller readers. Maybe just not of interest to legal-thriller readers who knew, as he did, that Grisham's version of the law is ratcheted up.

Or is it? Nothing like those plots ever happened to lawyers. Hold it. Maybe they did. Maybe something within those stretched parameters was happening now. To him – and, wow, if it was, if it was his own made-to-order legal thriller, then that was kind of, wow, exciting.

Excitement in his life? When did that ever happen?

Like, never.

But back to the papers he was sorting through. He seemed to remember a few others he had in there, but if he couldn't recall what they were, how important could they be to him? He wondered if even the supposedly important contracts were important to him. They were, but in the greater scheme of things, were they?

He didn't even try to suppress the returning thought that the Bad Mama Bears were right when whichever one of them said they were doing him a favor by deep-sixing the briefcase.

While he was musing on that, Mac returned with, in one hand, the eggs on a plate with some toast and home fries and, in the other, a mug of coffee from which steam was rising exotically.

"Hold these," he said, "while I get you a table to put them on and a fork. I hope you don't take butter or sugar. I don't keep any in the house. Not good for you." He left and returned right away with a wooden cart and a fork. He set the cart down in front of Skip. "There's the table. Sorry it's not too fancy."

He handed Skip the fork, sat down with his hands on his knees and leaned in to talk. Skip began to eat. The eggs were as good as Mac said they'd be. To let Mac know, he made non-verbal appreciation noises.

"Glad you like them," Mac said. "The secret ingredient makes the difference. It's not so secret. Paprika." He held up a fleshy hand. "But only a dash."

Skip ate more, while Mac, remaining on his bare feet, moved closer to him. "But that's not what I want to talk about. I got to get back in the hack shortly. To make up for what I didn't take in last night following you around."

With a mouthful of toast, Skip wasn't about to go find his wallet.

Mac picked up the look in Skip's eyes. "I don't say this to make you feel guilty. I say it because there's something going on with you, and you oughta tell me what it is. Nobody makes the cross-town trips like you made last night, ending up in a trash can, without something going on. You don't have to tell me if you don't want to, but it sure as hell might help if you did."

Mac stopped to wait for what Skip had to say. For his part, Skip thought about it, but what could he do? He plain and simple didn't want to go into the business with the overcoat. He'd sound like a grade-A fool, accepting the coat outright in the first place.

Mac, deciding the extending pause meant Skip wasn't going to say anything, said, "Okay, it's your funeral. I'd like to provide my services again today, but like I say, I can't. I'm getting out of here in about fifteen minutes. If you feel up to leaving with me, I'll drive you back to Manhattan. If not, you can stay here until you're ready to leave. I'll give you an extra set of keys. When you lock the three locks, you can push the keys under the door.

"Either way, if you want to shave, there's shaving cream and an extra razor in the bathroom." He pointed out the bedroom door and to the right. Before walking out of the room, he said, "I keep one there for whoever ends up spending the night."

Skip thought over the options. He wasn't going to stay here. If he did, he'd have to take a subway back to Manhattan, and in the best of times, which these weren't, he tried to avoid the subway whenever he could.

Look at me, he thought, worrying about subways when I have an overcoat in the next room with a stone burning a hole in its pocket – a stone that had already burned a hole in the other pocket.

He was now *compos mentis* enough to know that dealing with the stone – maybe it was Peruvian, maybe it was from another part of the world entirely – required finding a dealer who knew about these things. He had no doubt there'd be one or more or many more in Manhattan. But how to locate whoever it was or they were?

Besides which he felt fueled by the hot-off-the-skillet breakfast, renewed for what increasingly had the aspect of a stimulating assignment, one he wanted to prove he was up for and up to.

He decided to accept the shaving offer, and, wobbly as a toddler, followed the directions to a bathroom just large enough for a three-foot by three-foot shower, a toilet, a sink with a mirror. It was also just large enough for a man to turn around in.

The mirror was what got him – looking at himself in it, that is, not the fact that it needed some resilvering. His face wasn't bruised, but in his hazel eyes, his mouth, under the day's beard, he saw a man he only recognized as a slightly disoriented version of his former self. It wasn't that he looked older. He looked different, changed, uncertain. In his appearance he saw the earmarks of a quandary.

He didn't have to think hard to admit he was in one. He wanted to know how deep it went, how wide it ranged, how high it reached? That's what he couldn't decipher in that somewhat familiar face of his, in that somewhat familiar face he'd been told wasn't bad-looking, in that somewhat familiar face he'd often trade on with the ladies, the face he'd adjust for clients he was attempting to mollify, for adversaries he was angling to get around.

That somewhat familiar reflection got him reflecting not just on his face at the moment but on the many faces he'd seen of himself over his thirty-seven years plus five months and some days.

When he was a kid, up until ten or eleven, he hadn't spent much time looking in mirrors. He'd eyeballed images of himself in the professional photographs Bernice Sawyer Gerber had had taken by family portrait shutterbugs she and her friends (Gussie Slotnik, for one) passed around like valued possessions.

He could see the adolescent checking for zits or the fair-to-middling athlete checking for bruises acquired in a pick-up soccer game. (Those games may have been the best use to which he'd ever put his head.) He could see the student musician determining whether the lip he needed to play his trump.t was developing. (Where was that trumpet anyway? He'd gotten good at it, might have become a professional musician, if other things – parental disapproval – hadn't intervened.) He could see the smiling good boy he was and then wasn't when in seventh grade he went to Trinity and fell in with a crowd of joke-pullers, instructor-taunters, troublemakers of the imitating-teachers-behind-their-backs variety.

Mostly, he knew his face from when he started shaving. He never thought much about his Gerber-Sawyer visage then. It was just his face, made up of assorted parts of his parents' faces and their parents' faces. The features were familiar, features that never seemed reshaped dramatically by troubling thoughts.

More the opposite, features molded by the self-satisfaction of a kid raised with privileges, features of a young man totting up girlfriends and congratulating himself with boastful murmured phrases like "You rogue, you," "You, handsome devil, you," features of a chap for whom continued entitlement was a given, whose place in the wider sea of humanity was established as long as he rocked no metaphorical boats.

He saw that same face through college and had noticed it altering only when he was at Columbia law, after Harvard. As those three years went by and his real-world future approached, that's when he saw the early signs of a furrowing brow.

Only then did he discern the onset of misgivings. He recognized then that as time went by, those misgivings had accreted. But what were they? Did they have to do with what kind of job he'd be offered before or just after graduation, and where? Did they have to do with what field of law he wanted to enter? Did they have to do with pleasing Gabriel Martin Gerber by choosing real estate law, or – since he nonetheless admired his aloof father and so had become intrigued by real estate law – by choosing the discipline to please himself? Did they have to do with the pros and cons of joining Gabriel Martin Gerber's firm? Did they have to do with his unexamined reasons for choosing law in the first place? Did they have to do with law versus music, now that it had occurred to him?

He looked closely at the face again. He looked at the mouth and would have bet money there was a new set to it. He looked at the chin and noticed that despite the pain – or *because* of it – he was holding it a bit higher. Did he ordinarily hold it higher when he was shaving? Well, yes, but this was higher, maybe only millimeters, but higher.

He looked into his eyes. fAs always, they were hazel, which from childhood he'd thought of as a non-color, a neither/nor color. Now, however, he saw something new in them. It, too, might only be a manifestation of bodily discomfort, but that wasn't it. What he saw was what he'd seen in other people's eyes, never in his own: a glint.

No, he corrected himself. It was the light in Mac's claustrophobic bathroom thrown by the lone bulb with the stained shade over it, he thought. But as he regarded the bulb in the mirror, he moved his head this way and that, keeping his eyes focused in the mirror to see what might happen. No change – the glint was there.

At every angle.

And he didn't want to lose it.

But how not to?

For one thing: the overcoat.

Or for two things: the overcoat and the stone now in its right-hand pocket, keeping company with Halls cough drops, the lucky Indian-head penny and the (lucky?) Sheryl Sherman business card.

If any or all of the items remained there after the Loisaida fracas.

Wiping a last dollop of shaving cream from his shaved former/current face, Skip felt the only reflection that mattered to him just then was Mac's. He'd come to the bathroom door and was reflected dressed in a version of what he had on yesterday.

"Speaking of drag queens," Mac said, "this is my cabbie drag."

Skip took the remark as Mac's joke and, turning around to face the jokester, gave it enough of a laugh to show he'd gotten the reference. Then he quick returned to thoughts of the stone and the part of his quandary it represented.

"Do you happen to have a computer?" he asked. Glintily, he hoped. "I have to look something up." He didn't want any questions, and he assumed he saw Mac about to ask one. "Something work-related."

"I got one," Mac said. "Who doesn't these days? It's a Mac, as you might guess, like yours truly. It's in the living room with the rest of your things. But make it snappy if you're coming with me. I gotta get outta here."

Mac left the bathroom. He'd been holding Skip's breakfast plate and mug. Skip followed him out, watched as Mac put the crockery in his Pullman kitchen sink.

So this is the living room, Skip thought. A big flat-screen television and a club chair facing it and spilling some of its stuffing shared pride of place. (Did Mac furnish his cop's/cabbie's crash-pad out of Goodwill Industries? It had that slightly stale air.)

Skip saw his clothes lain more or less carefully on a card table that Mac obviously used for scarfing his fast-food meals.

Mac's Mac sat next to them. Before Skip got into his duds – and the overcoat which looked as it had when he first held it – he sat on a metal folding chair in front of the computer and Googled "Manhattan Antiquities Mexico South America."

Something came up.

Mac, who was standing at an angle where he couldn't read the screen, said, "Do you need to take anything down?" Skip nodded that he did and was handed a Bic pen and a piece of paper. He wrote down, "Hugo Penrose, Dealer in Central and South American Antiquities, Art & Artifacts Building, 222 East Fifty-eighth Street, (212) 535-3553, Monday–riday 9.30–5.30, Enquiries welcome."

He was about to log off when he thought about taking another minute or two to locate Gussie Slotnik's information – if only to get Bernice off his case – but Mac was standing there ready to leave.

He logged off.

"Find what you wanted?" Mac asked. In the terse sentence, Skip was fairly certain he detected suspicion. He didn't like lying to Mac, but he couldn't see any way around it. Curiously, he'd never minded dissembling in similar situations – not that there were any completely similar legal situations or otherwise – but he disliked it now.

"I'll get dressed, and we can get going," he said. When he made the remark, he heard in it determination and – flashing on being escorted down a Lower East Side Street by four burly men in women's clothes – liked what he was hearing. He let it ride as he started to dress in clothes that looked as if a good laundering and dry-cleaning wouldn't hurt.

Not so the overcoat, which Mac had gotten to look spiffing and which – when Skip felt in the pockets – held its enigmatic and, for some reason now, reassuring contents.

Within ten minutes, Mac and Skip were leaving the Astoria apartment and heading past garish storefronts for the taxi garage and Mac's trusty hack. After lugging Skip to bed, Mac must have parked the taxi there and then returned home to keep his vigil.

Aside from Skip thanking Mac for his impromptu hospitality and asking whether he'd gotten any sleep at all and, even if it amounted to a couple of hours dozing in a chair, why he wasn't tired, he said little. He didn't want to offer any openings for more questions he'd feel worse about evading.

And aside from Mac asking Skip where in Manhattan he wanted to be dropped off and Skip telling him anywhere on Second Avenue around East Fifty-eighth Street, Mac didn't say much, either.

Dropping Skip at Fifty-ninth and Second by the Roosevelt Island Tramway, Mac – while refusing to be paid – did remind Skip with conviction embellishing his craggy features that Skip had that convenient business card and shouldn't hesitate to use it "for whatever, whenever."

Unconvinced that Mac wouldn't keep tabs on him, Skip watched the cab – 3Q61 was the number he memorized on the taxi's roof – plunge into the morning traffic. He made a mental note to look for any cab carrying 3Q61. That would be Mac.

He checked his pseudo-Rolex, the one he now remembered the teen gangsters so knowledgeably recognized and refused to make off with: 9:44 am.

He pulled out the paper with the dealer Hugo Penrose's facts. It confirmed what he'd recalled. Mr Penrose had already begun his business day. His Wednesday business day, Skip told himself, having been hit with it being almost ten hours into Wednesday.

But before Skip dropped in on Mr Penrose, he realized he had at least one call to make. He'd also better check any phone calls and texts that might have come in.

The call to Brianna was quick and efficient, made while leaning against one of the pillars holding up the tram platform. (Leaning on the partially hidden side of the pillar was a way to minimize his exposure.) He told Brianna he was delayed, wouldn't be in until later and might not even make it. He asked her to duplicate the contracts he now knew were soiled and on some pages illegible and had her cancel his lunch with Garret Overmyer who, like many lawyers of his acquaintance, talked but never listened.

Such colleagues, as he'd accumulated! How he'd like to brush them off like lint on a collar, like Mac brushed off any dirt that had collected on the overcoat.

The two phone calls and the texts he'd missed (but his cellphone hadn't) surprised him and didn't. Bernice Sawyer Gerber calling not only about Gussie Slotnik but also because she sensed something was wrong. Throughout Skip's childhood and young adulthood she'd sense something was wrong. Throughout his childhood and young adulthood he denied it, though she was inevitably right. Not being in the mood to deny her correct guess, he decided not to return the call just yet.

The second call was more perplexing for him. His phone told him no number was recorded. There was a three-word message in a voice that he might have heard before or might not have. It said, "That overcoat rules." Or did it say, "Bad Rover drools." Or "The grocer's got tools."

Was it a wrong number? Right number?

The first text didn't surprise him either. It was from Faye – a follow-up to the (rash?) one he'd sent the previous evening. She'd texted about two and a half hours later. It read, "I've already forgotten I chose to send this. If lucky, I'll remember little or nothing of our past. What do you know? I've forgotten everything." No need to reply, he concluded.

The second text did surprise him. It was from Jerome and was terse. It read, "Luv u Bro."

Skip shut off the still trusty cellphone, stopped leaning against the pillar, circled it three or four times for good luck (where did that impulse originate?) but was jarred from his multifaceted reverie by shrill barking. He looked down. A yappy red Pomeranian was returning his gaze. Addressed to the dog, he heard, "Bethany, be quiet, Bethany." Addressed to Skip was, "You're standing too close to her favorite spot."

The speaker was a woman somewhere in her fifties wearing a bulky cut-off-at-the-waist black down jacket, tight black trousers and over-the-knee black boots. Curly dyed black hair poked out from a black knitted cap.

Looking at Skip under long false (mink?) eyelashes, she said, "I watch the dog circle this pillar a couple times a day. I've never seen a man do it. You aren't doing it for the same reason, are you?"

Making as if he got the joke and even found it funny, Skip committed something close to a laugh and moved away to make room for Bethany. He thought he'd just keep going when he heard, "Now that's a smart coat you've got on. My husband used to have one like it. Funny thing, it just disappeared one day. He left it somewhere or other. If I didn't know better, I'd say that's the coat."

It could be the coat, Skip thought, it *could* be the coat. He turned around and said, "How do you mean, that's the coat?"

Abashed, the woman looked at him. "I don't mean it really could be the coat. It just looks like it, is all."

Skip wasn't about to let this drop. He took a couple steps towards her. She took a couple steps back. Bethany stopped sniffing the pillar. "How would you know if it were really your husband's coat?" Skip asked. "Could you identify it?" He put down his briefcase and started to take the coat off.

Realizing what Skip was in the act of doing, the woman said, "I was just saying. It looks like my husband's coat. It can't be his coat. It's your coat. You're wearing it." Skip had the coat off now. "Or not wearing it. But it's yours. I was just kidding."

Skip held it towards her. She must have thought he was about to carry the demonstration too far and decided to cut it off by saying – with a strain in her voice – "If it was Reggie's coat, his initials would be in it. RAT. For Reginald Arthur Thatcher. 'Rat.' He took a lot of ribbing for it when he was a kid."

Skip knew he'd searched the overcoat for initials. None were there – certainly none that spelled "Rat." He put the coat back on.

The woman looked at Skip. He saw pity in her eyes. She said, "The way you're acting, anybody would think you're trying to get rid of the coat. I don't know why. It's a great coat. I keep telling Reggie to get another one like it." She must have anticipated what Skip might do then – loony as he must have appeared to her. "Not yours, of course. Not yours."

When Skip had gotten into the coat again, Bethany lost interest and did her business. Now the woman said, "Come on, Bethany. Mama's taking you home to Daddy." She hurried away.

As Bethany and she disappeared around the Fifty-ninth Street corner (Skip could hear Bethany barking at something or someone new), Skip had a bracing thought. He'd had word of a coat like it – could be a good omen.

He rounded onto East Fifty-eighth, looking for 222, and slightly more than midway down the block, there it was. He realized he'd passed it any number of times before but never had any reason to go in, his interest in art and/or artifacts never being very pronounced – unless they were somehow tied up in a real estate sale or acquisition. Which hardly ever happened – once, maybe, to his recollection.

He recognized the ground-floor show windows in which a fabric designer showed off what could be done with expensive upholstery, draperies, lampshades and the like.

He entered the building, went to the elevators, waited a minute or so for the first one to come down – resisting the urge to bet with himself. When it did, he touched the disc for the fifth floor.

He tried to ignore the others who got on it with him but couldn't stop himself from noticing two burly men in suits who got on after him and flanked him. One – or both – of them gave off the faint odor of perfume he might have sworn was the scent he now recalled emanating from one or more of the Bad Mama Bears.

But these two couldn't be Gertrude or Lulu or Gigi or Zelda. Could they? He almost wished they were. He was ready to take them on. How, he didn't know, but he could feel his fists clenching. When they got off at the third floor but not without jostling him from both sides so that he had the distinct feeling he'd been frisked (but checking, found he hadn't been), he was almost disappointed.

Alone in the fifth-floor corridor, he put his hand in the coat's right-hand pocket to make certain the stone was still there. He felt its jagged front and smooth back. He was aware of something else in the pocket and pulled it out. The Indian-head penny. He wondered if he should show that to Hugo Penrose, too.

There'd be no call to show the Halls cough drops.

He reached the fifth floor. Directly in front of him when the elevator doors opened was a double door, on one door of which was written in five-inch letters the name "Hugo Penrose." To the right of the door was a bell and a printed sign above it advising, "Please ring for admittance."

Skip pushed the button. After a minute's wait during which he put down his briefcase, picked it up again, patted his right-hand pocket a few times to assure himself the stone was there, the door opened.

A man in an old three-piece suit, an immaculate white shirt and foulard with a monocle hanging on a silver chain around his neck stood holding the doorknob. He was about five feet five inches tall with well-barbered russet hair that might have been a wig, had a high brow, dark bags under his eyes and a Van Dyke. His lips were pursed.

Behind him – Skip was looking over the man's head – were any number of étagères in which expertly illuminated objects were carefully placed and spaced for display. There were heads, sculptures of animals, bowls, utensils, masks, tools, boxes.

Against a wall to the right was a roll-top desk, at which a grey-haired woman, probably in her seventies, sat writing in a ledger with what looked to Skip to be an old Esterbrook pen of the sort his father had always insisted on using.

Next to her and the desk was a shelf of books with aged bindings. The few windows were covered with black gauze so that no light inched through. There was the distinct aroma of chemicals and dust. The large room was illuminated by six equally spaced fixtures with matching yellow-brown plate-like covers that had red capillary-resembling streaks in them.

"May I help you, young man?" the natty doorman said in precise, subdued tones.

"I'm looking for Hugo Penrose," Skip said.

"You have found him," Mr Penrose said. "I'm Hugo Penrose. What can I do for you? Are you interested in buying something from the past? Or are you selling something from the past? So often my visitors are sellers. I see you're carrying a briefcase. Am I to assume you have something inside you wish to show me? But first, won't you come in?"

He made a little bow and waved Skip in. When Skip had come inside, Mr Penrose closed the door and peered in anticipation.

Skip bit the bullet – admonishing himself for thinking the phrase – and said, "I have something I'd like to find out about. It may be nothing, but I thought that considering your business, you might be able to tell me something about it."

"I shall do my best," Mr Penrose said. "Why don't we sit over here, and you can show me what you'd like me to see."

Mr Penrose led Skip to a long brown leather couch that hadn't been visible from the doorway. It had been obscured by the étagéres. In front of it was a long and low wooden table with a straight-backed chair at each end.

On the way to it Mr Penrose said, "That's a fine overcoat you're wearing, young man. I know good material when I see it. My father was a tailor. He was an engineer in the old country, but he took up tailoring when he arrived here. He taught me about quality material. Quality is the essence of life, you know."

He motioned Skip to sit not on the leather couch but on the straight-backed chair at one end of the table, and he sat in the matching chair at the other end. "As you wish, young man, show me."

Skip put his briefcase on the floor to the left of him and reached in his right-hand pocket for the stone.

As he was doing that, Mr Penrose said, "But before that, would you be so kind as to tell me your name. I like to know to whom I'm speaking."

"Edward Gerber," Skip said. He chose not to say Skip Gerber. Well, he didn't usually when law or business was in process, but this time he heard "Edward Gerber" with new interest, with satisfaction even.

"I see, Edward. And Gerber. Like the baby food," Mr Penrose said. "Now Mr Edward Gerber, what are you holding in your hand?"

Skipped handed over the stone, saying, "I'm just wondering if this is of any value. I thought it might be an old relic or something like that."

With small, delicate hands, Mr Penrose lifted the monocle to his left eye, took the stone and said, "I see." He looked it over, asking, "How did you come by this stone, may I ask, Mr Gerber?"

Skip knew his answer would be insufficient but gave it. "I found it."

Mr Penrose stopped looking at the stone and looked at Skip. Through the monocle, his left eye was enlarged. Skip felt as if it was looking deeper into him – not judgmental but probing. He decided he ought to be more forthcoming. "To be perfectly honest," he said, although he knew "perfect" honesty wasn't what he was about to offer, "I found it in my pocket, as if someone had slipped it in there somehow."

"I see," Mr Penrose said and returned to looking over the stone. "You came by it – shall we say – by accident, and now you want to know its initial origin and perhaps its more recent provenance and whether it is of any value. Is that right, Mr Gerber?"

"That's right," Skip said.

Mr Penrose continued scrutinizing the stone, running his fingers over the front, turning it over to look more closely at the back.

Looking up from it, he said, "I regret to tell you, Mr Gerber, that there's not much I can tell you. I can say it is of no intrinsic value. It may be of *sentimental* value. As a talisman, shall we say. To you or someone. That is something someone like me can never appraise. The little I can tell you is that it was undoubtedly carved recently, in recognition of, for instance, the Mayan civilization, which I venture to say, you as a layman looking at it, may have thought it had come down to us from.

"It may have been carved by a young person eager to fool friends into believing he, too, had just been lucky enough to find an ancient artifact. But I shouldn't have to tell you that were it of value, no one would have scratched his name on the back. It's showing off, wouldn't you say – this 'Harold Smith,' it looks like to me.

"I can tell you that you're not the first person to come to me with something like this they hope is worth something, as if they're on 'Antiques Roadshow.' Sometimes it seems as if someone comes to my door daily with a stone just like yours he found – it's always a gentleman, never a lady – and wonders if it's Mexican or Peruvian or Incan or Mayan or Inuit. I can't say it's the same stone, but sometimes I think it could be.

"For all I know, someone somewhere in this big city is turning them out regularly for reasons only he or she knows. I can't even say if the same name isn't etched into the back of it. I can say, by the way, that it's limestone – good old reliable, adaptable, venerable, ubiquitous limestone."

Mr Penrose handed the stone back to Skip. "Maybe you should just regard it as a good-luck charm. Like a lucky penny, say an Indian-head penny – and I've seen my share of fake Indian-head pennies as well." He stood up and said, "Now, Mr Gerber, I must bid you a good day. It's been a pleasure meeting you."

Hugo Penrose put out his hand. Replacing the (lucky?) stone in with the (lucky? fake?) penny, Skip stood up, too. Again, he was aware of how sore he was and how fatigued. His head still hurt. Ignoring his discomfort as best he could, he shook Mr Penrose's hand and allowed himself to be led to the door.

Midway there, Mr Penrose stopped and addressed Skip. Picking up his monocle, he used it to point while he spoke. "You know, Mr Gerber, I'm always interested in what young people consider valuable. You come in here with a stone that has no intrinsic value. Perhaps it does to Mr Smith, if that's his name, but who can really tell?"

Hugo Penrose was holding the monocle in his left hand. With his right hand he reached over and took the lapel of the overcoat between his thumb and forefinger and tested the material. Then he patted the front of the coat.

He said, "This coat, on the other hand, is genuine quality. No, Mr Gerber, it wouldn't fetch in my establishment or at auction what a *bona fide* Mayan pot would bring. It's valuable all the same. I told you my father was a tailor, and I grew up learning what he taught me about the trade. So I know a bespoke coat when I see one. You must have bought it second-hand. You're too young to have acquired it when it was new.

"But this coat could have only been made by one tailor. Not my father. Oh, no. I know his styling idiosyncracies. Tailors had them in those days, and they knew each other's hand. As did I. If you ask me, this coat was made by the Jewish tailor Isaac Solomons, well-known and admired in his time. He always sewed two buttons on the inside breast pockets. If this coat has those, it's the object you should be valuing. Isaac Solomons of East Broadway, he should live and be well."

Astonished about the two buttons he knew were there on each inside breast pocket, Skip blurted, "But he can't still be alive, can he?"

Mr Penrose resumed walking to the door. "No, he can't, but in that coat his spirit *could* be. It might even be hovering over the East Broadway shop, rolling its eyes at the decline in tailoring since his day and my father's. It was 105 East Broadway, if I remember correctly. I know he had two sons. Whether one or both took up the trade, I couldn't tell you. But the building must still stand where Isaac Solomons toiled and tailored."

They'd reached the door. Mr Penrose opened it, offered his hand once again. As Skip shook it, Mr Penrose said, "If I may take the liberty to advise a young man as intelligent as you appear to be, the great achievement in life is to learn what quality is, what substance is, what enduring is, what worthwhile is. In all things public and private. And you're not the first young man in a good-looking overcoat to whom I've said as much."

He shook his monocle at Skip one last time and shut the door.

Skip stood there, not yet ready to turn left or right, sensing there was something he needed to absorb, sensing that whatever it was, he'd already absorbed it, and it would come to him, had already come to him, had settled inside him and would reveal itself when he was ready, had already begun revealing itself.

All he had to do was keep moving forward. Easy to do, no? His next move had already revealed itself. He was bound for 105 East Broadway, where – who knows? – Isaac Solomons or maybe a descendant was waiting for him with instructive overcoat lowdown.

Hearing the click of heels traversing a perpendicular corridor, he returned to the elevator before him and pushed the button to call for it. As he did, the clicking stopped. He deliberately took a couple of steps back and a couple of steps forward. The clicking, which sounded as if it could be made by a drag queen's fuck-me pumps, started again and stopped.

Skip looked toward the corner from which the person must be about to appear. The elevator arrived and opened with a certain amount of metallic scraping. Skip got on.

"Hold it, will you please?" a woman's voice said. Skip was inclined not to, but the elevator held itself, as a woman in high heels and a migraine-inducing chartreuse-and-orange plaid coat hurried into the cabin.

"Thanks," she said. For what? Skip thought as the doors clanked shut. "Sometimes you can wait forever for the elevators here," she said. She was heavily made up – thick mascara, flaming red lips, rouge that made her cheeks look as if she were a clown-school graduate. She looked Skip up and down and said, "Nice big coat ya got there. Where'd you get it? I'm looking for one like it to give my brother. Maybe in a brighter color."

Not inclined to make a thing of this exchange, Skip said, "I wish I could remember where I got it, but I can't. You might try Saks or Barneys."

"Maybe I will," she said, as the doors opened on the ground floor.

She preceded Skip and immediately said hello to a man about six feet four who must have weighed at least three hundred pounds. He had a neck tattoo peeking out from a motorcycle jacket with a dragon insignia on it.

She put her arms around him and kissed him on the mouth, then turned around to speak to Skip, whom she rightly assumed was directly behind her. "This is my brother, Cyrus." To Cyrus, she said, "See the coat this guy has on. That's the kind of coat you should get. You'd look good in it."

Cyrus wasn't interested. All he could contribute was, "Let's get out of here, Sis."

He took the woman by the arm and led her towards the door of the building. On their way out, he looked back with the latest sneer Skip had encountered, as if it was Skip's fault that his sister thought he should own a coat like the one Skip – entirely by accident, but more and more looking as if not by accident – had on.

Skip was ready to hand it over and might have if he thought Cyrus would take it. But he didn't. He thought it more likely the coat would be thrown back at him, and that – this was curious and curiouser – he'd be thankful to get it back.

He stayed where he was, acting as if he were thinking something over, while Cyrus and Sis cleared out. Then he left the building, went to the corner, flagged a cab from the cab cortege streaming down Second Avenue.

When he got in, having forgotten to check for the number 3Q61, he half expected Mac McAllister to be at the wheel and was disappointed he wasn't.

When the driver asked whether Skip wanted to go to East Broadway via the East River Drive, it was in an Indian accent. "Whatever's the fastest way possible," Skip said, "and the quietest. I have things I need to think through."

He did and he didn't. He'd made the remark as a pretext for quiet. He wasn't interested in cabbie-passenger conversation of any stripe. He also wasn't interested in looking out the taxi's side or rear windows at anyone possibly sneering his way or tailing him with whatever diabolical motives in mind.

All he wanted was a faux-Rolex check and then to close his eyes for, he hoped, an unimpeded catnap: 10:46 a. m.

"Mister, we're here," Skip heard, waking up from a dream in which he was being chased by his mother Bernice, brother Jerome, apparently ex-quasi-fiancée Faye and administrative assistant Brianna, the four of them wielding wooden hangers on which they demanded to hang an overcoat he was wearing that had burst into flames.

He was perspiring lightly. He hurt from the crick in his neck he'd gotten during his short slumber, but what was the additional discomfort from which his body was recoiling? He could only ascribe it to psychic discomfort, an affliction he couldn't recall ever experiencing before now – although perhaps he had but had never taken the time to notice.

He looked at the Rolexoid: 11:14 a. m.

"This is the address you give me," the cabbie said in his somnolently sing-song manner. "Is it not?" The "Is it not?" came out as "Ees eet nawt?"

"That's right," Skip said. "What do I owe you?" The driver told him. He paid it and alighted, briefcase in hand. He stepped onto the curb.

He was standing in front of a brownstone building, late nineteenth century, he thought. From the looks of the windows, the building had been and still was an apartment building. Below ground level, down three steps, was a shop.

Above a dirty window, in which a cat slept on a patch of old carpet, was a metal sign with letters in bas-relief saying "Jake's Jalopies U Call We Drive." Not far from the cat was a large piece of cardboard on which was a sign with the phone number "212 626-2353" and, handwritten in red ink, the words "Dont hesitat to call at any hr."

If this was once Isaac Solomons' store, it wasn't anymore. He looked to the right, where a similar building featured a Chinese laundry at the bottom with a handwritten poster in its cleaner window giving the rates for shirts folded or hung.

To the right of 105 East Broadway there was no building. It was an unattended empty lot, some dead weeds in clumps behind a chain-link fence. Skip walked left to look at 105 East Broadway from that angle and found what he was looking for, although he hadn't known it was what he was looking for.

At the top of the wall was a sign in faded paint. It included an artist's rendering of a turn-of-the-century, narrow-lapel two-piece suit and said:

Isaac Solomons & Sons

Expert Tailor

"We Suit You"

Only the Finest Durable Top Quality Fabrics

105 East Broadway

New York City

Visit for a Fitting or Call 62353

Established 1897

Something struck Skip between the eyes. He reached into the coat's right-hand pocket and felt for the yellowing ad he'd found the previous day in the West Forty-seventh Street office. He pulled it out. There they were, the words "top" and "quality." The words combined by no means added up to a unique phrase, but the match might mean something more than unimpressive coincidence. And there were the tops of the possible capital letters that could have been attached to the "I" of Isaac and the "S" of Solomons.

Carefully placing the fragile newspaper fragment back in the left-hand pocket, Skip turned to 105 East Broadway, where it looked as if neither Isaac Solomons nor either of his sons still occupied the commercial premises.

On the off-chance someone did who knew about them, Skip retraced his few paces, walked down the steps, aware of aching calf muscles as he did, and pushed open the door.

A chubby, bearded, sixty-something African-American man (was he Jake?) looked up, gave him a wide toothy grin and raised a finger to ask for a moment's indulgence. He was sitting at a table on which rested several landlines. There was also a microphone that appeared to be hooked up to a slightly obsolescent two-way radio with a two-way radio speaker.

Jake(?) was giving instructions for a pick-up at an address on West Sixty-eighth Street.

Skip heard a scratchy response.

When the bearded, coffee-colored dispatcher with the smile and the twinkling eyes over prominent bags finished, he looked at Skip and said, "I'm Big Jake. What can I do you for?"

Before Skip could answer, one of the phones rang, Big Jake (chubby, yes, especially big, no; was there a smaller Jake somewhere?) picked it up. Again he silently begged indulgence from Skip with his forefinger, got information and relayed it by way of the two-way radio, got a different scratchy response.

While he was doing that, Skip looked around him at a room whose walls were a jaundiced yellow. The room was furnished with a few ancient wooden armchairs, a poster of Willie Mays one corner of which was curling off the wall, a 1994 calendar advertising automobile parts, a few hooks on one of which a leather baseball jacket dangled.

The table Big Jake sat at also held remnants of a Chinese dinner in a corrugated aluminum plate. In one corner of the jaundiced yellow room, there was a second table with a burner on it supporting a dented coffee percolator. In another corner was a third table – a Singer sewing machine table with a pedal. A few phone books rested on it. Opposite the front door was another door, partially open, leading to a back room.

The sewing machine was what yanked Skip's attention. When Big Jake finished his business and again looked up with his sunny grin, Skip pointed at the machine and, hopeful help would be forthcoming, said, "I'm trying to get some information on a man named Isaac Solomons, a tailor who used to own this shop. Do you know anything about him?"

Big Jake – who had on a fleece vest, a green work shirt with metal snaps and brown workman's pants that had been laundered many times – stood up and shook himself out, first his entire body and then his limbs one by one. Skip got the impression he did this often.

Having completed the exercise to his satisfaction, Big Jake said, "Funny you ask. This must have been some business, 'cause it ain't unusual someone comes in about this old Jew – usually some dude dressed in a nice suit and coat, big like you got on – but there's not much I can tell."

Skip was glad to hear that much. He said, "You mean there's something you can tell?"

Big Jake sat down again and looked at the phones as if wondering why at least one of them wasn't ringing. He said, "I can tell you when my partner Otis and me – he passed a long time back – took over this shop in April, the year of our Lord nineteen-seventy-three – it was still a tailor establishment. We took it over from two old men." He chuckled. "My, they was old – who was the sons of this here Isaac Solomons. I can tell you they said they had two sons each of they own, who didn't want to be tailors nohow, and that's why they was giving up they store."

Skip asked, "Do you know where they went, how I could get in touch with them?"

Big Jake said, "I sho don't, and that's what I tell anyone who ask. The day they walked out and lef' me and Otis the key, they said they was glad to be shut of the place."

As he was saying that, the cat in the window must have awakened, because Skip heard paws hitting the floor and then saw the cat walk toward the door at the back, stop to stretch and then, its tail aloft with feline hauteur, pass through the door.

"He gone for his food," Big Jake said. "Anyway, those two old Jews lef' that sewing machine you see there, saying they be back fo' it. But they never was. They got the rest of they equipment out of here, but lef' that. Probably forgot about it. Why they want it anyway? They give up the tailorin'. I got mail fo' 'em fo' awhile, but I ain't seen any since I cain't say when."

This leaves me with what? Skip thought. For want of something else to do just then, he watched the cat strut back into the room with a regal air and visit here and there as if to make certain his (her?) kingdom had remained in order.

Skip looked out of the front window in time to notice the lower half of two figures in sweat pants and running shoes pass by, slow down and shamble out of sight. He heard a ringing he took a few seconds to realize was his cellphone.

He picked up for his mother. Before he finished "Hello," she said, "Where have you been? You know I wouldn't be hocking you if Gussie wasn't hocking me, but it's already tomorrow."

"I'll get to it when I get to it," Skip replied. "Gussie Slotnik isn't my only concern, I shouldn't have to point out."

"Concern?" Bernice Sawyer Gerber said. "You've got concerns. What concerns?"

"Nothing with which you need to *concern* yourself," Skip said, pleased with the way he'd turned the phrase. He was looking out the window. The bottom halves of two figures in sweat pants and running shoes shuffled by in the opposite direction from the previous two figures in sweat pants and running shoes.

Were they the same figures in sweat pants and running shoes from before? And the ones before that? And the ones before that?

"I can't stay on the line, Mother. I'll call you later."

He rang off.

During that abrasive minute, Big Jake answered a static-ridden two-way radio call and saw to dispatching. When he finished, he looked back at Skip and said, still cheerful. "The sewing machine ain't the only thing they never come back fo'. They never saw to the safe."

"The safe?" Skip said.

Big Jake pointed a thumb at the back room. "In there. They never come back fo' it. Prob'ly nothin' in it they wanted anymo'. Prob'ly too heavy to haul away." The two-way radio went again. Before answering it, Big Jake said, "You can see for yo'self. You won't be the firs'."

Skip went for the door, pushed it back and felt along the inside wall for a light switch. There was none, but the light from the outer room threw enough illumination into the back room that he could see a bulb hanging from the middle of the ceiling and the string hanging from it.

When he'd walked over and pulled, he scanned the room. On the cracked concrete floor, he saw old newspapers tossed haphazardly around, a couple pair of old boots, a deflated football, a water-stained tailor's form Big Jake hadn't mentioned (and maybe never took in anymore), a long table with an array of canned goods and a can opener on it.

Leaning in one far corner, he saw a red plastic bowl with dried catfood clinging to it, a broom with bristles worn down to what looked to be half their original size and not far from it – nearer to him – a door to a smaller room ajar, revealing sections of a sink with a dripping faucet and a toilet.

In the other far corner squatted on short, stubby legs a black safe with elaborate but flaking gilt decorations. It had a combination lock and a graceful handle shaped like an elongated teardrop.

It was shut. Crestfallen, Skip went over to it and crouched on his haunches. He noticed his overcoat (it wasn't his, of course) rippling round his bent legs. Confronted with the apparently locked safe door, he did what many people do when confronted with apparently locked doors – he did what he'd done at the spurious Miles Rogers Havilland office: He tried the handle.

It opened easily, as if floating on air. It was divided by a single shelf into an upper and lower section. On the bottom shelf was a ledger with a leather cover so old Skip was concerned that if he lifted it, it might crumble. The entire volume might turn to dust as thick as he noticed the dust was that lay in other parts of the room.

Nevertheless, he thought that if any information relevant to his expanding, even heady, investigation (thanks partly to whatever the Big Bad Mamas poured down his throat) could be found in what he assumed was a business ledger, he'd be foolish not to look for it. There could be clients' names, descriptions of made-to-order suits and coats, addresses to which they might have been delivered.

Ignoring the top shelf on which he noticed was a yellowing envelope, he carefully gripped the ledger with both hands, lifted it from the safe and, trying not to jar it, moved gingerly to the long table.

He set it on the table as if it were not just a ledger but something comparable to a Belleek teacup, a Fabergé egg, a Ming Dynasty vase. He ran his hand over the cover, over the raised word "Ledger."

Wanting to be as cautious as possible, he reached into the coat's right-hand pocket and pulled out the black kid gloves. He put them on, thinking how smoothly, how perfectly they fit, how handy they'd become, how smart he'd been to think of them.

With his left thumb and forefinger, he opened the ledger. On the first page, there were three names followed by three years "of our Lord" (to quote Big Jake), all of it written in flowing penmanship – skilled calligraphy, really – but each in a different handwriting.

They were "Isaac Solomons, January 1897," "Ezra Solomons, March 1932" and "Herman Solomons, June 1934."

They refer to the tailoring shop founder, Skip thought, and the sons

to whom the business had been passed. Remembering the faded sign
on the building's exterior, he reasoned that the years mentioned had to
mark, respectively, the shop's opening and then undoubtedly the younger
Solomons brothers' entry into the business.

Looking at the page, Skip had a feeling that perhaps he was observing
something he shouldn't be seeing. Though he knew he was alone in the
room, he looked around to check if he were being watched.

Big Jake was in the doorway. He said, "Find what yo' lookin' fo'?"

"I don't know what I'm looking for?" Skip said. "Something to do with
this coat, I think."

"You looking to get another like it?" Big Jake asked.

"Not exactly," Skip said.

"Then what you here fo'?" Big Jake wanted to know. Two-way-radio
static rasped. Leaving to get it, Big Jake said, "White folks. They come,
they go, they don' know what they lookin' fo'."

Skip absorbed the naturally rhymed couplet, thinking that on his
broadening chase he was now encountering street poets. He looked back
at the names on the first page. While his right hand steadied the ledger,
he carefully lifted the page with his left hand.

What he saw made his heart sink. It was the latest in the ongoing
series of heart-sinkings that weren't helping the heart-risings. At the
binding were the jagged remnants of pages that had been ripped from the
ledger. They looked as if they'd been torn out by the shark's teeth of time.

Not all the pages were gone. The page that remained at the top of
those still in place was blank. Skip turned it back, and a second blank
page appeared. Ditto the next few he looked at. Ditto all the rest he tried,
just in case on one of them he'd find something.

He found nothing to tell him whether the absent pages had been taken
at the same time or one by one – not that either circumstance would
disclose much. If they'd all been taken at the same time, that could mean
the ledger's owner(s) had taken them. But not necessarily. If taken one
by one, that might mean others looking for whatever he was after had
removed them singly. Or maybe not. Anyone preceding him on a similar
search could have taken all of them in order to leave nothing behind for a
subsequent hunt.

Skip could reach no conclusion.

He looked again at the first of those remaining pages to see if there were traces of an impression made by anything written on the last removed page. Again he could ascertain nothing. The vision didn't pan out of him rubbing over those impressions with pencil or pen to expose names, addresses, phone numbers.

Cary Grant does it with positive results in *North by Northwest*, he thought. How about if I'd been Cary Grant, he thought digressively. With reluctance that felt almost as painful as what was pulsing through the rest of his body, he closed the ledger and went to replace it in the bottom of the safe.

As he did that, he noticed the envelope on the top shelf. It was canted upward at the back, as if the flap weren't completely closed. Again on his haunches and still wearing the black kid gloves, he picked up the envelope.

He stood up.

On the front, handwritten in the same red ink that appeared on the first page of the ledger and in the same cursive handwriting as either the name Ezra Solomons or Herman Solomons – he'd have to check again to decide which – were the words "For our sons."

He turned the envelope over and, yes, the flap was unsealed. He flipped it back gently, and just as gently took hold of the folded paper inside – the enclosed letter. He removed it slowly. Looking around for a chair to sit on and seeing none where he'd seen none before, he went to stand-sit against the long table.

He unfolded the letter to find that one side of the single sheet of thick stationery has been written on and signed. At the top was a date, "April 5, 1973." The salutation said: "To our sons." The letter said:

"It is important to us and more important to you that the career you choose is one in which you will thrive and be happy. It is true we followed our father into his business and continued its success even though neither of us were at first tailored (cut out, hoo-ha!) for it. Yes, we learned to take pride in it, just as he had after coming to this golden land and forsaking his previous trade as a textile merchant. But times have changed, and what we want for each of our sons is that he be a beneficiary of our toil, not a slave to it. What profiteth a man if he labor only for profit, turning his back on his favored pursuits? We would rather you preferred to follow our wishes for you than to follow obsequiously in our footsteps. For that purpose we have sold our exclusive patterns to the Sandford Clothing Manufacturers at 617 West Sixtieth Street. They are now in full knowledge of what wiser men than we call the tricks of the trade. This was not an easy decision. We made it after having observed what others in our position failed to do for sons who, despite their dreams, assumed ownership of their fathers' businesses only to have them founder and go under.

Signed your loving fathers,

Ezra Solomons

Herman Solomons

Skip finished the letter, looked up from it without focusing on anything in the room, then read it again – pausing more than once to ask himself if Gabriel Martin Gerber, who loved the law more than Skip could claim of himself had ever written anything comparable for him to read – could have, would have, perhaps actually had and discarded it.

If Dad had, would he, Skip, have heeded it? If he thought he should heed it, were there dreams he'd since abandoned that he might have pursued? Music? The trumpet? Where was that trumpet, anyway?

He dismissed the thoughts, or thought he did.

He read the letter again, this time not for its sentiments but for the directions contained in it. Implicitly, it pointed at Isaac Solomons' sons Ezra and Herman. Were he to find them, they might be able to affirm that the coat had been made by their father or by them. Explicitly, it gave an address. And whereas finding Ezra and/or Herman Solomons now seemed chancy at best – were they even still alive, they'd be in their very late nineties, likely with failing memories – a factory on West Sixtieth Street sounded a more effective stratagem.

Folding the letter, putting it back in the envelope and then returning it to the shelf from which he'd taken it, Skip closed the heavy safe door. He didn't bother spinning the combination-lock dial. He did bother to take off the black gloves and return them to the coat's left-hand pocket, careful not to damage the Isaac Solomons (?) ad.

(He'd reasoned that neither the gloves nor the ad would fall through the hole.)

He pulled the light-bulb's string and, leaving everything as he found it, walked out of the room. He left the door to the room partially open – also as he found it.

"There he is," Big Jake said, finishing up some good-natured dispatching, "large as life and twice as good-lookin'. You seen my back room now. Find anything in that ol' safe? You was back there long enough."

"Nothing much," Skip lied.

"Not much else to see *here*, either, that you ain't already seen," Big Jake said. "Anything else I can oblige you with?"

His mind more on his next move, Skip said, "No. I just have to head uptown now."

Big Jake's grin widening, he said, "How far uptown?"

"Way west on West Sixtieth Street," Skip said, not seeing why he shouldn't say.

"Then there is something I can do fo' you. You need a car. I got one." He spoke into his two-way. Skip tried to stop him with a wave of both glove-less hands, but Big Jake was a man who knew his mind.

He was saying, "Pick-up needed, home base to go way west on West Sixtieth Street. Rider's a tall white man in a *boss* overcoat. Who got it?" There was a crackling Skip couldn't make out. Big Jake turned to him, "Yo' char'yot arrives faster 'n you can say 'Ben-Hur.'"

So Skip, without asking, was taken care of.

Big Jake said, "Anything else you need, you let me know. Otherwise, I'm gonna sugges' you stand outside in that bad coat of your'n."

Leaving Big Jake smiling like a commercial for Uncle's Ben's rice, Skip walked out of the Jake's Jalopies office and up the three steps to stand at the curb more concerned that he was once again exposed to whatever might come along.

He wasn't exposed for long. Chugging his way was a long automobile with a grill like the maw of an advancing Kodiak bear and tail fins practically stretching the length of the block. He knew it had to be from the nineteen-fifties, but he didn't know the make. The closer it

David Finkle
125

approached, the clearer it was that not for nothing did Big Jake revel in jalopies.

For that was what the Buick rolling up was. He could see it was a Buick now. The window by him was down, and the driver said, "You gotta be the man in the boss overcoat?"

Skip didn't look around for someone else in a coat anything like the one he had on. He knew there wouldn't be. He nodded yes.

"Climb aboard," the driver, wearing a threadbare infantry jacket, said. He pushed open the shotgun-seat door with a thick, firm hand.

Why Skip wasn't meant to sit in the back seat he couldn't surmise, but he was getting too inured to the non-stop bundle of surprises being thrown his way not to do as instructed. He was too disposed by now not to take advantage of them. He climbed aboard and yanked the door the three times he needed to get it to close.

"Where on West Sixtieth Street?" the driver said above the two-way-radio crackling. "The six hundred block?"

How he knew the block, Skip couldn't figure out. He recalled that Big Jake hadn't specified as much. "Yes, what made you say that?"

"Somebody's going way west, that's usually the block," the driver said. Skip realized he had a Southern accent thicker than a slice of Georgia pecan pie and that his head and neck were just about as thick. "You cain't go no further west without landing in the Hudson River."

"Oh, right," Skip said, thinking he could just as easily have said a self-deprecating "Duh." He didn't. He said, "617 West Sixtieth Street."

"Go up the West Side Highway?" the driver asked. "The fastest route, given today's traffic, and you look like a guy in a hurry."

Do I look like a guy in a hurry? Skip asked himself. He was in a hurry. He definitely was, but why should it be so obvious to everybody he met, like having two heads or three arms? He didn't like being so easily sussed out.

To undermine that impression, he said, "I'm not in that much of a hurry. You know, I need to get there, but..." He let the sentence trail off.

The driver said, "We'll take the West Side Highway anyway." Keeping his eye on the street, he took his right hand off the wheel and extended it towards Skip. "Harlan Rawlings," he said. "We'll get you there in no time flat."

Skip shook hands, although shaking hands with drivers wasn't
something he made a habit of. Rather than committing entirely to it, he
pointed up his low-grade enthusiasm by looking at the cheapo Rolex: It
was 12.01 pm – afternoon already.

"Traffic on the West Side Highway can be bad some days," Harlan
Rawlings said, "but it's nothing compared to driving a truck around
Baghdad. Oh, yeah, I was an Army truck driver – two tours. Never hit.
Not myself. One of the gunners riding with me was once. Not bad. Minor
wound, but still. No, sir, guiding this baby around the five boroughs is a
day at the beach compared to that."

Skip saw Harlan Rawlings glance over at him to see what kind of
attention he was commanding. Skip nodded, just so he wouldn't have to
say anything.

"Besides which I don't have to sleep *under* this vehicle," Harlan
Rawlings, satisfied, said. "Oh, yeah, we slept under our trucks some
nights. Some days, too. Sleeping under them when we weren't
maintaining them. That fell to us, too. You wanted to. That way you knew
the vehicle was good to go and hadn't been given a lick and a promise by
somebody too tired to think straight. That's what makes me valuable to
Big Jake. He knows this jalopy of his is being taken care of proper. And
I'm glad *he's* taking care of *me*."

He glanced at Skip again. Skip returned a second reassuring nod.

"What line of work you in?" Harlan Rawlings asked. Skip had enough
rattling him that he didn't want to travel this bumpy conversational
route. His pause didn't deter Harlan Rawlings. "From the look of you in
that expensive-looking coat – I'm going to guess it was your dad's – I'm
going to say you're white collar. No doubt about that. Business man,
lawyer, maybe government. Am I close?"

Skip had no wish to drag this out. "Lawyer," he said as he watched the
West Side slide by for the second time in twelve hours – only by daylight
this time.

"Honest profession," Harlan Rawlings said. "What kind of lawyer, you
don't mind my asking?"

Skip did mind but said, "Real estate law."

"Real estate law," Harlan Rawlings repeated, savoring the words with his accent as if savoring that Georgia pecan pie. "That interests me. You happy at it?"

Far from blissful playing "Twenty Questions," Skip said, "Happy as I want to be."

He said it, but was he?

"Now me," Harlan Rawlings said, "I'm happy, but I can't say I'm happy as I want to be. Don't get me wrong. I'm glad to be driving for Big Jake. When he gave me the job, I wasn't sure what the future held for me. It wasn't looking too bright. I got back from Iraq after the second tour – my wife ditched me during my first tour – and there was nothing for me in Alabama, in where I'm from and where I was a mechanic before the war. Little town outside of Birmingham you never heard of. Maybe you heard of it. Boaz?"

Harlan Rawlings glanced Skip's way again, to see if Skip had heard of Boaz. Skip didn't know if he had or he hadn't. The name was familiar but probably not as an Alabama town but as someone in the Bible, something to do with Ruth – something that as a Jew with only a tentative grasp of the Old Testament he didn't remember.

Not moved to sort out Boaz's origin, he turned his attention to the passing urban scene and noticed that, having exited the West Side Highway at West Fifty-fourth Street, Harlan Rawlings hadn't turned left towards West Sixtieth Street but was doubling back.

Did he know a better way?

There wasn't a better way.

Skip was about to say something when Harlan Rawlings turned east on West Fifty-second Street and was pulling over to the curb. What was going on? Why was Harlan Rawlings idling in front of an empty white building with a large corrugated garage door on which was a "For Sale" sign?

Feeling a chill traveling up from his feet, Skip decided he wouldn't show fear. That might be the worst thing he could do. On the other hand, maybe this was another frisson he was mistaking for a chill, and he'd begun to like those frissons. "I think you may have misunderstood me," he said. "I said 617 *West Sixtieth* Street. You're on *West Fifty-second*

Street."

"I know we are," Harlan Rawlings said.

He knew? Then why were they where they were? Was Harlan Rawlings even who he said he was? Thinking fast, Skip decided he didn't want to wait to find out.

He needed to take action. That was what he was about now, wasn't it? Action. He slid his left hand down to grab his briefcase. With his right hand, he took hold of the door handle.

He twisted it, but the door wouldn't open. He twisted it two more times before it gave. When it finally did, he jumped from the car and pushed the door shut after him as hard as he could.

He intended to get away quickly, but as he stepped from the car, he felt himself being held back. When he slammed the door, he'd caught the overcoat in it. He pulled at the coat but it wouldn't come free. He could pull it harder, but if he did, he might tear it, and something in him refused to do that.

Without his doing anything, the door swung open. Harlan Rawlings had leaned over and opened it. "Hey, man," he said, puzzled. "Where're you going? You don't have to run up to Sixtieth Street on your own. I'm going to drive you there."

Trying to sound calm, Skipped asked, "Then what are we doing here?"

Still leaning over and looking up at Skip, Rawlings said, "You want to get back in the car, and I'll tell you?" Skip moved a foot towards the car but didn't get back in.

Rawlings shrugged, almost imperceptibly. "You said you weren't in a hurry to get where you were going. You told me you're a real estate lawyer. So I thought you wouldn't mind a little detour. To look at this building. I've got my eye on it. I thought as a real estate lawyer you might give me your opinion. I'm happy now driving this jalopy, but like I said, I was a mechanic, and I think I'd be happier owning my own body shop. If I can put the money together, this could be it. Hey, I'm sorry if I surprised you by coming here. I probably shoulda said something."

Rawlings' sincere face looked even more sincere, and Skip felt there was nothing else to do but relent. He got back in the jalopy – without closing the door.

"I don't know how I can help you," he said and looked at his – quotes – Rolex to underline the point: 12:26 p. m., it advised him.

Rawlings got it and said, "I'll have you where you're going in green-apple quick-time, but I just wanted to show you the place. I'm probably going to need a lawyer. So it's a stroke of luck you got into my vehicle. I have to raise capital, and I figure I'll need advice on that, just for starters."

Skip felt his muscles relaxing even as the car was humming underneath him. Rawlings, he saw, was unthreatening and had been all along. Just because he had a thick neck and hands that could probably bend steel – and maybe had already bent more than their share of fenders – didn't mean Skip had to jump to conclusions. Besides, for a few minutes now, nobody had issued out of the building in front of which they'd been parked to sneer Skip's way or otherwise harass him.

He pulled the door shut, which happened on the first try this time, and said something that, after saying it, he wasn't certain had come out of his mouth. "I might be able to help you figure a few things out, but I'm not sure I'm going to be practicing real estate law long enough to see you through to any body shop you're able to open."

"Wow," Rawlings said, turning the key in the ignition to a cacophony of scraping parts. "You're thinking of giving up the law?"

"Just a thought," Skip said. "Nothing concrete."

Giving up the law? What made him think such a thing? What made him say such a thing? What would he do if he gave up the law? Become partners with Harlan Rawlings in his West Side Manhattan body shop? Become the modern-day Chet Baker or Miles Davis? The new Wynton Marsalis? Skip didn't think so.

But he could dream, couldn't he?

Why shouldn't he?

"Okay," Rawlings said, putting the Buick in gear and pulling away from the curb. "You've seen the place. We're off to West Sixtieth Street."

He headed to Eleventh Avenue, made the appropriate left turn north, drove to West Sixty-first Street, made another left in order to circle the block onto West Sixtieth.

"Yeah," he said, "My own body shop would make me happy, and we all deserve to be happy. Right? I'll shut up now. I see you have other things to think about."

Skip was glad for the relief but at the same time realized one of the things that had just entered his mind was a loaded question: If like everybody on the face of the earth, he deserved to be happy, what would catapult him to that elusive zone?

It was followed by the ancillary thought that at present he wasn't happy, a condition he never gave much consideration – possibly because he was too busy to consider it. Or maybe because he *kept* himself too busy to consider it.

Skip looked down at the coat for the umpteenth time. And while he was looking at it – at the discreet herringbone pattern, at the wide lapel, at the pockets with their evocative, ostensibly arbitrary contents – and agreeing with himself that the coat was the cause of whatever practically palpable unhappiness he was experiencing at the moment, he had to concede the coat might also be the cause of the sneaking sense of something he was tempted to call happiness.

What's with this coat? he asked himself. I know I'll find out – I think I know I'll find out – when I get to the bottom of all this or, better yet, when I get to the top of all this.

"Looks like you're here," Harlan Rawlings, who'd shut up for several minutes, was saying. "617 West Sixtieth Street."

Skip snapped to and looked at the building where the Jake's Jalopy had stopped. He saw that though it must have been a factory at one time, it was no longer the outfit to which Isaac Solomons had sold his patterns, his secrets, his everything that might have constrained his sons' sons from goals loftier in their minds than tailoring.

He was looking through the windshield at a factory that had been converted into an apartment building in which a sign attached to it promised "luxury apartments" but, while looking sufficiently reputable, wouldn't fit most connoisseurs' definitions of luxurious.

It was brick and, he assumed, wood, now undoubtedly reinforced by steel. It featured arched windows commonplace at the time and fashionable again for a certain stratum of New Yorkers with money. It came replete with a canvas marquee that possibly had tenants believing they were entering something posh when they arrived under it. But there was no doorman, just a glass door requiring a tenant's key.

Taking it in, Skip was apprehensive that whatever he hoped he'd find there he wouldn't find. But then again, you never know.

He went for his wallet to pay Rawlings. "How much do I owe you?" he said, since neither Big Jake nor Rawlings had mentioned a hired-car fare.

"Twenty," Rawlings said.

Skip took out a twenty and a ten, noticing he was beginning to run low on immediate funds. He handed the bills to Rawlings and gave the door one effortful and almost too successful shove. The door swung wide with a metallic thump, pulling Skip with it.

Just before he fell out of the seen-better-days Buick completely, he righted himself, and parted with briefcase and dignity mostly intact – some of the dignity, he surmised, conferred by the coat.

Behind him, he heard Rawlings saying, "I can't accept this." He was trying to hand the ten back to Skip. "I took you out of your way. I owe you."

Feeling slightly guilty about misjudging Rawlings earlier, Skip waved the bill away. This set off some back and forth hand movements about accepting or not accepting the tip.

It ended with Rawlings conceding. "But this was my pleasure," he said. "By the way, do you have a card? If I need a lawyer anytime soon, I'd like to call you."

Skip wasn't going to say no. Why stop the business-card swap in which for hours now he'd been so freely participating? He went about setting down his briefcase, bending over to open it, locating a card and handing it over to Rawlings.

"I hope you'll hear from me," Rawlings said. "Don't forget. Harlan Rawlings."

Skip wasn't likely to. "I won't," Skip said without, he hoped, any sarcastic slant.

Before he could close the door, Rawlings leaned over and with his thick right hand firmly shut the door. "One day," he said through the open window, "this door'll fall off, but until then all systems are go."

The next second he'd streaked noisily away and Skip was left to walk across the sidewalk under the canvas marquee to the building's disappointing door and its small metal directory on the left metal post.

Giving the directory some thought, Skip realized that reading the tenants' names wasn't likely to be enlightening but that if a superintendent oversaw the premises, he might be able to pass along information.

And there it was – not a he but a she: Agnes Pawlenski, Superintendent, 1F.

Skip found the proper button and pushed it. He waited for a response to the ring and while he did, glanced right, left and behind him just in case.

Nothing, but no response to the pushed button, either.

He'd barely had time to ask himself what he'd do if no answer came when he saw through the glass doors two barrel-chested young men in wife-beaters, soiled trousers and partially laced work boots approaching the door through the small lobby.

They were obviously brothers and, for all Skip knew, twins. They had the same flat-plane faces with hard mouths, hard eyes and noses that looked as if they'd been broken – could they have done that to each other?

When they reached the inner door, they hesitated to see who'd go through first – like a World-Wrestling-Federation Alphonse and Gaston. They decided. The one in soiled black trousers preceded the one in soiled brown trousers.

As if trying to rip the door off its hinges, the one in the lead opened it to Skip. He said, "We was wondering...," and the other one charged in with "...if you'd arrive on time. "But you're...," the first one said, as the second one appended, "... early."

Taking this in and wondering why he'd be expected – he was instantly worried that he *had* been expected – Skip had no time to answer them, let alone back away. The overgrown boys took him by one arm each, Big Bad Mamas-like, and wriggling back through the doors, marched him through the lobby, with its one potted, six-foot-tall artificial ficus plant lashed to a slab of cheap-looking wood, up two steps and down a corridor towards a door at the end.

It was ajar. One of the big boys shoved the door, which was marked 1F, fully open with a pumped-iron shoulder and boomed, "He's here, Ma." The other one boomed, "Here he is, Brenda."

"Here" was a living room stuffed with more mismatched furnishings than you could shake a stick of furniture at. It was as if anytime a tenant in the building moved out and left a chair or table behind, the Pawlenskis lay claim to it.

Ma was a doughy heavy woman in a shapeless black widow's dress. Her grey hair was pulled back in a bun. She was seated straight-backed at a dining-room table on which pieces of crockery had been pushed to the end away from her. Brenda was a doughy younger woman in a shapeless black dress sitting straight-backed next to her mother. Her hair was also pulled back in a bun.

Busy finding his tongue, Skip was about to say something when Brenda said, "Show him here, Max." She pointed to the chair next to her. "Take his coat, Gus," she said. "Such a nice coat, too," she said. "Don't throw it just anywhere."

Gus said, "I won't."

Noting that the three younger Pawlenskis spoke as if they had large agates in their capacious mouths, Skip felt himself being guided through the furniture obstacle course by the one called Max. The one called Gus was pulling the coat from his shoulders.

Up until this moment, ridding himself of the coat was, from Skip's vantage point, what he'd devoutly thought he wanted. But maybe not anymore. Unless this is where the coat belonged – though it didn't look as if it did. Who were these people? Why were they expecting him? Had someone alerted them to his arrival? What were they preparing to do for him? Or *with* him? Or *to* him?

He found the wherewithal to resist. He hunched his shoulders so Gus couldn't easily remove the coat. He tried to slow Max's progress towards the table where Agnes Pawlenski and daughter Brenda were giving him hard looks.

"What are you expecting me for?" Skip exclaimed as he was lowered (not gently) into a seat at the table and the overcoat was finally lurched from him and thrown on a metal hook jutting from one of three coat racks amid the furniture clutter. "Why do you want me here?"

In unison, Max, Gus and Brenda said, "The *life-insurance* policy." Brenda tacked on, "*Ma*'s life-insurance policy."

"Life-insurance policy?!" Skip asked. He was caught way off guard. "What have I got to do with a life-insurance policy?"

The wide-bodied Pawlenskis looked at each other as if surprised, aggravated and suspicious all at the same time. "You tell us," Gus said. "You're the insurance man."

"No, I'm not," Skip said, not knowing whether to be relieved or frightened.

"Yes, you are," Brenda said,

"You showed up for the appointment," Max said.

"Even early," Gus said, "eager-like to do business."

"Wearing a suit and a tie and that big-ass coat and carrying one of those bigtime cases you're about to open to take out some papers for Ma to sign," Max said.

"You may be expecting an insurance salesman," Skip said, "but I'm sorry to tell you I'm not he."

"Hear that," Gus said to the others, "*He's* not *he*."

"Him," Skip said. "That's not me. I. Me."

Brenda rose half-way from her chair, "What are you saying, you're not the life-insurance man? *Who* the *fuck* are you? Pardon my French. And what the *fuck* are you doing in our house? Pardon my fucking French again."

When Brenda heaved herself part-way out of her chair as if not wanting her French to be pardoned at all, Max and Gus moved in on Skip from each side. "You're not telling us you're a repo man, are you?" Gus said. Max said, "You're not some collection-agency guy weaseling his way into our place, are you?" Brenda demanded. She was standing now and, Skip observed, not exactly a slip of a girl. She went on with beady wide eyes flashing, "Is this some undercover cop thing, you barging in here pretending to be an insurance salesman?"

As they bombarded him with the questions, Skip noticed all three siblings forming hammer-like fists.

"Hold on," Skip said, "hold on, I'm not anything like that. I'm a lawyer."

"A *lawyer*!" came another unison cry from the fearsome three. "What makes you think we need a *fucking lawyer*?" Max asked. He inched closer to Skip "Why would we need a fucking lawyer?" Gus asked. "The law is a fucking ass." He also inched closer to Skip.

"Now you say you're a fucking lawyer," Brenda said. "You're one of those ambulance chasers looking to make money off the little guy's miseries?"

With the brothers and sister Pawlenski edging in on him, Skip realized he'd never before seen himself as others see him. Worse, he wasn't certain the image he'd gotten in his addled head of himself chasing an ambulance down Park Avenue would ever fade.

"No," he said, "I'm a real estate lawyer."

Brenda's pillow-cheeked face was closing in on his. "What?" she said. "You come here thinking to con us out of our property?"

"Nothing doing," Gus said. Max said, "You can't fool a fooler." They were both looming over him, if "looming" adequately described their towering presence.

"That's not it at all," Skip said, at that moment again experiencing just about every bruising and pummeling he'd undergone throughout this unending contest he inadvertently seemed to have entered. "I'm not here to sell you anything. Believe me, I don't want to take advantage of you in any way. I'm here for something else entirely."

"Oh, yeah?" Max said. Gus said, "What would that be?"

Skip was about to answer when a raspy buzzer sounded.

All four Pawlenskis turned their heads towards the door, which is when it dawned on Skip that Agnes Pawlenski had never spoken. She'd sat there, a black-clad mountain of seemingly dissolving flesh and bones.

"Who's that?" Max said.

"If this guy isn't the insurance guy," Brenda said, "then whoever's out there now's gotta have Ma's life-insurance policy."

Mom Pawlenski and the three younger Pawlenskis looked at Skip.

Gus said, "What do we do with this one?"

Brenda said, "You get rid of him." The "get rid" part didn't ease Skip's mind. Brenda added, "Show him out the way you showed him in."

With that, Max and Gus each grabbed one of Skip's arms and lifted him out of his seat so that his feet were barely skimming the ground. The routine was again familiar from the night before and couldn't be doing any good for the toes of his loafers.

As he was being led out the door, he heard Brenda ask, "What the fuck *didjoo* want here anyway?"

Waiting for the answer, the brothers lowered Skip onto his feet and turned him around.

Having been given the floor, in a manner of speaking, Skip said, "This building was once a clothing factory."

"We know that," Brenda said. "So what?"

"They manufactured coats here."

Brenda looked at Skip with scorn beetling her wide brow. "What? Isn't the fancy one you came in here with enough for you, you need another one?"

Fed up, Skip said, "I don't *need* another one. I'm trying to find out more about that one." He tilted his head towards the coat rack on which the coat had been tossed. "I thought if I came to the factory where it was made, I could get some information. Possibly. Maybe."

"If you're looking for information," Agnes Pawlenski said, speaking up finally but not putting much inflection into her mezzo voice, "why don't you look in a secondhand clothing store? If I was you, I'd go to the one around Seventy-second Street on Third Avenue. That's where we send all the clothes that get left behind here, and that's no small bundle, I can tell you."

"You tell 'im, Ma," Brenda said. Max and Gus echoed, "Yeah, you tell 'im, Ma."

Seventy-second Street, Skip was thinking as the buzzer went again with the impatient sawing resonance buzzers get. He thought he knew a thrift shop there. He'd passed it a million times without paying much attention. He had the impression it was a store to which some of his mother's friends gave used clothes, like Mimi Freedman, who lived across the street from it.

When the buzzer rasped again, Ma Pawlenski looked at her offspring. "That's enough outta you three." She pointed at Skip. "Now get that one out of here, and bring the right one in for a change." To herself she said, "Life insurance, is it? All those three want is to see the last of me."

But no time was being lost by Max and Gus. They faced Skip towards the door, got him through it, down the corridor, through the inner and outer doors – past a startled man in a business suit grasping a leather briefcase not unlike the one he wasn't holding – and onto the street.

Letting go of Skip, they each punched him on a shoulder. Max said, "Good riddance to bad rubbish." Gus said, "And don't bother us again with your phony excuses."

Skip stood where he was and felt something hit him in the back. He heard something else hit the pavement. He turned around. The overcoat was on the ground. A few feet farther off was his briefcase. Brenda had thrown them.

When he bent over to pick up the case and coat and brush them off, the three fighting Pawlenskis, as one, gave him the bent-arm fuck-you sign and galumphed back to the door, carting the man cowering at the door with them.

Skip put the coat on again, surprised – as he contemplated his next move – by how much he appreciated its warm embrace.

Agnes Pawlenski had mentioned the secondhand thrift shop on Third Avenue and having shipped clothes from the building to it. Maybe, just maybe among those shipments had been Sandford Clothing Manufacturers stock. Depending on how many bundles the Pawlenskis might have sent and how long ago they'd started, a sizable portion of the donations had undoubtedly been sold, but Skip wasn't about to forgo any possibilities.

On to Seventy-second and Third, he told himself. He began to jog towards the two-way Eleventh Avenue traffic and another cab. He slowed the pace when his body reminded him it had been taking a repeated beating and wasn't completely ready to cooperate on a competitive jog.

When he reached the corner, he flagged a cab on the uptown side. It stopped. It wasn't 3Q61. He got in without looking at the driver but consulting his watch – 1:05 p. m., the generally trusty Rolex replica told him. He said, "Seventy-second and Third, please."

"You're checking your watch," the driver said. "Are you in a hurry?

Someone following you?"

"What makes you say that?" Skip asked. "Do you think I'm being followed?"

"Wow," the driver said. "Nerves. No, I don't think you're being followed. It's just that you guys in a hurry always act as if you're being trailed. Maybe it's just that you're following yourselves. Maybe it's you're being followed by a guilty conscience. But who am I to say?"

Other than to note that the hurry he was in appeared extremely easy to spot, Skip ignored the remark and said, "As a matter of fact, I am in a hurry."

"That's what I'm saying," the driver said. "You guys always are. I see it in your faces. What's the big hurry, I want to know?"

Skip looked at the driver, who was looking back at him in his rear-view mirror. He was a man whose wavy hair fell below his ears and who was wearing an Oxford shirt fraying at the collar.

Skip felt a flush of annoyance rush through him. He remembered looking at himself in Mac's mirror. What was going on with his face now? Wasn't the new glint also apparent to this guy? So he was in a hurry. So? Every other person in New York City is in a hurry.

"Everybody in this city is in a hurry," Skip said. "That's how cabbies count on making a living."

"I don't mean any harm," the driver said. Skip looked at the man's name on the license – Phipps, Douglas. "I only know about your face. I used to have one just like it. Brow furrowed, mouth set tight, chin tucked in. All because I was in such a hurry all the time. But where was I going? What was I in such a hurry to get to? That's the sixty-four-million-dollar question."

"Okay," Skip said, mainly because there was nothing else he could do before they reached Seventy-second and Third, "I'll bite. If that's the question, what's the answer?" It came to him that he sincerely wanted to know.

"You tell me," Douglas Phipps said. "You're the one in a hurry."

There was a pause while Skip thought about whether or not he was going to think about it.

"See," Phipps said, "you don't have the answer. Only you do. I did.

What are you? Don't tell me. Let me guess. Judging by the briefcase you're carrying and the fancy overcoat you're wearing, I'd say you're an accountant? Lawyer? Insurance salesman? Not CIA. They dress to not stand out. Doesn't matter. I was the chief financial officer at a startup that had really started up, but the pressure was on, and I gave in to it. Until, that is, I got into a cab one day in a tearing hurry – just like you got in here today – and the driver asked me the same questions I'm asking you."

The taxi was stopped at Central Park West and Sixty-fifth Street, waiting to enter the transverse. Phipps turned around. Skip was looking at a man he would guess was somewhere around his own age and whose blue eyes, straight nose, cleft chin and relaxed mouth added up to a picture of ease.

"That was it," Phipps said as the light changed and he put the taxi in gear. "Remember that sixties term? 'Tune in, turn on, drop out'? That driver tuned me in. I turned on – not with drugs. Hell, no. I turned right around and made for the two-way corporate door. I dropped out so fast heads spun. Most of the spinning heads were my colleagues' and my family's. What was I going to do instead, they wanted to know. 'I don't know,' I said. 'I'll drive a cab.' I thought I was making a joke then, but it's three years now, and here I am, happy as a clam. But that's me. I can't really speak for you, can I?"

They were at another light. Phipps had gone silent and stayed that way. This allowed Skip to ask himself whether Phipps was speaking for him. And where was Phipps coming from anyway?

Not in the literal sense. In the literal sense he'd probably come from dropping off a previous fare. In the figurative sense. In the figurative sense, why was he asking Skip all these questions, making all these observations? You'd think he'd been deliberately put in Skip's path.

Had he been?

No, Skip told himself. So much of what had been going on seemed somehow premeditated. Not by him, of course, by someone else. But why? Who would go to the trouble? No, if so much had been going on that he was losing touch with reality – and it had been – whatever that reality was at this point, he better get back in touch, and pronto.

"This is it," the driver said.

Skip looked out the window. He'd been parsing his situation long enough that they'd reached the southwest corner of Seventy-second and Third. See. He was back in touch. He opened the door, stepped out, snagged his rapidly thinning wallet and paid driver (and ex-CFO) Phipps.

Phipps said, "Sorry if I talked your ear off, but by the way, you might be interested to know that in my spare time, I'm auditing philosophy classes at Columbia. Do I want to go into that for real and teach, which is about the only thing you can do with a philosophy degree? Not on your nelly. I'd only be substituting corporate politics for academic politics." He nodded good-bye.

Skip shut the cab door, and driver Phipps, the traffic light now green, pulled left and headed to Seventy-second and Lexington.

It was only when Skip crossed to the north side of the street, looked right and saw the St Boniface's Charity Store three doors in from the northeast corner that he sensed something missing. He looked at his hands. Empty. He looked down at the street, then behind him, then across the street at where he'd gotten out of the cab.

Nothing.

He'd left his briefcase in Douglas Phipps' cab. He looked west on Seventy-second Street. Gone, but he wasn't going to worry. At some point Phipps would become aware of it. Probably the next person he picked up would say almost verbatim, "Somebody left a briefcase in your cab."

Phipps would know it was Skip's. Phipps undoubtedly knew that men in a hurry have a habit of forgetting briefcases. Phipps himself had probably forgotten a briefcase or two before he ankled that two-way corporate door.

Skip hadn't given his name, of course. Nevertheless, he was easily identifiable. For one, his cards were inside the case. For two, the contracts were there and traceable, if potentially embarrassing for certain confidential information being exposed.

Not that Skip cared right then. What's more, Skip was glad to be relieved of the briefcase. He was happy to have it off his hands, so to speak – not that anything but off-loading the overcoat was going to make him truly happy.

As a man continuing to ache in every joint and muscle but relieved of an encumbering briefcase, he blithely shoved his hands in his coat pockets – his for the nonce (how long was a nonce, anyway?) – and crossed to St Boniface's Charity Shop.

As he did, he grasped the Halls packet in his right-hand pocket where the gloves, the Harold Smits (Smith?) stone, the Indian-head penny, Sheryl Sherman's business card remained. He rubbed the stone, jiggled the penny and, what's this?, fondled Sheryl Sherman's card.

He reached the St Boniface's Charity Shop quickly, took his hands out of the pockets, opened the door and entered to the tinkling of bells.

He was looking around the surprisingly large store for the area where men's clothes were displayed when a short and very thin woman in a dress of lavender lace with long sleeves and a skirt almost to her ankles came up to him. Taking her in from top to bottom, Skip noticed she had black hair with grey streaks and wore sensible black shoes with lavender shoelaces.

Placing herself directly in front of him as if she were a strict high school teacher – which, for all Skip knew, she could have been at one time – she pointed and said, "Oh, I remember that overcoat."

At last, Skip, startled, said to himself. At last what? He said to her, "You do?"

"Oh, yes," she said, "or one like it." Skip's hopes, on the crest of a wave, crashed. "Don't tell me you've come here to donate it back," she went on. "You look too handsome in it."

Right, Skip thought for a split second, I could just give it to the St Boniface's Charity Store. But was it his to give? He couldn't see that it was. Feigning confusion at her comment, he said, "You say you've seen this coat before. Or one like it? What can you tell me about it?"

He heard tinkling behind him. He hadn't moved away from the door, and someone was coming through it. The saleslady beckoned him to one side. He obliged. They moved next to two mannequins. The male was in a yachting outfit – blue blazer, white polo (Polo?) shirt, ascot, captain's cap. The female wore a long floral frock and had on a picture hat. She held, incongruously, a tote with the pink-and-blue St Boniface's Charity Shop logo on it.

Skip felt as if he and the saleslady had become part of a boating foursome. "What I can tell you depends on what you want to know," the saleslady said.

She was about to continue when another thin, short, grey-haired saleslady in a blue lace dress almost to her ankles called from several feet away. "Rose, in which closet did you put away the beaded handbag Mrs Langton wanted?"

Rose called back, "The left one, Lily. I told you last week when she left." She turned to Skipped and said, "My sister." She angled her head her sister's way. "Sometimes I think I'm the only one here who knows anything. That'll teach me to keep close tabs for decades now on everything that comes in and goes out of here. Of course, that's why I can tell you about that coat. Or one very much like it."

"I'd appreciate if you'd tell me anything at all you know about it," Skip said.

Rose was about to answer, when Skip's cellphone sounded.

He picked it up to his mother, who said, "Mimi Friedman just saw you going into the thrift shop at Seventy-second and Third, the one where she's always unloading what she calls her designer clothes, although we know better. Where you get the time to go in there I'd like to know when you can't even find the time to call your mother or do Gussie Slotnik a tiny favor."

Skip said, "There's a perfectly good reason why I'm here, Mother." He didn't yet believe there was a perfectly good reason, but he said it anyway. "I'll tell you when I see you."

"And is that likely to be anytime before Shavuos?" Bernice Sawyer Gerber asked. "Mimi is also wondering who the two men in those hoodie things are who she says seem to be with you but stayed outside when you went in. Or are they just following you in that smart coat Mimi says you've got on that I've never seen?"

"Good-bye, Ma," Skip said and clicked off. He glanced past the forest of tchotchkes in the front window to see what he could see. Not much. No two men in "hoodie things." That didn't mean that if they were there, they hadn't moved out of range. To Rose, he said, "Please forgive the interruption. Do go on."

Rose, obviously a woman who believed patience was a virtue, said, "That's quite all right. We must all be good to our mothers while we have them, mustn't we? As I was about to say, this coat is familiar. I suspect it was made either by a tailor named Isaac Solomons or his sons. Or it was made at the Sandford Clothing factory that was once on West Sixtieth Street. If I don't miss my guess, the two inside breast pockets have two buttoned-down tabs."

She raised a right hand and made a testing-fabric gesture. She said, "Do you mind?" Skipped nodded that he didn't. She took the left lapel between her right thumb and forefinger and rubbed. "Oh, yes," she said, "I think this was made at the factory. The fabric they used there was actually slightly finer than the fabric Isaac Solomons was able to obtain. The factory shut down in the late eighties. Quality goods were less important to Yuppies is how I see it. Flashy, that's how they wanted it. But I'd say this coat was made in the late seventies. We see a lot of them, but they go out as fast as they come in. Or maybe they come in more."

"A lot of them?" Skip asked.

"Oh, yes," Rose said, patting the lapel before lowering her hand. "Men often come in with them, thinking to sell, but when I tell them what I've just told you, they leave still wearing them." She looked at him with the eyes of a woman who rarely doubts herself. "But I'm tempted to say I'm close to certain I've seen the one you have on before. I think we may have sold it some time ago. Or one like it."

"You wouldn't by any chance happen to remember whom you sold it to, would you?" Skip prodded, lengthening the "by any chance" with the intention to instill the phrase with a mix of charm and need. He put a little extra into the "'would you?" too.

Rose regarded him as if he'd insulted her very being and said, "Of course, I would. Here at St Boniface's we keep immaculate records of all our acquisitions and sales. I keep immaculate mental notes as well." She clasped her bony hands with their crepe-like backs. "If you'll excuse me for a moment. I'll return with the information on the provenance of the exceptional overcoat you're carrying off so well."

She swiveled smartly on her sensible heel and disappeared into the second room. Skip looked around and noticed that Lily and the woman for whom she had evidently retrieved the beaded bag were observing him while whispering to each other.

They noticed him noticing them. The customer yelled across the room to him, "We couldn't help saying how handsome you look in that coat." The saleslady added, "You obviously take good care of it." "You must never expunge it from your wardrobe," the beaded-bag lady said.

"Thanks," Skip said. "I'll make certain I don't."

He listened to himself and wondered, What am I saying? No time to answer himself, though. Rose had returned, holding a business card. She said, "I've written the information on our card."

Skip took the card from her and turned it over. On the back Rose had written in a flowery hand, "ROL Haven" and below it "11 East 95 Street."

"I have no telephone number," she said, "or any other contact information that so many people seem to have in great supply these days. If they want to tell us when we ask, that's fine. If they don't, that's fine, too. We still understand the value of privacy and respect it." She winked at him. "I could go on about respect and the current lack of it, but I won't."

Skip was disinclined to wink back but responded with a respectful "Thank you for your help."

Rose put out her hand and said, "I hope it is indeed helpful. By the way, our records show we sold Mr Haven the coat – or one almost exactly like it – several years ago, and if I recall correctly, it looked almost as good on him as it does on you."

Although he hadn't even turned away from her, Skip had backed himself halfway out the door. He thanked her again and went about completing his leave – not without, when he'd closed the St Boniface's Charity Shop door behind him, looking left and right to see if anyone he might or might not recognize was monitoring him. Any hoodied personage or two. Was it possible he was being watched from some concealing doorway or from behind or inside a parked car?

He also looked across the street and up at the building where he knew Mimi Friedman lived on the fourth floor. Might she still be looking? If so, he gave a general wave. If so and from her vantage point, might she be aware of anyone trailing him?

He even thought about calling her to ask if she saw anyone or anything suspicious. He had her phone numbers. He also had Gussie Slotnik's. His mother liked his having her friends' numbers so that if the urge to call her came over him, he could reach her.

(He'd had them from before his mother had gotten her cellphone. Not long after she had it, he'd mentioned no longer needing any of the numbers and could eliminate them, but Bernice had said he must do nothing of the sort in case he had to contact her wherever she was and for some reason her cellphone was on the blink.)

But no, he wasn't going to call Mimi Friedman and set off a domino series of calls that would only irritate him when he was already sufficiently up to here in intangible irritants coming between him and his elusive goal. Content for the moment he wasn't being surveilled, he walked into the street to catch the first cab he encountered.

He spotted none as far down as he could see. Many occupied cabs passed in the first seconds he stood there, but no empties.

In the near distance, he saw a couple or three buses bonding, as they so often did on their routes. He could hop on a bus, of course, but was that a good idea? Probably not. What if he needed to alight in a hurry and the bus was between stops? In that case, he could be up shit's creek without a paddle, a slang situation he hadn't contemplated seriously (or jokingly) since he was a teenager.

He looked at the rogue Rolex – 1:39 pm in the sunlit afternoon. Near as he could tell, he was going to have to hoof it, at least until he spotted an unoccupied cab. The question was, What was the quickest route? It was a two-part question, the second half of which was, What was the safest route?

The answer was he had no time to think about that now. He'd better just start running – or scurrying fast – in something resembling broken-field movement. He'd also better keep an eye out for streetside nooks and crannies into which he could duck if the need arose.

He wondered what Mimi Friedman would make of him if she could see what he was up to. He imagined her on the phone not just to his mother but to all the women the two of them had in common, saying, "You'll never guess what that nice real-estate lawyer boy of Bernice's is doing outside my window."

But why was he thinking about Mimi Friedman, when there were other pressing concerns – such as the two young men in hoodies who were running up East Seventy-fourth Street as he headed to Lexington Avenue, which ran south, of course, and on which the cabs would be going in the wrong direction.

Trying to advance with speed while looking behind him, he kept his eye on the two beanpole kids long enough to satisfy himself they'd stopped running and walked up the steps of a brownstone.

No sooner had he surveyed them doing that than his cellphone went, bannering an unknown number. He said, "Hello" and heard, "Don't assume that we've forgotten your coat." Or was it, "Don't let the Siamese cat get your coat"? Or was it, "Donna Sue wove her cotton coat"?

Traffic noise was too clangorous for him to be sure, and now that he was heading up Lexington and turning into East Seventy-fifth Street on which cars headed west – or, that is, in the direction he was going – he was uncertain about the man looking out the window of a passing black limousine.

The limo was pulling into a parking spot just ahead of him. He didn't like the look of this at all and dodged to the north side of the street. He heard behind him, "Edward?" Then "Edward Gerber – Edward – is that you?"

He stopped in his tracks. He was aware he was breathing heavily but didn't want to look as if he was for whoever this was. He gazed across the street and saw Marcus Nealon for whom he'd handled a real estate issue as a favor a few years earlier. In fact, it was in regard to the very property he'd just run past without noticing.

"Marcus," Skip yelled back but didn't move from where he was standing and attempting to breathe naturally. "Just late for a meeting," he yelled. He hoped that would be explanation enough for his not being more cordial.

It wasn't. Marcus, a short and compact guy who had his suits made to emphasize his toned physique, was crossing the street with his hand out. "The way you're racing, you must be very late," Marcus said. He shook Skip's hand as if meaning to crush it. "Where do you need to get to? My driver's free for the time being. He can drop you. Great coat, by the way, but isn't the weather a little warm for running in it?"

Skip thought fast, but not fast enough.

Marcus was looking down to where Skip was doing something with his left hand. Skip looked, too. He was fidgeting with a piece of paper. It was the business card with the East Ninety-fifth Street address on it. Without thinking about what he was doing, he'd taken it from the left-hand pocket where he'd put it when saleslady Rose gave it to him and was turning it over, flipping it between his fingers as if trying to master a trick with a disappearing coin.

He transferred it to his right hand so he could slip it into his right-hand pocket, where he felt not a disappearing coin but the Indian-head penny and the other accumulated *objets d'aventure*.

Marcus watched him without comment but with just the merest pursing of his lips in amusement, "What about the car? You can use the lift, can't you?"

"Thanks for the offer, Marcus," Skip said, "but I'm only due right around the corner. If I were going any farther, I'd jump at the chance to use it, but I'm not."

He was going farther and might have benefited from the lift, but if he accepted the ride, he'd have to tell the chauffeur his destination, and something told him – well, he told himself – that he didn't want the chauffeur knowing something he might then relay to Marcus. Even if he had the chauffeur drop him at the corner of East Ninety-fifth and Madison Avenue or a few corners sooner, it was still, as he gauged it, disclosing too much information.

"Thanks, anyway," Skip said, "and thank your driver."

Marcus, who was observing him as if he knew something was askew, said, "You're always welcome, as you know."

"I'll see you then," Skip said. "Always a pleasure."

He started away, noticing his right hand was still in the coat's right-hand pocket and was not only holding the Indian-head penny but rubbing the St Boniface's Charity Shop business card against it. As he let go of both objects and removed his hand, he heard Marcus call after him.

"Edward, wait a minute, if you don't mind." Skip stopped and walked back a few steps but not all the way back.

Marcus raised his voice to compensate for the remaining distance and said, "Actually, it's lucky running into you. I've been meaning to call. I have a little deal I want to talk to you about. It's in the early stages, but I'd like your opinion."

"Can you give me a ring at the office?" Skip said, beginning to back up and turn. "In kind of a hurry now."

"Sure thing," Marcus said. "I'll call first thing tomorrow morning."

As he began moving faster, Skip thought of being in the office first thing tomorrow morning. The concept seemed no less likely to him just then than had he said that first thing tomorrow morning he'd be dog-sledding in Siberia. Would he ever see his office again? Did he want to see his office ever again?

He turned on to Park Avenue, calculating he still had eighteen blocks to go north and a block and a half west. He ran through his mind's Rolodex and his mind's iPhone contact slate to see whom he knew along this wide boulevard that could waylay him and he'd therefore want to avoid. He compared this to the lists of possible relatives, friends and/or business associates who could cross his steady path were he to use Madison Avenue.

He could think of no one, knowing that, on the other hand, there had to be any number of candidates but he was pulling blanks because he was so rattled. He decided to split the Park Avenue-Madison Avenue difference. When he got to Park and Eighty-third Street – hadn't he been near there recently?; oh, yes, only last night – he'd go west to Madison.

He got there in a matter of minutes and breathed relief that he'd progressed that far spotting no one who knew him and no one whom he knew but hadn't spotted who'd spotted him.

Eighty-fourth, -fifth, -sixth, -seventh – the greatcoat's tails whipping about his legs. He tried to keep up his pace as he hit the Carnegie Hill grade and realized his body was still wracked, and he was hungry. He hadn't eaten since Mac's short-order breakfast.

He was on the east side of the street between Eighty-eighth and Eighty-ninth when he heard a high, shrill voice behind him. "Yoo-hoo," it tooted. "Edward Gerber. Skip. Skip Gerber."

He knew the voice and, in a second, placed it. It was Gussie Slotnik's voice. Now was no time for Gussie Slotnik. He saw a break in traffic and veered to the west side of the street. As he did, he turned back and waved. He yelled, "Can't talk now, Mrs Slotnik. Sorry about the information you want. Try Googling it."

Would she know what he was talking about? He hoped so, but all he heard as he made feet away from her as fast as possible was, "Handsome overcoat, Edward. You look..." She was fading, and the rest of her compliment, if that's what it was going to be, never reached his ears.

And wouldn't you know that as he crossed and checked he was all right to do so, he saw a vacant cab coming towards him? Drawing nearer, the driver edged towards the left side of the street in obvious hope the running man was looking for a taxi.

Now you come along, Skip thought, when a three-block ride was hardly what he needed. Fuck you and the horsepower you rode in on, Skip thought. Without looking at the cab, he waved it on.

Buoyed by his anger at cabs that aren't there when you need them and cabs that are there when you don't, Skip reached East Ninety-fifth Street. Checking his – er – Rolex as he rounded the corner, he saw it was 2:12 pm He'd reach 11 East Ninety-fifth by 2:13 p. m., which is what counted right then.

Not wanting to look too desperate as he approached number 11, apparently the home of ROL Haven, Skip slowed his pace. He thought of it as a post-workout cool-down. Although he was breathing so heavily as he approached his destination that his chest hurt – in addition to his other pains and pangs – he believed himself to look passably respectable.

That's how he wanted to look as he got to 11 East Ninety-fifth Street. He also thought it might be a good idea not to look too obviously interested in it. He didn't want to look as if he were casing the joint, which was exactly what he was doing.

His first maneuver was to walk past the building nonchalantly, giving it a quick once-over. Eleven East Ninety-fifth Street was a five-story limestone – yes, limestone – edifice with a limestone stoop leading to a parlor-floor-level and graceful bay-windowed front accented in marble. The bayed front extended to the top of the second story.

The windows on all floors gave little away in the few seconds he allotted to examining them as he sauntered by. Curved black bars covered the below-stairs windows. Beyond them, he could make out the accoutrements of a modern kitchen. The parlor-floor bay windows seemed to be framed inside by draperies of a deep color and in the middle was a large vase holding a bouquet of white flowers that didn't seem to match the season.

Glancing with studied nonchalance at the top of the building, Skip saw a copper cornice unadorned by, he was thankful to see, gargoyles or any other sort of grotesque statuettes.

For safety's sake, Skip kept walking towards the Fifth Avenue corner, stopping only when he reached it. He reckoned he'd stand there a moment as if he were mulling something over, snap his fingers as if the something had come to him and then double back – but not on the same side of the street.

He crossed to the south side and walked east to grab another look-see at the ROL Haven abode. For this pass, he slowed down even more and, looking up at the cornice, noticed that tucked underneath it at each end was a partially hidden camera.

The building being watched was watching back. That's to say, unsuspecting citizens walking by the house were being observed. What were they being watched for? The overcoats they wore?

This irked Skip. He decided he'd had enough. If the edifice was an embassy, cameras would be understandable, but this was no embassy. That was clear. Or was it? Then he noticed something else he hadn't seen before – a metal plaque to the right side of the large double-door.

He was bound and determined to read that plaque. Not wasting another second in joint-casing, he looked right to see if a car was coming. There was none. He crossed the street, moving through two parked black limousines that each, unsurprisingly, he took in, had one-way windows in the back.

Just then he had no time for black limos, either.

He was a man on a mission.

He marched up the steps to read the plaque by the carved double-door with its matching lion-head knockers. It said: "This building was constructed in 1893 for Roland Everett Herbert Haven by Richard Morris Hunt after the railroad mogul saw Marble House, the 1888 domicile Hunt constructed for William K. Vanderbilt. It is representative of Carnegie Hill limestone architecture during the period."

Hmmm, Skip hmmmed to himself, REH Haven. The Haven he was seeking had to be a Haven of whatever generation by now and, it was highly likely, had the given name Roland.

Is that what it would say on the black speaker at the right of the door? It said nothing on the black speaker at the right of the door. There was a single button placed above the vented speaker.

"Here goes," Skip said aloud, although not too loudly. He pushed the button, and as he did, he thought he saw movement in the window nearest him – as if a curtain had momentarily been held aside an inch or two and then let fall back in place. He tried to ascertain whether the curtain was still fluttering but couldn't be sure. He leaned over to see if a gap might have been left between an edge of the casement and the curtain.

He could make nothing out but thought he heard something. It wasn't coming from inside the Haven mansion, however, but behind him. He turned and thought he saw the curbside front and back doors of both black limousines open a crack.

His scrutiny was interrupted by a scratchy voice, though Skip couldn't distinguish whether the scratchiness was a quality of the person speaking or a faulty system. "May I help you?" the disembodied voice asked. From the desiccated timbre, Skip would have guessed it belonged to an older woman.

"I'm looking – ." Skip's own voice cracked on "looking," but he persevered. " – for ROL Haven. I've been given this address."

"Is he expecting you?" the voice responded.

The way the question was asked implied to Skip that whoever ROL Haven was, he must be somewhere behind the heavy double-doors. What was left of his pounding heart lifted.

"I don't think so, but maybe," Skip answered, thinking that over the last twenty or more hours he'd lost all grasp of when and where he was expected and who might be expecting him. As far as he knew, anyone could be expecting him anywhere. How many of those he thought he was encountering arbitrarily might have been expecting him?

"I'm sorry," the voice carried on, "but Ambassador Haven only sees people by appointment made through the mail."

So was this an embassy, or wasn't it?

"I'd only have to see him for a minute or two," Skip said and heard deference in his inflection. But he was okay with it. Deference can be a useful tactic, and, as he factored it, it had become incumbent on him to be a tactician.

"Can you tell me what this is about?" the woman's (?) voice said.

The phrase "I want to see a man about a coat" flew like an arrow through Skip's head, but he couldn't imagine saying it or any variation of it. How stupid it would sound spoken on this limestone – wouldn't you know it? – stoop.

Instead, Skip said, "I have to tell him in person."

This was true, no? He didn't picture himself telling the person on the other side of the speaker that he was wearing an overcoat he had reason to believe belonged to Mr – Ambassador? – Haven. He might only have slim reason to believe it, but reason nonetheless.

Shown to the man's inner sanctum, he might, however, come face to face with someone who delivered an affronted form of "That's my coat. How did you come by it?"

This wasn't to be.

The voice said, "I'm sorry, but that's not possible. The ambassador isn't home right now and won't be for some time." Why hadn't the voice told him that before? "He's giving a talk at The Cloisters."

"He's at The Cloisters!" Skip exclaimed.

"That's what I said, young man," crackled through the speaker. "I suppose if you wanted to speak to him, you might be able to approach him when he finishes."

"Do you have any idea when that will be?" Skip asked. There was no answer. The connection, he could tell, had been cut off.

He pushed the button again. Nothing. He pushed again and again. With great effort. Still nothing.

Still nothing from the speaker that is, but again he heard sounds from the curb. The black limousines' doors were clicking open. He saw a man's shoe and pant leg angle out from one of the limos. He didn't like the look of that and decided the best thing he could do would be to get out of where he was. The active verb he was looking for was "scram."

He did. Towards Fifth Avenue. Looking back long enough to see four broad-chested men in grey suits, grey shirts, grey ties and dark glasses chasing him. Cumulatively, they looked like a ton of muscle. What's more, three of them were waving their arms at him to stop. One of them seemed to be waving a piece of paper. One held a cellphone to his ear.

Oh, my god, Skip thought, and then, at least they're not waving pistols. Not yet.

They were gaining on him – might have caught up with him, too, if one of them hadn't fallen and two hadn't stopped to get him back on his feet. The third stopped to continue his cellphone conversation.

Skip reached the corner and raced into the street to stop a cab.

What if there were none free?

But there was, and not only was it free but as it pulled over to him, he could see the driver reach behind him and release the rear door.

Looking east on Ninety-fifth Street as he slid in the back seat, he saw the four goons on his tail reverse their pursuit and race to their limousines.

They were going to follow him. Of course, they knew where he was going. The one on the cellphone had contacted the woman at the inside speaker and learned his objective.

Shutting the door, he said to the driver, "The Cloisters, and make it quick. I think I'm going to be followed by two black limousines. Do whatever you can do to elude them." He thought for a moment, then added, "Thanks."

"Anything for you, Mr Gerber," the cabbie said. "You wouldn't be you if someone wasn't snapping at your heels."

The driver knew his name. How did he know it? He knew someone was after him again. How did he know that? Is everyone in the city on to him?

As if there's something about him to be on to.

He leaned forward to get a closer look at the driver. Dermot

McAllister. Mac. "Mac," Skip said, thinking that once again he hadn't looked at the number on the taxi's roof light. "What are you doing here?"

"I could ask you the same thing," Mac said. "When I saw you a few minutes ago, you were running up Madison Avenue. I tried to stop for you, but you waved me on. You looked like you had a pack of wolves after your ass. I decided you might need me. So I've circled the block twice."

The cab was making right turns to get to the East Ninety-sixth Street transverse and, Skip guessed, the Henry Hudson Parkway.

"Have you been monitoring my every move today?" Skip asked.

"No way," Mac said. "I gave up when I dropped you at the tram this morning. Just my luck – or yours – that I left a fare at Eighty-sixth and Madison when I saw you on the hoof. I recognized the coat from two blocks away. It's this city, man. You never see a person in your life, and then you see him twice in two days. That always happened to me when I was on the force, but in those days, they were usually criminals. Which I don't take you for, although I'm starting to wonder."

Skip was listening to this and realizing he was finding comfort in Mac's gritty voice, but he was also peering out the back window to see whether two or maybe just one black limousine was behind them and if so, how far behind and how rapidly catching up.

Two were in view, but Mac was now crossing West Ninety-sixth, and there was traffic. What's more, there were other cabs in the group now stopped by a red light at Ninety-sixth and Amsterdam. He saw a broad-shouldered heavy step out of one of the limos to see what he could see of the taxis in front of him.

Skip could slink down so as not to be seen, but he was damned if he was going to do that. Something in him signaled he had to do something radical – and while they were still held at the light.

Not stopping to think about what he was doing, he opened the door on his side of the car, and, as he shut it, he said to Mac, "Move over, I'm driving now."

Running around the front of the car and shaking a fist over the cars separating him and the grey-suited posse, he opened the door on the driver's side.

"I can't let you do this," Mac said. "It's illegal."

Skip wasn't convinced it was, although Mac was probably right – hack permits being as comprehensive as they were. But his dander was up. He said, "Mac, you know I'm a lawyer. If anything happens, I'll get you out of it."

"Can you even drive?" Mac said.

"Of course, I can drive." The light had changed. "And ever since we met you've been doing all the driving. It only seems fair that I take on some of it." Cars behind him were honking. Skip saw Mac looking through the rearview mirror, shrug his thick shoulders and move over reluctantly, reaching for the two parts of the seat belt there.

Skip bolted into the cab, shut the door, fastened the seat belt as hastily as he could, took the wheel and threw the cab into gear. The lurch pressed Mac and him into the seats and just as quickly jerked them forward.

"You said you could drive?" Mac said.

"I can drive," Skip said. "See. I'm driving." He was already getting the feel of the wheel. "This way you can watch what's happening behind us and let me know what to do about it."

"Who's after you?" Mac asked.

"I don't know," Skip said.

"Who do you *think* is following you?" Mac pressed.

"I don't know," Skip said.

"Then why do you think anyone is following you?" Mac went on.

"I just know I'm being followed,' Skip said, "and they know I'm going to The Cloisters?"

"What's at The Cloisters," Mac asked, "besides a lot of paintings of Mary and the baby Jesus and a bunch of sculptures and things on the stone walls?"

Skip couldn't decide how much he wanted to tell Mac, but the guy was owed some information for all the trouble he'd taken – and was still taking, having just had the driver's seat usurped from him. He said, "There's someone there giving a talk I need to meet. I'm pretty sure the men in those limousines don't want me to meet him."

"Why not?" Mac asked.

"I wish I knew," Skip said, his eyes on the road as he pulled out of the left lane into the right, "I only know that when I found out back there on East Ninety-fifth street where the guy who lives there is speaking and started uptown, they chased me down the street. If you hadn't been there, who knows where I'd be now?"

"Now we're getting somewhere," Mac said. "If they know you're going to The Cloisters, they're going to assume you're going to take the fastest route, right?" He didn't wait for an answer. "They'll think you're going up the Henry Hudson Parkway. Maybe we take an alternate route. No, that's no good. If we take longer to get there than they do, they'll be waiting for you. When's this guy talking, and how long's he talking for?"

'I can't answer that," Skip said, still watching behind him.

"Do you know anything about him?" Mac asked.

"I know his name," Skip said. "I know he lives at 11 East Ninety-fifth Street." He debated with himself as to whether he should add that the overcoat he was wearing might belong to the man. He decided what-the-hell, he would. "You see the coat I'm wearing?"

Mac said, "Affirmative to that. I've seen it plenty over the past two days. I even cleaned it once. It's a sharp coat. What about it?"

"I think it's his," Skip said. "I think it belongs to him."

"If it belongs to him," Mac asked, "what are you doing with it?"

"That's what I'd like to know," Skip said.

"How'd you get it?" Mac asked. "Why don't you just give it back?"

"That's what I've been trying to do," Skip said, "but it's not that easy. Every time I try, something goes wrong. Something stops me. Like those four guys after me in the limousines."

"Maybe you're supposed to have it," Mac said without turning around. "Did you ever think of that?"

"Not really," Skip replied, and as he said it, he saw that the traffic had cleared. Worse, in the rearview mirror he saw the two limousines passing the cars separating them from Mac and him. If they pulled alongside Mac's cab and saw him, things would likely take a turn for the worse.

For the much worse.

"They're behind us," he said in a mild panic that he recognized had an upside – a proactive upside.

"I know," Mac said, "but I didn't drive a patrol car all those years for my health. 'A course, you're driving now."

Skip took his eyes from the road long enough to see Mac's face. It was a mixture of surprise and – this was interesting – excitement. Why wouldn't it be? Mac was an ex-cop and would likely be wired by suddenly reliving the kind of everyday – or at least occasional – events he hadn't realized he missed.

With Mac unable to keep his hands from pointing in the right directions, they'd reached the Henry Hudson Parkway. Now he pressed his foot on an invisible pedal, and Skip pressed his on the real pedal. As he climbed the ramp, he picked up speed.

"I hate to tell you this," Mac said, "because I don't know how you're going to take it. You haven't taken much well since I first picked you up. 'A course, you're driving now, and that's gotta be some sign of change."

"Just tell me," Skip, for whom the difference between good and bad news had begun to blur, said.

Mac said, "It looks like the speed you're going at has tipped the limos that we're in the hack they're after. Maybe if you sort of ambled along at a normal speed, they might get confused. It could be any of the ones on the parkway. 'A course, they can't be sure you're in this one, but they're after us like two bats outta hell after one bat who got outta hell with a head start."

"What do you suggest we do?" Skip asked, noticing he was taking shorter breaths but more of them.

"I think the thing to do is for us to keep doing what we're doing. If we slow down, and they go ahead of us without seeing you, and we let them, they get to The Cloisters before us. I don't think that's what you want. Not if you need to get inside to find the guy you're after."

"I'm thinking the same thing," Skip said.

"I'm also thinking," Mac said, "maybe we can have a little fun."

"What kind of fun?" Skip inquired. Fun. Yes, that's what his new car-chase self wanted.

"Fun teaching them a lesson about taking on Mac McAllister," Mac said, "and Edward Gerber."

"What do you have in mind?" Skip said.

"You'll see," Mac said.

The as yet unspecified suggestion sounded good to Skip, who was hearing a distant tinkling. It wasn't so distant. It was his cellphone. Fishing it out of his pocket with his right hand while he kept his left hand on the wheel was a little awkward.

"H-h-h-hello," he stuttered into it in a low tone, as if the limousines' occupants would hear him if he spoke at a normal volume. It was Brianna, whose first remark was an incredulous "Mister Gerber?"

"Yes," Skip said.

"You okay? You sound funny."

"I'm fine, Brianna," Skip replied. "Why wouldn't I be?"

There was every reason in the world why he wouldn't be, but he wasn't going to let her know that.

"I don't know," Brianna said, "but I just got a creepy phone call. Some cab driver called the office to say he had your briefcase. He said you left it in his cab. At Third Avenue and Seventy-second Street. But you never do anything like that."

Skip thought he'd never done anything in the last day like anything he'd ever done. Ever. He'd never done what he was doing at that very moment, but that wasn't what he was about to say to Brianna. What he said, as another sound from outside the speeding cab reached his ears, was "I guess I'm more unpredictable than you thought, Brianna. It so happens I did leave my briefcase in the cab."

"Oh, I know that, Mr Gerber," Brianna said, surprise still in her manner. "When I said it couldn't be your briefcase, he said it had your cards in it. He opened it up again and listed some of what was inside, including three soiled contracts I knew I typed. It's yours, all right. Although why the contracts are soiled I can't say. They weren't when I put them on your desk. I told him to come right over. I'll meet him downstairs. I think I'd better give him a tip out of petty cash. Is that okay?"

During this exchange, Mac was showing signs of consternation that it was taking place at all. He kept gesturing that he was ready to man the steering wheel.

"You always know what to do, Brianna," Skip said, trying to let Mac know he could talk and steer at the same time, although he wasn't convinced he could.

"Gee, Mr Gerber, that's the first time you ever said anything like that," Brianna said, now sounding a trifle breathier than usual. "Better be careful, I could hit you up for a raise. Are you sure you're all right?"

"I'm fine, Brianna," Skip said, as the cab went over a bump and lifted him and Mac about six inches. He landed with a body-long thump. "I'm just fine. No need to worry about me."

"If you say so, Mr Gerber, and by the way, when I called Mr Overmyer, he said to remind you this is the second lunch you've postponed with him. He said he's beginning to think you're avoiding him. I said I didn't think so. Anyway, I better go now. The taxi might already be downstairs."

"You do that, Brianna," Skip said and rang off, thinking that Garret Overmyer was right, even though he was wrong. Skip was trying to avoid him, although this time he had a legitimate reason.

The bigger issue was, How much more of his life had he been trying to avoid without obsessing on it? How much of it was he running on cruise control? When was the last time he'd enjoyed – *really enjoyed* – himself, when was the last time he'd deviated from routine? Not that his was a bad routine, but it was a routine. It was limited, constricted, left little room for himself.

Now he – Edward Raymond "Skip" Gerber" – was deviating from his routine.

No doubt about that.

He had to laugh. It was a sardonic laugh, and he tried to hold it back before letting it go and getting a harmonizing chuckle from Mac. It's just that at the black wheel of Mac's cab, he reflected that whatever it is about the coat that had him there, in a bizarre way it's an improvement.

"Sorry about the bump back there," Mac said, noticing Skip had put the cellphone back in his pocket. "I should have told you it was coming up. On the other hand, there's good news. The taxi's small and the limos are bigger and trying to keep out of each other's way. Easier for you to weave through traffic than it is for them."

Skip wanted to be buoyed by good news, but he was apprehensive – and correct to be. The noise that had provided background for his conversation with Brianna was more distinct, louder, and he realized it was a police car. Now not only was he being followed by two limousines but he had the cops after him, too.

And catching up. About to take him over.

"What do I do now, Mac?" he said, letting up on the gas.

"Not to worry," Mac said. "Just lean back a little, will ya?"

The cops were coming even with them, but Skip saw Mac's arm reach a bit in front of and over him. He looked fleetingly at Mac and saw him give a confident nod at the cop riding shotgun, who smiled and nodded in return. The cop turned to his partner, said something, and suddenly the cop car pulled ahead of them and headed to an off-ramp.

"What did you do?' Skip, astonished, asked. In reply, Mac said, "I flashed my badge. I still got one." Skip made another short look and saw the badge. "There are certain courtesies the public doesn't know too much about. Are they legal? That's for me to know and you to find out. They won't bother us again, and maybe you haven't realized it yet, but when the limos saw the cops they slowed down so's not to be noticed."

"Great," Skip said. "Do you think I can stand to slow down, too?" Not that he wanted to. He was getting too much of a kick out of the whole shmear.

"I wouldn't if I were you," Mac said. 'When the limos saw the cops leave, they stepped on the gas again. And here they come. You think you know what you're doing, doncha fellas? You don't know who you're dealing with – Dermot 'Mac' McAllister. That's who. Mac McAllister and Eddie 'Speed Demon' Gerber."

Skip, again putting the pedal to the metal, realized he had never mentioned the name Skip to Mac and liked the sound of a different diminutive.

Savoring both his ease behind the wheel and his being Eddie "Speed Demon" Gerber, he continued heading the cab north on a dizzying parabola he hoped would stump the limos. The entire time Mac emitted any number of pleased comments.

Then his cellphone tootled again. Freeing it with some effort in his current position, he said, "Hello, Mom, I really can't talk now."

To which Bernice Sawyer Gerber said, "I'm only calling now to say you can forget about getting Gussie Slotnik those answers. She got them herself, no thanks to you. Sometimes I wonder what you do with your time. Your father never practiced law the way you do. He bent over backwards to make himself accessible."

Skip said, "I bend over backwards." The cab hit another bump, again embedding him and Mac in the front cushions for a split second. "As a matter of fact, I'm bending over backwards right now." Skip said. "I promise I'll call you when I straighten up. If I ever do. Good-bye for now."

He heard Bernice Sawyer Gerber shouting, "Wait a minute. Evelyn Janoff called and needs – ," but he couldn't have cared less what Evelyn Janoff needed and clicked off. Rather, thinking the minutes were only flying by as they might to a tortoise but not a hare, he checked the Rolexoid: 3:03 p. m.

Mac said, "We're almost there. Take that ramp. I wish I could tell you we ditched the limos, but I can't. They're still close behind us."

Skip had been tracking them in the rearview mirror all along, and said, "We gave them a good run for their money, though, didn't we?"

"You betcha," Mac said, "and maybe bought us enough time to get to whoever it is you need to get to before they do."

"That would be nice," Skip said.

"Okay," Mac said, "there it is, looming ahead of us like one of those fortresses you see in movies. You better get ready to stop. I been here many times before. I know the drill. Pull up to the entrance and hop out. I'll slide back in the driver's seat and park in the space directly opposite where you'll go in."

Skip did as told. He screeched to a stop. Just like they do in the movies, he thought.

Mac said, "Jump out, run inside. I'll park and follow you."

Skip was surprised at how reassured this made him feel. "What about the guys in the limos? Where are they?"

"Behind us," Mac said, reaching past Skip to open the door and get him out, "but only about a quarter mile."

Skip got out, brushing the car shmutz off his coat – not his coat, the coat – as he sprinted madly. It wouldn't do to return ROL Haven's overcoat (if it was ROL Haven's) in a more soiled state than it was when he got it, and it had appeared immaculate.

The last minute had been so jam-packed that only as he headed towards the door mere feet away did he take in a bus that had discharged passengers. He couldn't say, but it looked like a line of young kids, students maybe, maybe twenty or thirty of them, all rushing him in spite of admonishing shouts from teachers and/or chaperoning parents.

No time to panic, he told himself – especially since, looking down the driveway from whence they'd just issued, he saw the limousines rounding it.

Skip didn't hesitate. He hastened to open the door, when, as fate – or luck – would have it, the youngsters (teenagers, they were, a class trip maybe?) had collected around him.

Skip tried to push through the door before them, but a tall woman in a kerchief and raincoat – obviously a teacher – stopped him, saying, "Excuse me, but we were here first."

She didn't stop him for long. A uniformed Cloisters employee materialized to explain to the imperious woman that groups are required to enter by a different door. Apparently, most of the massing bunch heard the employee and began to walk towards the door at the top of the cobblestone drive.

They did so just as two black limousines arrived and had to stall to let them pass.

Skip, realizing he could now proceed, saw three of the men in grey suits eject themselves from the limos and, pointing, rush towards him like so many grey tarantulas. He hurried through the doors, up a wide flight of stairs with one thought: to get up that flight of stairs as fast as he could.

No, with two thoughts: the other being that he'd been here before. When the woman in the speaker at 11 East Ninety-fifth mentioned The Cloisters, he only took in the word, the destination. He hadn't bothered to picture it.

Now that he was on the premises, however, and had already viewed the sand-colored edifice (not limestone?) with its square tower and walls, he knew he knew it to an extent. A former girlfriend – what was her name? Anita something. Was it that long ago? Anita Rolfe. That was it.

She was an art historian with an interest in art of the Middle Ages (she wouldn't use the word "Renaissance," except to disparage it, for a reason he'd forgotten), and had brought him to The Cloisters at least twice.

Here he was again, under different circumstances, after maybe a dozen years. This time not to be lectured at about the art. No room for that, not if he had a minute or two at most to get to ROL Haven without being tackled by at least one of his tenacious pursuers.

He reached the top of the stairs, listening for fast footsteps behind him. So far nothing. The men must have been waylaid while trying to get through or around the school kids.

He was at the ticket counter, reached for his wallet and extracted a lone twenty. There were three or four people in line ahead of him, including a grey-haired couple in matching lightweight anoraks, but they'd have to accept his cutting in front of them. He threw the twenty down by one of the tills and kept going.

"Wait a minute," he heard behind him, rising above a jangle of comments about his rudeness. "You need the sticker." He knew the person yelling after him referred to the detachable sticker with the "M" on it that anyone entering the Metropolitan Museum or its branch must display somewhere on his or her clothing.

He turned around, thinking he'd better grab the thingie. Just as he did, the first two men materialized at the top of the stairs. He ran through a door to his left.

"Hey," a guard said. "You need a sticker."

"I'm just here for a minute," Skip yelled behind him, hoping that the piece of news would satisfy the guard, knowing it wouldn't.

"Hey," the guard said and started running after Skip. "You need a sticker, and you're going the wrong way. You're supposed to start the exhibit the other way. Through the Romanesque Hall."

Skip passed another guard and then another, both of them hip to the fact that something was up and joining the chase, shouting phrases like "Stop that man," "He doesn't have a sticker" and "No running in the galleries." Behind them the four men in the grey suits were also on the move but shouting nothing.

By this time, Skip was doing more of his recently reinvigorated fancy broken-field running, dodging patrons who were appreciating art in the traditional museum-goer manner. He saw he could use them to his advantage, was on to something when he spotted another school group, this gaggle in uniforms – the boys in white shirts, plaid ties and dark trousers, and the girls in white shirts, plaid ties and short plaid skirts.

Thank god for school groups, he thought In the past he'd found them inconvenient, disruptive. Now he loved them singly and en masse.

The more en masse, the better.

He pushed through to a chorus of "Watch where you're going, watch what you're doing." Skip knew exactly what he was doing but not exactly where he was going.

Where was ROL Haven?

Skip and the pursuing entourage were now causing a ruckus as they charged through the room with the Unicorn tapestries.

Passing through in this manner was not the ideal condition under which to peruse the seven tapestries, but racing past them at (fill in the blank) miles per hour, Skip saw enough to recall they depicted medieval huntsmen tracking a white unicorn they finally cornered and either penned into captivity – with the help of blood-thirsty hounds – or killed.

I'm a unicorn, Skip thought as he exited the room. If there's a medieval cudgel handy in any of these rooms and one of the dark-suit foursome snatches it, I could meet the unicorn's fate, my blood liberally splashed on paintings, sculptures and walls.

He was just turning into another room when someone coming from another direction grabbed his right arm. He looked down at the arm holding his. It wasn't encased in dark material or a guard's uniform grey.

Mac had snared him.

"It's over here," Mac said. They were both running abreast and breathing like mountain climbers reaching the rarefied air on top of Mount Everest. It seemed to Skip that some of the portraits and carvings of the Madonna, with or without her infant son, were regarding him with scorn, others with pity, others mourning his plight, others smiling at how dashing he appeared.

Those last were the ones he liked.

"I asked at the desk if a lecture was being given here," Mac said between hearty inhales. "They said the only one is in a room with a funny name. The something Chapel. From what I can tell, it's somewhere over here."

"Where's the funny-name chapel?" Skip yelled at one of the guards running after him.

Looking back to get the answer and the direction – whatever the right direction was – Skip saw the pursuing guards followed by the limo men and, trailing them, several young male students who'd decided this was their idea of a hoot. They were being tailed by agitated teachers visibly determined that The Cloisters weren't intended for hoots, not on their watch.

Skip also noticed the activity was accompanied by a certain amount of pushing and shoving from museum-goers in mounting dudgeon that the quiet they undoubtedly associated with The Cloisters was being so summarily disregarded.

Wasn't the origin of the word "closus," Latin for "closed," "peaceful"? This was only one more scrap of trivial information he'd packed away – maybe from Anita Rolfe – but why was he thinking that at a time like this? What he should be thinking about was the men in grey suits who'd just passed the huffing, puffing guards and were now gaining on him.

Not only gaining on him but the bruiser in the front-most position was reaching towards him.

And had him by the left arm.

Mac got on the other side of the guard to pull him off, so that now Skip was the rope in a Cloisters tug-of-war. It was a situation he deplored so heatedly that he felt previously unsuspected power surging in him. He wrested himself loose from both and put extra heft into his gait.

Sprinting into the lead of the madding Cloisters pack and unconcerned with any nearby gargoyles or grotesques that might be sneering at him, he looked back at Mac. Mac was animatedly pointing to a doorway framed by matching wooden doors with some kind of animal carved on each of them.

"That's has got to be it," Mac shouted, and, Mac be praised, he was right. Skip made a hard left turn into a longish, not-too-wide-ish room in which several rows of chairs had been placed. At its far end was a raised stone platform where to the left was a lectern and behind it a silver-haired gentleman speaking into a microphone.

The man had clearly been talking, had stopped and now was wearing a surprised expression, along with a three-piece blue suit and a regimental tie.

Skip didn't have to think hard to understand why. When he'd been man-handled into the high-ceiled room – high enough so that a crucifix holding an elongated, emaciated Christ figure hung well above the speaker's head – Mac had stopped short. So had the man who'd been gripping Skip's left arm. So had the considerable retinue that had collected behind him.

Everyone involved in the unchoreographed Do-the-Cloisters conga line had stopped short. They were bumper to bumper, some slamming indelicately into one another – except for one guard who approached him, handed over a pale blue "M" sticker and indicated Skip should attach it somewhere on his overcoat. Backing away, he said in a low whisper, "Nice coat."

What surprised Skip most wasn't that he had to right himself but that the four men in grey suits – all of whom he could now account for when he looked around – had also halted in their tracks and were standing stock still with the docile expressions of Catholic school students given an unblinking stare by a suffers-no-fools nun.

Skip understood. The speaker wasn't looking at him but had cast glances at them. Of course, Skip thought, he knows them. They work for him. They wouldn't want to be caught causing him trouble, certainly not getting in the way of the lecture he was giving.

Skip sensed he could make the most of this lull. He looked around the room for another exit. Not one. He couldn't leave the way he'd entered. The four could back out and follow him.

He looked at the rows of seats and saw there was an empty seat in the right end of the front row. Why not fill it? He motioned to Mac that he was going to sit. He walked slowly to it, and as he did, he saw the speaker had shifted his gaze.

The overcoat, he thought. He sees me in the overcoat. Will he recognize it? Has he recognized it? If so, will he somehow signal he recognizes it?

As Skip neared the seat, he fondled the overcoat. He rubbed his hands down the front of it. He unbuttoned it. He took it off. He slowly arranged it on the back of the chair in which he was about to sit.

He looked at the speaker. No sign of recognition from him, but he noticed he'd captured the attention of those in attendance. A few were turning to those next to them and mimicking his coat-fondling gesture, as if he were a self-styled clotheshorse who'd come late to the lecture and was attempting to make a flashy entrance – as if he were trying to impress the assembly with his expensive overcoat.

Skip thought about hunkering down in his seat, but that didn't seem the thing to do if he wanted ROL Haven to remain aware of him. Indeed, any kind of hunkering was beneath him now. Whoever he was now was diametrically other than a hunkerer.

He looked at Mac, who'd gone to stand in a corner at the back of the room and was watching the grey-suit quartet, each of whom had stationed himself significantly apart from the others and was watching Skip like a gargoyle with prey in sight.

So he went to sit and as he did, noticed a sheet of shiny eight-and-a-half-inch-by-eleven-inch paper on the seat. He picked it up and realized it was a biography of speaker ROL Haven.

Reading it over quickly, he learned that the man, an ambassador who'd served in several second- and third-world countries over several decades "after coming relatively late to the diplomatic corps," was "an expert on limestone and its history." He was also "an avid collector of arts and crafts" and had "dedicated his time to many social causes, including the betterment of communal and individual well-being."

Just as Skip finished scanning the nicely reproduced background material, ROL Haven cleared his throat and adjusted the microphone before him.

He gave Skip another quick glance, adjusted papers on the lectern and said, "As I was saying. The three thousand limestone blocks lent by the Spanish government to construct the chapel in which we find ourselves – the Fuentiduena Chapel – represent not only building materials common to the twelfth century. Limestone has a distinguished history.

The pyramids are constructed of limestone. Limestone has been used through the centuries for many of our most important landmarks. St Paul's Cathedral in London is constructed of limestone. I've mentioned that my home is constructed of limestone, but more significantly, if you ask me – and you have – the Empire State Building at Fifth Avenue and Thirty-fourth Street, for many years the tallest building in Manhattan and the entire country, is constructed of limestone."

Skip was listening with half an ear. Limestone again. What was limestone to him, or he to limestone? The coat he'd hung over the back of the chair he sat on was made of cloth, not limestone. He heard the Empire State Building mentioned and thought, Not another potential destination to which Mac would have to conduct him.

Nevertheless, he was stuck where he was for the time being. He'd better listen some more.

ROL Haven shuffled his papers again and said with what Skip thought of as a patrician smile, "Still, limestone isn't only seen in great public structures such as the now-fragile limestone making up this Fuentiduena apse, but you find it in small artifacts as well."

He reached into the left-hand pocket of his suit jacket and pulled out a small piece of stone. He held it up and said, "This is a limestone carving. I can't speak for what it represents exactly – a head of some sort, yes, but I've never been able to determine its origins. It may have no value at all. I carry it as a lucky charm. It reminds me of the service limestone has done for humanity since pre-recorded time. It reminds me of one of those things for which I am – and I hope all of us are – eternally grateful."

With that, ROL Haven tidied his papers and closed a leather folder in which he must have brought them. He straightened himself up to an imposing height and looked over the audience with another of his benevolent smiles, although when his glance met Skip's, Skip thought he saw a flicker of another, less kindly attitude.

Then ROL Haven said, "In conclusion, I hope I've proved my point that although limestone is hardly the first thing we think of when we hear the term 'precious stones,' perhaps it should be. Limestone has made its immeasurable contribution to humankind. How many of us can say as much?"

ROL Haven held his two-inch-high lucky charm up for the audience to see, passing it in front of him in a wide, horizontal arc that paused – but imperceptibly – when his gaze again caught Skip's.

Or so Skip thought.

"And now," ROL Haven said, returning the stone to his pocket, "I'm happy to take questions."

Hands shot up around Skip, who wondered, How many questions could there be about limestone? Still, here was his chance. He shot his left hand up and, without giving it too much thought, reached behind him for the overcoat and with his right hand felt in the right-hand pocket for the stone he'd stored there.

As his hand went into the pocket, however, he saw peripherally that one of the guards drew even closer to him. Maybe they all did, but he wasn't going to gaze around to find out. He left the stone where it was and raised his left hand to draw attention to himself – again.

He debated whether to ask a question about the stone but also didn't fail to take in that when he raised his hand, each of the four men in grey suits moved a foot or two closer to him.

So did Mac.

Skip looked at ROL Haven, who'd already pointed at someone else and was fielding a query about limestone quarries, a quarry query. He waited for ROL Haven to finish with that one and again put his hand up. ROL Haven scanned the room, allowing his glance to rest on Skip. He'll point at me, Skip thought.

ROL Haven didn't, and Skip had to wait for several more questions to be dealt with, at which time ROL Haven said, "If there are no more questions, I would like to thank all of you for – . Oh, no, I do see one more hand up."

He pointed at Skip. Skip had the floor – the limestone floor, that is. And now that he had it, what was he going to ask? He contemplated taking out the stone, holding it up and, calling it his lucky charm, inquiring whether the speaker could identify it as limestone.

But he hadn't surmounted innumerable obstacles to come to this airy room – with its wall hangings, stained-glass windows, Mary-is-risen-to-Heaven mosaic and the crucifix hanging menacingly above (the second of the day that would have Bernice Sawyer Gerber shaking her head in dismay) – to learn about limestone, no matter that limestone appeared to be the order of the day.

He stood, took the overcoat from the back of the chair and held it up for ROL Haven to see. He didn't care that the four men in grey edged closer to him as did a couple guards.

As did Mac.

At this point, nothing was going to intimidate Skip, and he asked, brazen as you please, "What can you tell me about this overcoat?"

A momentary hush fell on the room, and then subdued laughter, led by ROL Haven, who said, "I can tell you it's not made of limestone." At which point the subdued laughter became raucous.

Along with it, ROL Haven for the first time recognized the four hulking men by simply, almost imperceptibly waving them back.

They followed his subtle command, as he looked at Skip and added, "I believe the young man has come to the wrong lecture. He obviously wants the talk on the origin of cloth. Perhaps one of the staff here – ." ROL Haven peered through the room. " – could inform him when that lecture is being held, and where, if it isn't being given here in the Fuentiduena Chapel."

He took another deep, patrician-like breath and said, "Or he might want to consult the British Woollens Board – the BWB – the American branch of which is located in the garment district midtown. That is undoubtedly what he wants to do."

That last sentence delivered as if issuing a command, ROL Haven brusquely and dismissively picked up his leather folder and signaled one of his henchmen to take it while he spoke congenially with the attendees gathering about him, the ones indisputably there to hear about limestone.

Skip thought of going to join ROL Haven and his fervent sycophants but didn't see where that would get him. He was stopped from mulling that thought over by a tap on the shoulder. A Cloisters staff member, a young woman in a pony tail, a leotard and wearing an identifying badge, was asking if she could have a word with him.

She said, "I'm sorry to inform you that you've missed the talk on medieval clothing and its depiction in paintings of the Madonna. It was given last week and was quite a success."

Skip made as if he were listening intently, although he was looking around to see whether those four men were still keeping him under their rude surveillance.

The young woman in the leotard said, "You can find the speech online, and now if you would follow me."

Skip realized that despite his displaying the Met Museum sticker on the overcoat he was putting on yet again, he was being shown the way out of The Cloisters. The museum was now cloistered against him.

He was about to resist when he saw one of ROL Haven's retainers converging on him through the dispersing auditors. Mac saw the converger as well and stepped between him, the pony-tailed Cloisters staffer and Skip.

The man so shortly before in hot pursuit of Skip gestured to show he had no intentions other than to give Skip a note he held in his raised right hand.

Was he the one who appeared to be waving a piece of paper at him before, Skip wondered?

In the kind of constricted voice that frequently comes out of thick-necked, thick-armed men, he said to Mac, "I only want to give this to your friend. It's from Ambassador Haven. It's what we've been trying to give him all along."

Mac took it on himself to accept the note and then passed it to Skip. The man in grey watched the relay and said to Skip, "That's some outrageous driving you did on the way here, pal. If we wasn't so sure you might have misinterpreted our intentions where the Ambassador's good graces is concerned, we would have enjoyed it more."

Then he turned, but before retreating said, "By the way, we all like the coat. Wear it in good health. You know, the Ambassador has one a lot like it."

That's when Skip, who hadn't known what to say, found his tongue. He asked, "He has a coat like it? How do you know he still has it? What makes you so sure this isn't it?"

Mac and the Cloisters factotum looked at Skip. In their eyes was the obvious question, "Why would you be in possession of a coat belonging to Ambassador ROL Haven?"

But the Ambassador's man just winked and said, "I know, because this morning I took it myself to the cleaner's on Madison Avenue. I have the ticket right here in my pocket."

He fished in a pocket and produced an easily recognized yellow cleaner's ticket. "See," he said and read, "Deluxe Cleaners, 'We care about your wardrobe as much as you do.'" He waved the paper at Skip and put it back in his pocket, made a military about-face and returned to Ambassador ROL Haven, who was leaving the Fuentiduena Chapel accompanied by the three other men in grey suits and a handful of limestone devotees.

What startled Skip, however, was that as ROL Haven left the room, he looked back in Skip's direction and held up his lucky charm – the limestone object that appeared from a distance to resemble the one Skip temporarily (he hoped) possessed.

What did he mean by the obviously deliberate gesture? He couldn't know what Skip had in his own pocket – that is, in the pocket of the coat he was wearing again. Or could he? If they somehow had both come by matching coats, why not matching coats' contents?

And what was this about the British Woollens Board? What would they know about a specific coat? Maybe they'd know something. Maybe ROL Haven knew they knew something. He must know something, and when he held up his lucky charm, he was sending a signal.

That's it, Skip thought, he'd received a signal he had to act on.

He was also receiving another signal. A more immediate signal. The pony-tailed Cloisters worker was standing by him looking as if, on behalf of the management, she was not going to brook his standing his ground for much longer.

With only a modicum of politesse, she was waving her arm towards the chapel entrance and by implication towards the main entrance – or perhaps towards an exit reserved for giving obstreperous visitors an unceremonious heave-ho.

Skip felt the need to oblige. So nodding at her and then at Mac, he began walking briskly. On this trudge, he unfolded the note Ambassador

(ambassador to what?) ROL Haven had had conveyed to him.

On it was an address: "1431 Broadway. Suite 1701"; a comment: "They could very well answer whatever question or questions you have. If you decide to go that far."

Skip had several questions. They'd been massing for some time. One was, How was a woollens board going to answer any question he had? Another was, What did Ambassador ROL Haven mean, or know, by sending the note via burly messenger that – if Skip was right – he was supposed to receive on East Ninety-fifth Street? What did he mean about a decision to "go that far"?

As Skip read the note and read it again, Mac was looking over his shoulder. He said, "1431 Broadway. The garment district. I know it well. Broadway and Fortieth Street. Is that where we go next?"

The garment district, the British Woollens Board, Skip thought, putting one and one together to make a possibly feasible two. Why hadn't he thought of this before? He'd been saddled with a garment – why not hit the garment district?

"Yes, the garment district," Skip said, "and fast."

"You know I can do fast," Mac said, "but maybe we take it a little easier this time." He waved the car keys at Skip. "And I drive."

They both looked around. As they were led out by the pony-tailed young woman who was keeping her counsel and a rapid pace, the museum had quieted down. Museum-goers circulated either silently or talking softly among themselves. Not a single school group – in or out of uniform – was visible. The guards had gone back to their regular vigils. No sign of the Ambassador or his keepers.

"Slower, yes, but I don't want to waste too much time getting there," Skip said and felt something was telling him – he couldn't say what – that the next stop would be the last one.

"Leave it to me, Eddie 'Speed Demon' Gerber," Mac said, a comment Skip assumed could mean anything but most likely held within it the promise of some effective endeavor and surely more than a sly innuendo about Skip's recent king-of-the-road display. Skip took the remark as a compliment – from an ex-cop patrol-car driver, no less.

The young woman had brought them to the top of the flight of stairs by which they'd entered, pointed down and stood with arms akimbo as Skip and Mac descended.

They were outside. They were at Mac's parked cab. Mac regained the driver's seat. Skip, after gazing around to see what possible assailants lurked and sighting none – though he'd been fooled before – regained the front right-hand seat, where he sat resolutely upright.

He looked at the sub-par Rolex – 4:05 pm Time flies when you're having fun, Skip thought. Then he thought, Time also flies when you're not having so much fun.

But, as Mac pulled out of his parking spot and navigated away from The Cloisters, Skip was again weighing fun and no fun on his imaginary scale and concluding that over the most recent hours the former had it over the latter by no small amount.

"Looks like no uninvited guests along this time," Mac said.

Peering around, Skip verified this for himself. The other cars on the road as Mac returned to the parkway and then those on the parkway didn't seem to have him targeted.

He was tempted to sit back and enjoy the scenery but couldn't convince himself to give over fully to temptation. Too much had gone on – could possibly continue going on as long as he was in possession of the overcoat – for him to settle against the seat and act as if he were on a ride through the New England countryside.

How right he was to have sneaking misgivings. Mac had hardly driven twenty or maybe thirty blocks when the occupants of perfectly ordinary Fords, Chevrolets and Lexuses, when they passed Mac – now driving within the speed limit – started trying to get Skip's attention. They were pointing at him and then pointing behind him.

He saw them, but decided to blow them off. If they were trying to compliment him silently on the overcoat, he'd had enough of that. But the more he took in of the pointing and moving mouths, as if their owners were trying to say something meaningful, the less Skip felt he could disregard them.

He said, "Mac, do you have any idea why people keep pointing at the car and then pointing behind it?"

As he was saying this, Mac seemed to be slowing down, and said,

"Yeah, I noticed that, too, but this baby tends to get a lot of attention. More today than usual, of course, but now I'm thinking something might be wrong. Holy shit!"

The "Holy shit!" disoriented Skip. He said, "Why did you say that? What's wrong?"

"I'm running out of gas," Mac said, "and I shouldn't be. Something's gotta be wrong with the gas tank."

This clicked with Skip. He said, "Holy shit is right. That's why people in other cars have been pointing at us." They weren't just mocking him for reasons he couldn't fathom but to which he'd grown accustomed. "They must have been pointing at a trail of gasoline behind us."

"Fuck," Mac said, "I have to pull over. No, check that. We're close enough to a gas station at One-hundred-twenty-fifth Street. Just a couple blocks shy of it. We should be able to make it. As long as no one lights a match."

For a minute or so, they fell silent, as if any kind of banter would affect their progress negatively. Skip filled the uneasy lull with thoughts of reaching 1431 Broadway, specifically how he was going to get there as quickly as he'd like.

Mac had other thoughts – or maybe just one – which he expressed by exclaiming in his thick Queens accent, "Those *fucking* bastards!"

"What fucking bastards," Skip blurted in response.

"Who do you think?" Mac said, impatience coating his words. "The men in the grey suits. I shoulda figured they'd do something to pay us back for the race we – you – ran them. Don't you see, before they left with your hifalutin limestone-loving gasbag, one of them must have poked a hole in my tank."

"But you can't prove it," Skip said.

"I don't need to prove it," Mac said. "I know it."

Skip wanted not to believe it, especially in light of the friendly signal ROL Haven sent him on departing. Then again, ROL Haven probably wasn't let in on the cute little prank. The men in grey undoubtedly thought that what he didn't know wouldn't bother him.

"Can't do much about it now," Mac said. "Anyhow, it is a kind of homage to you." Skip couldn't stop himself from breaking into a wide grin, but he cut it short out of deference to the situation. "I'll just have to eat it," Mac said as he reached the gas station – safely – and was pulling in on momentum alone.

He brought the car to a halt and started to climb out. "Unless I miss my freakin' guess, this isn't something I'm going to be able to fix myself. For this I'm gonna need a mechanic."

Skip had more or less come to the same conclusion, which left him high and dry and feeling out of gas himself. He wasn't completely high and dry. Harlan Rawlings, mechanic, came to mind, and the prospective West Fifty-second Street body shop, but what good did that do him or Mac right then? He opened the left-hand back door and said to Mac, "So what should I do, do you think?"

"Sorry to say, my friend," Mac said, looking around for the closest attendant, "this may have to be the parting of the ways. I'd like to see you right to that garment-center door, but it ain't gonna happen. You need to flag another cab."

"You know what," Skip said, "I think I've had enough of cabs for a while. I'm not even sure I have enough money for another ride, which reminds me, how much do I owe you?"

"You don't owe me a cent," Mac said. "I've had more entertainment with you last night and today than I've had in months." He held out his hand.

Skip shook it and said, "I wish I could say the same thing." He reconsidered that. "Maybe I *can* say the same thing. One thing I can definitely say is I've sure appreciated your help. I couldn't have done without it."

"You never told me exactly what's going on with you," Mac said. "Maybe you will the next time I pick you up."

"I only hope I can," Skip said. Wishing in part that he could remain shmoozing with Mac – who felt to him like a dyed-in-the-wool new friend – he was tugged more strongly by the urge to get downtown.

He shook hands once again with Mac and walked away, looking back only for a second to see Mac in conversation with a mechanic who was wiping his hands on a dirty cloth. Mac was pointing under the taxi with animation Skip recognized and had even come to envy.

Skip thought, The subway's my solution now. He headed towards the stop at Broadway and One-hundred-twenty-fifth Street, which wasn't, he soothed himself, that far off.

It was far enough off, however, for him not to have gone more than half a block when a group of eight men in hoodies obscuring their faces began pointing at him and in no time at all were surrounding him.

"Great coat," one said. Another said, "I could use a big coat like that." "How 'bout letting me try it on?" a third said. A fourth came up behind Skip, reached around and attempted to remove the overcoat, which Skip had buttoned up when leaving The Cloisters. The others laughed at the attempt.

Skip, startled at what was happening, also found himself furious. For so long he'd thought of nothing but unburdening himself of the coat. Now he was resolved that the last thing he was going to do was allow these hoodlums to pinch it.

When another of the assailants moved in on him to unbutton the coat, he managed to say, "Believe me, you don't want this coat. It's old and it may not look like it, but it's falling apart. I'll tell you what. I've got a Rolex." He tried to hold his hand up but couldn't. The kid behind him had too tight a lock on his arms.

"Let's see it," a different menacing adolescent said and lifted the coat's left sleeve to examine the watch. When he had, he said, "Who you fooling, man? This ain't no Rolex. It's a cheap knock-off. You get 'em on Canal Street a dime a dozen."

Another one, putting his half-covered face in Skip's, said, "You trying to take advantage of us? We don't take kindly to that." He raised a fist.

Cognizant of traffic going past paying no mind to him and these hoodied hoods, Skip was thinking about the difficulty of passing off fake Rolexes as the real thing and wondering if he was right or wrong, in the present circumstances, to own the bargain-basement copy. Maybe he should forget the Rolex manqué entirely and check time on his iPhone, like everyone else he knew.

At the same time, he was preparing himself for the blow – a blow that would for certain be the first of many he realized he was prepared to resist as well as he could.

It didn't come. Instead, a voice he instantly recognized as Mac's blared. "Off-duty cop here, boys, and I'm holding up this badge so you know I'm not connin' you. You'd better be able to explain what you're up to or you're in deep shit. And by the way, I have a gun I don't want to pull out yet. If you don't believe it, test me. I guarantee you'll be sorry."

As Mac made his threat, Skip felt the grip on him loosen and saw all of the boys move away. He also remembered the Halls packet in his left-hand pocket. He reached in, grabbed it, pushed it against the coat and surprised himself by saying, "Undercover cop here, too, boys. Back off or suffer the ugly consequences."

At that, every one of the One-hundred-twenty-fifth-Street eight put up his hands. One of them said, "Just joshing, fellas." Another said, "We was just havin' some fun. Didn't mean no harm." The octet moved back even farther. Another one said to Skip, "Boss coat. Definitely phat."

"You boys, on your way now," Skip said in a low register he had no idea he possessed.

There was a chorus of "Thass right" and "Yessuh" and one muffled "muthafuckah."

They hightailed it off in a pack, as Mac and Skip watched them turn north at the next corner. Mac said to Skip, "Nice work, Eddie. If you're heading to the subway, you ought to make it without anything else happening. Just in case, I've got your back. They don't need me at the gas station right now."

"Thanks again, Mac," Skip said. "You're a life-saver."

"Don't mention it. For a cabbie or a cop, it's all in a day's work."

Skip made it to the subway without incident. When he got there, his worthless Rolex appropriation – not entirely worthless; it did tell the time no less well than the real thing would – said 5:09 pm That's good, Skip thought, it'll be helpful if I get to the British Woollens Board before the close of the working day.

When he arrived at the ticket booth, he found two dollars in his wallet and two quarters in his pants pocket (along with a couple dimes and some pennies) and bought – he almost never took a subway – a Metro card for a single ride.

Nobody paid him any out-of-the-ordinary attention as he went

through the turnstile and reached the downtown subway platform. He
looked up and saw that a number one train to New Lots Avenue was due
in seven minutes. It'll be almost 5:20 pm when the train arrives. Still
good time.

He found a bench with an empty seat and sat between a young girl and
a woman in a large knitted hat. "Ooh," the woman in the hat said when
he was seated, "That's a nice coat you have on." She reached over and
rubbed the sleeve. "I hope you don't mind. Good fabric always says things
to me."

What did she mean by that? Skip wondered. Was she getting at
something? What could fabric possibly say to her? Could it be telling her
the name and/or location of the true owner? Or did she just admire the
coat?

He said, "Does it? What's it saying to you now?"

"Ooh," she replied, shaking her head so that her knitted hat wiggled,
"It's saying it's top quality, like I said." While Skip was thinking about
that, the woman leaned across him and said to the young girl. "Top
quality, Shaniqua." She pointed at the coat. "That's what you need to
understand." The girl said nothing but got up and walked to the edge of
the platform to look for the train.

The woman said to Skip, "There's a lot of young people today don't
understand. And she's talking about becoming a lawyer. How she gon' do
that if she don't understand quality?"

The woman in the hat may have been addressing Skip, but she was
speaking loudly enough for the young girl, who had to be either her
daughter or granddaughter, to hear her.

"I don't want to be no lawyer," the young girl said, not taking her
eye from the track on which the train would arrive. "I want to be a
policewoman and bust people."

"Doesn't want to be a lawyer, when she has the smarts," the woman in
the hat said. "Did you ever hear such a thing?"

Skip didn't say so, but he had heard such a thing. He had heard such
a thing as not wanting to be a lawyer. It had been echoing in his head for
untold hours. It was an inner voice that had steadily risen in volume.

The train pulling in couldn't drown it out.

Along with the woman in the hat, the young girl and other rush-hour riders, he boarded the train. No seats available, he noticed immediately. The car was packed. He jostled himself within grabbing distance of a center pole, and planted himself in the midst of a bunch of women who sounded as if they worked together.

One of them suddenly said, "Girls, look at this *overcoat*." Within a split second, Skip was the cynosure. The woman who'd made the exclamation was fingering the fabric, while the others were oohing and aahing and calling attention to Skip.

The first woman said, "Wouldn't you die for a coat made of this tweed?" She looked Skip in the face. Since he was trying not to notice what was happening – although he knew full well what was – this had required her to twist herself around in front of him. "Where *did* you get this *coat*?"

Skip wanted this to be over. It didn't take a second for him to say, "Funny you should ask, but I don't remember."

"He doesn't *remember*," the fabric-fingerer said, "That's men for you. Can you imagine a woman ever forgetting where she bought *anything*?" The group agreed that such an occurrence was impossible.

The train had reached the next stop, and Skip decided to depart that car and walk to the next one. On it, he found a seat between a woman with a toddler and a young man holding a guitar. When Skip sat, he put his head down to pretend he was sleeping. That way he'd catch no one's eye who might be impelled to say something to him about the coat.

He only heard the woman say, "Byron, don't dribble on the man's coat." Skip raised his head and looked at the coat for any signs of drooling. Then he looked at the mother and child. The mother said, "Sorry, Mister, nothing happened. I only thought it might."

When they reached the next stop, Skip again changed trains, where he sat undisturbed until the Seventy-second Street stop where the doors opened and remained open for an inordinate amount of time Skip only noticed after minutes had crept by.

A static-riddled announcement was broadcast. "We apologize for the delay," it went. "We're being held in the station for an investigation. A passenger has reported a stolen coat. The police are requesting that no one leave the train."

An investigation! A stolen coat! The police want no one to leave the train! He patted the overcoat he had on. He looked at his not-exactly-a-Rolex – 5:43 pm. What if the stolen coat looked anything like the one he was wearing and had been wearing for some time? What if the police hauled him in? What if the stolen coat was actually the one he was wearing and had been the one he'd been wearing for some time? And this entire post-Bogart overcoat escapade he'd been on had been leading to this?

For the moment, he was sitting quietly but was afraid he noticed other passengers looking at him and then turning to each other to whisper. He knew what they were thinking. They were thinking he was wearing the kind of coat that someone might steal, whereas no one would help himself to what most of them had on, which was any old worn-looking jacket or town coat or shapeless raincoat good enough to put on for the subway.

They'd seen him get on the car and try to look nondescript, try to pretend he was sleeping. And weren't there passengers in other cars who'd seen him rush out of one car into another as if attempting to be elusive? What about those secretaries – executive assistants? – who'd asked him where he'd gotten his coat and he'd said he'd forgotten? How fishy did that sound?

His head still bowed, Skip saw two transit policemen boarding the train with a man wearing a suit and holding a briefcase. The trio moved down the car. As they neared Skip, he could put together what they were saying as they asked passengers whether they'd seen any suspicious characters carrying a coat. One piece of information he picked up was that the man now bereft of his overcoat had taken it off and placed it on the empty seat next to him before reading his newspaper.

As they reached Skip, who'd straightened himself up and was trying to look nonchalant but not too nonchalant, he heard one of the policemen say something about a Burberry trench coat. A Burberry trench coat! Sigh! Phew! It wasn't an overcoat like his.

Nevertheless, the first policeman stopped in front of Skip, forcing the other two to halt. The first policeman said, pointing at Skip for all to see,

"Now that's a coat." He turned to the overcoatless man and said, "Are you sure this isn't your coat? If you say yes, you could be trading up."

The man, in no mood to be kidded, said, "It's not my coat. I told you. Mine's a Burberry."

The first policeman said, "I was just trying to lighten the mood."

The second policeman said, "Bucky, this ain't no time for mood lightening."

"I guess not," the first policeman said.

The trio moved on, and when they reached the end of the car and after quizzing a few more passengers, they left it, presumably to enter the next one to the south and then the next and so on.

As they did, Skip noticed a man opposite him open a large Banana Republic box he'd been holding on his lap. As he did, he looked towards the open subway-car door that the policeman and the overcoatless man had just vacated.

Assuring himself they'd gone and letting a cat-that-ate-the-canary smirk crease his face, he pulled out a man's Burberry trench coat and stood up to put it on. Skip knew it was courtesy of Burberry, because he got a sneak peek at a sliver of Burberry-plaid lining.

What was a Burberry trenchcoat doing in a Banana Republic box? That's what Skip wanted to know. He bet himself that when the guy got on the train, the box was empty, and who brings an empty box to a subway ride, if not ready to find a way to fill it? The guy comes prepared. Not only that. He counted on the cops not finding the box suspicious.

Now that Skip was a man of action, it was time to act. "Hey, you," he hollered as loudly as he could, realizing at his involuntarily emitting the reverberating howl that having a coat stolen is much worse than having one handed to you – not the kind of quality overcoat that bestows the kind of full day, night and day again that had been bestowed on him.

At the "Hey, you," the man tying the Burberry trench coat belt as shamelessly and as suavely as all get-out, darted dagger looks at Skip, rose, threw the Banana Republic box at Skip and raced towards the nearest open subway-car door and through.

Skip knocked the box aside and, knowing what he had to do, ran after the man, shouting, "Stop him. Stop the thief." Pandemonium broke out like a rash. Several men waiting on the platform headed towards the man in the lifted Burberry. Others dodged this way and that.

Skip reached the scoundrel first, glory be. He grabbed the miscreant – a legal term, he didn't mind remarking to himself – by the shoulder with his right hand and circled the man's waist with his left arm. The move came to him from his not-so-hot football days as if from long-suppressed muscle memory. The momentum the two of them had worked up combined with the abrupt stop sent them both tumbling to the grimy subway floor.

It was a camera-worthy tackle.

"That's the guy," Skip, dazed, heard. "That's my coat, and that's the guy who took it." Within seconds the Burberry trench coat owner and the cops who'd been doing the interrogating arrived to the sound of applause and cheers.

What Skip didn't immediately understand was that the clapping and the cheering was for him. He wasn't sure how to take it, but as the cops were seeing to stripping and hand-cuffing the "alleged perp" – Skip knew that's how it would be termed, if the owner pressed charges – they nodded at Skip to do something in the way of accepting the acclaim.

He made a sheepish nod – in his head he pictured himself raising his arms and clasping his hands over his head – and backed away from where he stood. He hadn't moved far, though, when he felt a tap on his shoulder and turned to see the Burberry trench coat owner holding out a hand.

"Thanks, pal," the guy said, looking Skip in the face and then up and down. "I guess we both know the value of a good coat."

You don't know the half of it, Skip thought to himself as he shook the man's hand.

Just then, as if responding to an unheard cue, an express train pulled in. The crowd – now contented the excitement was over and they could move on – began assigning themselves doors to wait by.

Skip glanced at his make-believe Rolex: 6:06 pm. He also needed to move on. He signaled the cops that he wanted to go, and they signaled he was free to do so. So with the others, he stuffed himself into the express. Next stop: Forty-second Street, Times Square, which the train reached at imposter-Rolex time 6:12 pm – and after several people who had witnessed Skip's deed and were now on the subway car with him had made a few congratulatory comments like "Nice going, fella."

As Skip accepted them with what he hoped came across as good-fella humility, he was positioning himself strategically by the doors. When they parted, he fairly flew out and up the stairs to the next level. Seeing a sign saying "Southwest corner Broadway and 40th Street," he fairly flew up that stairwell, too.

And there, looming in front of him, was 1431 Broadway.

Was he too late to catch the British Woollens Board? Only one way to find out. He dodged the people streaming out of the building, any one or more of them possibly from the BWB office, Skip figured, but he wasn't going to poll them.

As he moved towards the building, he did a three-hundred-sixty-degree swing round to see if he was being ogled by anyone whose gestalt he didn't like. No one near, but when he looked at the cars tearing down Broadway with rush-hour intent, he saw among them a black limousine. The windows were black, but he could see a driver with a familiar thick, round head in a grey suit. He only saw the jacket, but it could have been part of a suit.

He thought he saw the driver sneering at him or maybe smiling. He thought he saw the back window roll down and behind it the top half of a silver-haired head that must have belonged to a patrician personage holding up perhaps a cellphone in one hand and in the other a small object that could have been made of limestone.

Aside from thinking for the fraction of a second that the man's expression and the object reminded him of ROL Haven, he had no time to fix on it further. Anyway, the limousine just kept going and he needed to get into the building on the double.

Which is when his cellphone played its erstwhile Top-40 tune. Why now? Skip asked himself while answering. He heard, "How's the coat? Or was it, "Who's the goat?" Or was it, "House a-float?" Or was it, "Sow your oats"?

"Who is this?" Skip demanded to know, but once again all he heard in response was a metallic click.

By now he'd paused by one of the series of revolving 1431 doors. He
pushed through. Reaching the elevator banks and the direct route to
Suite 1701, he saw they were divided as: 1–11, 12–22, 23–34. He readied
himself in front of one of the 12–22 elevators. A digitalized sign above the
door indicated the elevator was heading down. It was at the fourth floor.
He pushed the button for all that bank's cars.

And waited.

While he did, the events of the last day rewound in his head, not
necessarily in chronological order. He seemed to see them in a glow, as
if radiant from the light often glimpsed in the kind of religious paintings
that flattered the stonewalls of, say, The Cloisters.
Everything about dealing with the overcoat that had seemed burdensome
– beyond the sheer weight of the overcoat itself – seemed to fall
away (including the head-to-toe aches and pains) – leaving only the
overwhelming magnetic pull of the past almost twenty-four hours to the
minute.

The instant that the experience as he'd undergone it transformed into
something different and yet the same, an idea tightly tied to the wide-
ranging expedition Skip had been on, pierced his consciousness as if
someone had snapped a rubber band at the back of his neck.

He thought about boarding the elevator that would take him to the
17th floor, where he might actually and finally learn something authentic
about the coat he had on. He also thought about the echoing phrase on
the note ROL Haven dispatched to him: "if you decide to go that far."

Perhaps he didn't want to go that far. Perhaps he didn't need to find
the owner of the overcoat. Perhaps he didn't have to determine whether
so many of the coincidental experiences he'd notched in the preceding
twenty-four hours – in no particular order: the garbled phone calls, ROL
Haven and the limousine boys, the limestone head, Sheryl Sherman, Mac
McAllister, Ambrosius Manley Sturtivant, Jake's Jalopies, the Central
Park thin man, The Bad Mama Bears, Hugo Penrose's apercus, Harlan
Rawlings, Harold Smits, Jr., teenagers in hoodies and running shoes, the
other what-all – were cumulatively too coincidental to be coincidental.

Perhaps there was an alternative to determining who the unidentified
coat owner is. Perhaps there was something else he could do with the

overcoat – was even intended to do with it – something much more significant than locating the owner.

If there even was/is an owner.

That's when he knew what was required of him, what he had to do.

Skip unbuttoned the overcoat. He took it off and held it, reaching only in the right-hand pocket but not for the stone head or the Halls cough drops or the black gloves or the lucky Indian-head penny but only the business card Sheryl had given him.

The elevator had reached the ground floor.

The elevator doors opened.

The first person getting off the elevator was a man in a business suit carrying a briefcase. He looked as if he had things on his mind.

As he passed Skip, Skip held out the overcoat and handed it off to the man. He said, "Here you go, and be *very* careful with it."

The man took it.

Skip immediately bolted to a revolving door at the other end of the lobby and pushed his way through. As he rotated out, he could see the man to whom he'd given the coat staring at it and then glancing around with a quizzical expression on his thin, flushed face.

Presumably, he was looking for Skip.

But it was 6:18 pm on a very atypical late October Wednesday, and Skip (really Edward Raymond Gerber) was feeling lightheaded and light-shouldered. As he flicked Sheryl's card in his right hand, he had an inkling he was already well on the way to a totally unknown and completely promising future.

CPSIA information can be obtained at www.ICGtesting.com
Printed in the USA
LVOW11s0818140515

438451LV00028BA/742/P